THE MAID OF MAIDEN LANE

A Sequel to "The Bow of Orange Ribbon"

A Love Story

AMELIA E. BARR

The Maid of Maiden Lane

Amelia E. Barr

© 1st World Library, 2007
PO Box 2211
Fairfield, IA 52556
www.1stworldlibrary.com
First Edition

LCCN: 2007935348

Softcover ISBN: 978-1-4218-9303-7
Hardcover ISBN: 978-1-4218-9403-4
eBook ISBN: 978-1-4218-9203-0

Purchase *"The Maid of Maiden Lane"*
as a traditional bound book at:
www.1stWorldLibrary.com/purchase.asp?ISBN=978-1-4218-9303-7

1st World Library is a literary, educational organization
dedicated to:

- Creating a free internet library of downloadable ebooks

- Hosting writing competitions and offering book publishing
scholarships.

Interested in more 1st World Library books? contact:
literacy@1stworldlibrary.com

Check us out at: www.1stworldlibrary.com

1st World Library Literary Society

Giving Back to the World

"If you want to work on the core problem, it's early school literacy."

- James Barksdale, former CEO of Netscape

"No skill is more crucial to the future of a child, or to a democratic and prosperous society, than literacy."

- Los Angeles Times

"Literacy... means far more than learning how to read and write... The aim is to transmit... knowledge and promote social participation."

- UNESCO

"Literacy is not a luxury, it is a right and a responsibility. If our world is to meet the challenges of the twenty-first century we must harness the energy and creativity of all our citizens."

- President Bill Clinton

"Parents should be encouraged to read to their children, and teachers should be equipped with all available techniques for teaching literacy, so the varying needs and capacities of individual kids can be taken into account."

- Hugh Mackay

CONTENTS

I. THE HOME OF CORNELIA MORAN.................................7

II. THIS IS THE WAY OF LOVE 16

III. HYDE AND ARENTA...33

IV. THROWING THINGS INTO CONFUSION....................50

V. TURNING OVER A NEW LEAF.......................................80

VI. AUNT ANGELICA 99

VII. ARENTA'S MARRIAGE.. 121

VIII. TWO PROPOSALS 139

IX. MISDIRECTED LETTERS... 159

X. LIFE TIED IN A KNOT 178

XI. WE HAVE DONE WITH TEARS AND TREASONS.. 206

XII. A HEART THAT WAITS.. 231

XIII. THE NEW DAYS COME 251

XIV. HUSH! LOVE IS HERE! 269

CHAPTER I

THE HOME OF CORNELIA MORAN

Never, in all its history, was the proud and opulent city of New York more glad and gay than in the bright spring days of Seventeen-Hundred-and-Ninety-One. It had put out of sight every trace of British rule and occupancy, all its homes had been restored and re-furnished, and its sacred places re-consecrated and adorned. Like a young giant ready to run a race, it stood on tiptoe, eager for adventure and discovery—sending ships to the ends of the world, and round the world, on messages of commerce and friendship, and encouraging with applause and rewards that wonderful spirit of scientific invention, which was the Epic of the youthful nation. The skies of Italy were not bluer than the skies above it; the sunshine of Arcadia not brighter or more genial. It was a city of beautiful, and even splendid, homes; and all the length and breadth of its streets were shaded by trees, in whose green shadows dwelt and walked some of the greatest men of the century.

These gracious days of Seventeen-Hundred-and-Ninety-One were also the early days of the French Revolution, and fugitives from the French court—princes and nobles, statesmen and generals, sufficient for a new Iliad, loitered about the pleasant places of Broadway and Wall Street,

Broad Street, and Maiden Lane. They were received with courtesy, and even with hospitality, although America at that date almost universally sympathized with the French Republicans, whom they believed to be the pioneers of political freedom on the aged side of the Atlantic. The merchants on Exchange, the Legislators in their Council Chambers, the working men on the wharves and streets, the loveliest women in their homes, and walks, and drives, alike wore the red cockade. The Marseillaise was sung with The Star Spangled Banner; and the notorious Carmagnole could be heard every hour of the day—on stated days, officially, at the Belvedere Club. Love for France, hatred for England, was the spirit of the age; it effected the trend of commerce, it dominated politics, it was the keynote of conversation wherever men and women congregated.

Yet the most pronounced public feeling always carries with it a note of dissent, and it was just at this day that dissenting opinion began to make itself heard. The horrors of Avignon, and of Paris, the brutality with which the royal family had been treated, and the abolition of all religious ties and duties, had many and bitter opponents. The clergy generally declared that "men had better be without liberty, than without God," and a prominent judge had ventured to say publicly that "Revolution was a dangerous chief justice."

In these days of wonderful hopes and fears there was, in Maiden Lane, a very handsome residence—an old house even in the days of Washington, for Peter Van Clyffe had built it early in the century as a bridal present to his daughter when she married Philip Moran, a lawyer who grew to eminence among colonial judges. The great linden trees which shaded the garden had been planted by Van Clyffe; so also had the high hedges of cut boxwood, and the wonderful sweet briar, which covered the porch and framed all the windows filling the open rooms in summer time with the airs

Amelia E. Barr

of Paradise. On all these lovely things the old Dutchman had stamped his memory, so that, even to the third generation, he was remembered with an affection, that every springtime renewed.

One afternoon in April, 1791, two men were standing talking opposite to the entrance gates of this pleasant place. They were Captain Joris Van Heemskirk, a member of the Congress then sitting in Federal Hall, Broad Street, and Jacobus Van Ariens, a wealthy citizen, and a deacon in the Dutch Church. Van Heemskirk had helped to free his own country and was now eager to force the centuries and abolish all monarchies. Consequently, he believed in France; the tragedies she had been enacting in the holy name of Liberty, though they had saddened, had, hitherto, not discouraged him. He only pitied the more men who were trying to work out their social salvation, without faith in either God or man. But the news received that morning had almost killed his hopes for the spread of republican ideas in Europe,

"Van Ariens," he said warmly, "this treatment of King Louis and his family is hardly to be believed. It is too much, and too far. If King George had been our prisoner we should have behaved towards him with humanity. After this, no one can foresee what may happen in France."

"That is the truth, my friend," answered Van Ariens. "The good Domine thinks that any one who can do so might also understand the Revelations. The French have gone mad. They are tigers, sir, and I care not whether tigers walk on four feet or on two. WE won our freedom without massacres."

"WE had Washington and Franklin, and other good and wise leaders who feared God and loved men."

"So I said to the Count de Moustier but one hour ago. But I did not speak to him of the Almighty, because he is an atheist. Yet if we were prudent and merciful it was because we are religious. When men are irreligious, the Lord forsakes them; and if bloodshed and bankruptcy follow it is not to be wondered at."

"That is true, Van Ariens; and it is also the policy of England to let France destroy herself." "Well, then, if France likes the policy of England, it is her own affair. But I am angry at France; she has stabbed Liberty in Europe for one thousand years. A French Republic! Bah! France is yet fit for nothing but a despotism. I wish the Assembly had more control—"

"The Assembly!" cried Van Heemskirk scornfully. "I wish that Catherine of Russia were now Queen of France in the place of that poor Marie Antoinette. Catherine would make Frenchmen write a different page in history. As to Paris, I think, then, the devil never sowed a million crimes in more fruitful ground."

"Look now, Captain, I am but a tanner and currier, as you know, but I have had experiences; and I do not believe in the future of a people who are without a God and without a religion."

"Well, so it is, Van Ariens. I will now be silent, and wait for the echo; but I fear that God has not yet said 'Let there be peace.' I saw you last night at Mr. Hamilton's with your son and daughter. You made a noble entrance."

"Well, then, the truth is the truth. My Arenta is worth looking at; and as for Rem, he was not made in a day. There are generations of Zealand sailors behind him; and, to be sure, you may see the ocean in his grey eyes and fresh open face. God is good, who gives us boys and girls to sit so near

Amelia E. Barr

our hearts."

"And such a fair, free city for a home!" said Van Heemskirk as he looked up and down the sunshiny street. New York is not perfect, but we love her. Right or wrong, we love her; just as we love our mother, and our little children."

"That, also, is what the Domine says," answered Van Ariens; "and yet, he likes not that New York favours the French so much. When Liberty has no God, and no Sabbath day, and no heaven, and no hell, the Domine is not in favour of Liberty. He is uneasy for the country, and for his church; and if he could take his whole flock to heaven at once, that would please him most of all."

"He is a good man. With you, last night, was a little maid—a great beauty I thought her—but I knew her not. Is she then a stranger?"

"A stranger! Come, come! The little one is a very child of New York. She is the daughter of Dr. Moran—Dr. John, as we all call him."

"Well, look now, I thought in her face there was something that went to my heart and memory."

"And, as you know, that is his house across the street from us, and it was his father's house, and his grandfather's house; and before that, the Morans lived in Winckle Street; and before that, in the Lady's Valley; so, then, when Van Clyffe built this house for them, they only came back to their first home. Yes, it is so. The Morans have seen the birth of this city. Who, then, can be less of a stranger in it than the little beauty, Cornelia?"

"As you say, Van Ariens."

"And yet, in one way, she is a stranger. Such a little one she was, when the coming of the English sent the family apart and away. To the army went the Doctor, and there he stayed, till the war was over. Mrs. Moran took her child, and went to her father's home in Philadelphia. When those redcoats went away forever from New York, the Morans came back here, but the little girl they left in the school at Bethlehem, where those good Moravian Sisters have made her so sweet as themselves; so pure! so honest-hearted! so clever! It was only last month she came back to New York, and few people have seen her; and yet this is the truth—she is the sweetest maid in Maiden Lane; though up this side, and down that side, are some beauties—the daughters of Peter Sylvester; and of Jacob Beckley; and of Claes Vandolsom. Oh, yes! and many others. I speak not of my Arenta. But look now! It is the little maid herself, that is coming down the street."

"And it is my grandson who is at her side. The rascal! He ought now to be reading his law books in Mr. Hamilton's office. But what will you? The race of young men with old heads on their shoulders is not yet born—a God's mercy it is not!"

"We also have been young, Van Heemskirk."

"I forget not, my friend. My Joris sees not me, and I will not see him." Then the two old men were silent, but their eyes were fixed on the youth and maiden, who were slowly advancing towards them; the sun's westering rays making a kind of glory for them to walk in.

She might have stepped out of the folded leaves of a rosebud, so lovely was her face, framed in its dark curls, and shaded by a gypsy bonnet of straw tied under her chin with primrose-coloured ribbons. Her dress was of some soft, green material; and she carried in her hand a bunch of

Amelia E. Barr

daffodils. She was small, but exquisitely formed, and she walked with fearlessness and distinction Yet there was around her an angelic gravity, and that indefinable air of solitude, which she had brought from innocent studies and long seclusion from the tumult and follies of life.

Of all this charming womanhood the young man at her side was profoundly conscious. He was the gallant gentleman of his day, hardly touching the tips of her fingers, but quite ready to fall on his knees before her. A tall, sunbrowned, military-looking young man, as handsome as a Greek god, with eyes of heroic form; lustrous, and richly fringed; and a beautiful mouth, at once sensitive and seductive. He was also very finely dressed, in the best and highest mode; and he wore his sword as if it were a part of himself. It was no more in his way than if it were his right arm. Indeed, all his movements were full of confidence and ease; and yet it was the vivacity, vitality, and ready response of his face that was most attractive.

His wonderful eyes were bent upon the maid at his side; he saw no other earthly thing. With a respectful eagerness, full of admiration, he talked to her; and she answered his words—whatever they were—with a smile that might have moved mountains. They passed the two old men without any consciousness of their presence, and Van Heemskirk smiled, and then sighed, and then said softly—

"So much youth, and beauty, and happiness! It is a benediction to have seen it! I shall not reprove Joris at this time. But now I must go back to Federal Hall; the question of the Capital makes me very anxious. Every man of standing must feel so."

"And I must go to my tan pits, for it is the eye of the master that makes the good servant. You will vote for New York,

Van Heemskirk?—that is a question I need not to ask?"

"Where else should the capital of our nation be? I think that Philadelphia has great presumptions to propose herself against New York:—this beautiful city between the two rivers, with the Atlantic Ocean at her feet!"

"You say what is true, Van Heemskirk. God has made New York the capital, and the capital she will be; and no man can prevent it. It was only yesterday that Senator Greyson from Virginia told me that the Southern States are against Philadelphia. She is very troublesome to the Southern States, day by day dogging them with her schemes for emancipation. It is the way to make us unfriends."

"I think this, Van Ariens: Philadelphia may win the vote at this time; she has the numbers, and she has 'persuasions'; but look you! NEW YORK HAS THE SHIPS AND THE COMMERCE, AND THE SEA WILL CROWN HER! 'The harvest of the rivers is her revenue; and she is the mart of nations.' That is what Domine Kunz said in the House this morning, and you may find the words in the prophecy of Isaiah, the twenty-third chapter."

During this conversation they had forgotten all else, and when their eyes turned to the Moran house the vision of youth and beauty had dissolved. Van Heemskirk's grandson, Lieutenant Hyde, was hastening towards Broadway; and the lovely Cornelia Moran was sauntering up the garden of her home, stooping occasionally to examine the pearl-powdered auriculas or to twine around its support some vine, straggling out of its proper place.

Then Van Ariens hurried down to his tanning pits in the swamp; and Van Heemskirk went thoughtfully to Broad Street; walking slowly, with his left arm laid across his back,

Amelia E. Barr

and his broad, calm countenance beaming with that triumph which he foresaw for the city he loved. When he reached Federal Hall, he stood a minute in the doorway; and with inspired eyes looked at the splendid, moving picture; then he walked proudly toward the Hall of Representatives, saying to himself, with silent exultation as he went:

"The Seat of Government! Let who will, have it; New York is the Crowning City. Her merchants shall be princes, her traffickers the honourable of the earth; the harvest of her rivers shall be her royal revenue, and the marts of all nations shall be in her streets."

CHAPTER II

THIS IS THE WAY OF LOVE

Cornelia lingered in the garden, because she had suddenly, and as yet unconsciously, entered into that tender mystery, so common and so sovereign, which we call Love. In Hyde's presence she had been suffused with a bewildering, profound emotion, which had fallen on her as the gentle showers fall, to make the flowers of spring. A shy happiness, a trembling delightful feeling never known before, filled her heart. This handsome youth, whom she had only seen twice, and in the most formal manner, affected her as no other mortal had ever done. She was a little afraid; something, she knew not what, of mystery and danger and delight, was between them; and she did not feel that she could speak of it. It seemed, indeed, as if she would need a special language to do so.

"I have met him but twice," she thought; "and it is as if I had a new, strange, exquisite life. Ought I tell my mother? But how can I? I have no words to explain—I do not under-stand—I thought it would break my heart to leave the good Sisters and my studies, and the days so calm and holy; and now—I do not even wish to go back. Sister Langaard told me it would be so if I let the world come into my soul—Alas! if I should be growing wicked!"

Amelia E. Barr

The thought made her start; she hastened her steps towards the large entrance door, and as she approached it a negro in a fine livery of blue and white threw the door wide open for her. Answering his bow with a kind word, she turned quickly out of the hall, into a parlour full of sunshine. A lady sat there hemstitching a damask napkin; a lady of dainty plainness, with a face full of graven experiences and mellowed character. Purity was the first, and the last, impression she gave. And when her eyes were dropped this idea was emphasized by their beautiful lids; for nowhere is the flesh so divine as in the eyelids. And Ava Moran's eyelids were full of holy secrets; they gave the impression of a spiritual background which was not seen, but which could be felt. As Cornelia entered she looked up with a smile, and said, as she slightly raised her work, "it is the last of the dozen, Cornelia."

"You make me ashamed of my idleness, mother. Have I been a long time away?"

"Longer than was unnecessary, I think."

"I went to Embree's for the linen thread, and he had just opened some English gauzes and lute-strings. Mrs. Willets was choosing a piece for a new gown, for she is to dine with the President next week, and she was so polite as to ask my opinion about the goods. Afterwards, I walked to Wall Street with her; and coming back I met, on Broadway, Lieutenant Hyde—and he gave me these flowers—they came from Prince's nursery gardens—and, then, he walked home with me. Was it wrong? I mean was it polite—I mean the proper thing to permit? I knew not how to prevent it."

"How often have you met Lieutenant Hyde?"

"I met him for the first time last night. He was at the

Sylvesters', and I danced three times with him."

"That was too often."

"He talked with father, and father did not oppose my dancing."

"Your father thinks of nothing, now, but the Capital question. I dare say, after he had asked Lieutenant Hyde how he felt on that subject he never thought of the young man again. And pray what did Lieutenant Hyde say to you this afternoon?"

"He gave me the flowers, and he told me about a beautiful opera, of which I have never before heard. It is called Figaro. He says, in Europe, nothing is played, or sung, or whistled, but—Figaro; that nobody goes to any opera but—Figaro; and that I do not know the most charming music in the world if I do not know—Figaro. He asked permission to bring me some of the airs to-night, and I said some civilities. I think they meant 'Yes.' Did I do wrong, mother?"

"I will say 'no,' my dear; as you have given the invitation. But to prevent an appearance of too exclusive intimacy, write to Arenta, and ask her and Rem to take tea with us. Balthazar will carry the note at once."

"Mother, Arenta has bought a blue lute string. Shall I not also have a new gown? The gauzes are very sweet and genteel, and I think Mrs. Jay will not forget to ask me to her dance next week. Mr. Jefferson is sure to be there, and I wish to walk a minuet with him."

"Your father does not approve of Mr. Jefferson. He has not spoken to him since his return from France. He goes too far—IN HIS WORDS."

"But all the ladies of distinction are proud to be seen in his company; and pray what is there against him?"

"Only his politics, Cornelia. I think New York has gone mad on that subject. Madame Barens will not speak to her son, because he is a Federalist; and Madame Lefferts will not speak to HER son, because he is NOT a Federalist. Mr. Jefferson, also, is thought to favour Philadelphia for the capital; and your father is as hot on this subject as he was on the Constitution. My dear, you will find that society is torn in two by politics."

"But women have nothing to do with politics."

"They have everything to do with politics. They always have had. You are not now in a Moravian school, Cornelia; and Bethlehem is not New York. The two places look at life from different standpoints."

"Then, as I am to live in New York, why was I sent to Bethlehem?"

"You were sent to Bethlehem to learn how to live in New York,—or in any other place. Where have you seen Mr. Jefferson?"

"I saw him this afternoon, in Cedar Street. He wore his red coat and breeches; and it was then I formed the audacious intention of dancing with him. I told Mrs. Willets of it; and she said, 'Mr. Jefferson carried the Declaration on his shoulders, and would not dare to bow;' and then with such a queer little laugh she asked me 'if his red breeches did not make me think of the guillotine?' I do not think Mrs. Willets likes Mr. Jefferson very much; but, all the same, I wish to dance once with him. I think it will be something to talk about when I am an old woman."

"My dear one, that is so far off. Go now, and write to Arenta. Young Mr. Hyde and Figaro will doubtless bring her here."

"I hope so; for Arenta has an agreeableness that fits every occasion." She had been folding up, with deliberate neatness, the strings of her bonnet, as she talked, and she rose with these words and went out of the parlour; but she went slowly, with a kind of hesitation, as if something had been left unsaid.

About six o'clock Arenta Van Ariens made a personal response to her friend's message. She was all excitement and expectation. "What a delightful surprise!" she cried. "To-day has been a day to be praised. It has ticked itself away to wonders and astonishments. Who do you think called on me this afternoon?"

"Tell me plainly, Arenta. I never could guess for an answer."

"No less a person than Madame Kippon. Gertrude Kippon is going to be married! She is going to marry a French count! And madame is beside herself with the great alliance."

"I heard my father say that Madame Kippon had 'the French disease' in a dangerous form."

"Indeed, that is certain. She has put the Sabbath day out of her calendar; and her daughter's marriage is to be a legal one only. I wonder what good Dr. Kunz will say to that! As for me, I lost all patience with madame's rigmarole of philosophies—for I am not inclined to philosophy—and indeed I had some difficulty to keep my temper; you know that it is occasionally quite unmanageable."

Cornelia smiled understandingly, and answered with a smile, "I hope, however, that you did not put her to death, Arenta."

Amelia E. Barr

"I have, at least, buried her, as far as I am concerned. And my father says I am not to go to the marriage; that I am not even to drink a cup of tea with her again. If my father had been at home—or even Rem—she would not have left our house with all her colours flying; but I am good-natured, I have no tongue worth speaking of."

"Come, come, Arenta! I shall be indeed astonished if you did not say one or two provoking words."

"I said only three, Cornelia. When madame finally declared— 'she really must go home,' I did answer, as sweetly as possible, 'Thank you, madame!' That was something I could say with becoming politeness."

Cornelia was tying the scarlet ribbon which held back her flowing hair, but she turned and looked at Arenta, and asked, "Did madame boast any afterwards?"

"No; she went away very modestly, and I was not sorry to see the angry surprise on her face. Gertrude Kippon a countess! Only imagine it! Well, then, I have no doubt the Frenchman will make of Gertrude—whatever can be made of her."

"Our drawing-rooms, and even our streets, are full of titles," said Cornelia; "I think it is a distinction to be plain master and mistress."

"That is the truth; even this handsome dandy, Joris Hyde, is a lieutenant."

"He was in the field two years. He told me so this afternoon. I dare say, he has earned his title, even if he is a lieutenant."

"Don't be so highty-tighty, Cornelia. I have no objections to military titles. They mean something; for they at least imply, that a man is willing to fight if his country will find him a quarrel to fight in. In fact, I rather lean to official titles of every kind."

"I have not thought of them at all."

"But I have. They affect me like the feathers in a cock's tail; of course the bird would be as good without them, but fancy him!" and Arenta laughed mirthfully at her supposition. "As for women," she continued, "lady, or countess, or Marquise, what an air it gives! It finishes a woman like a lace ruff round her neck. Every woman ought to have a title—I mean every woman of respectability. I have a fancy to be a marquise, and Aunt Jacobus says I look Frenchy enough. I have heard that there is a title in the Hyde family. I must ask Aunt Jacobus. She knows everything about everybody. Lieutenant Hyde! I do wonder what he is coming for!"

The words dropped slowly, one by one, from her lips; and with a kind of fateful import; but neither of the girls divined the significance of the inquiry. Both were too intent on those last little touches to the toilet, which make its effectiveness, to take into consideration reflections without form; and probably, at that time, without personal intention.

Then Arenta, having arranged her ringlets, tied her sash, and her sandals, began to talk of her own affairs; for she was a young lady who found it impossible to be sufficient for herself. There had been trouble with the slaves in the Van Ariens' household, and she told Cornelia every particular. Also, she had VERY NEAR had an offer of marriage from George Van Berckel; and she went into explanations about her diplomacies in avoiding it.

"Poor George!" she sighed, and then, looking up, was a trifle

Amelia E. Barr

dismayed at the expression upon Cornelia's face. For Cornelia was as reticent, as Arenta was garrulous; and the girls were incomprehensible to each other in their deepest natures, though, superficially, they were much on the same plane, and really thought themselves to be distinctly sympathetic friends.

"Why do you look so strangely at me, Cornelia?" asked Arenta. "Am I not properly dressed?"

"You are perfectly dressed, Arenta. Women as fair as you are, know instinctively how to dress." And then Arenta stood up before the mirror and put her hand upon Cornelia's shoulder, and they both looked at the reflection in it.

A very pretty reflection it was!—a slender girl with a round, fair face, and a long, white throat, and sloping shoulders. Her pale brown hair fell in ripples and curls around her until they touched a robe of heavenly blue, and half hid a singular necklace of large pearls:—pearls taken from some Spanish ship and strung in old Zierikzee, and worn for centuries by the maids and dames of the house of Van Ariens.

"It is the necklace!" said Cornelia after a pause, "It is the pearl necklace, which gives you such an air of mystery and romance, and changes you from an everyday maiden into an old-time princess."

"No doubt, it is the necklace," answered Arenta. "It is my Aunt Angelica's, but she permits me to wear it. When she was young, she called every pearl after one of her lovers; and she had a lover for every pearl. She was near to forty years old when she married; and she had many lovers, even then."

"It would have been better if she had married before she was near to forty years old—that is, if she had taken a good husband."

"Perhaps that; but good husbands come not on every day in the week. I have three beads named already—one for George Van Berckel—one for Fred De Lancey—and one for Willie Nichols. What do you think of that?"

"I think, if you copy your Aunt Angelica, you will not marry any of your lovers till you are forty years old. Come, let us go downstairs."

She spoke a little peremptorily—indeed, she was in the habit, quite unconsciously of using this tone with her companion, consequently it was not noticed by her. And it was further remarkable, that the girls did not walk down the broad stairs together, but Cornelia went first, and Arenta followed her. There was no intention or consideration in this procedure; it was the natural expression of underlying qualities, as yet not realized.

Cornelia's self-contained, independent nature was further revealed by the erect dignity of her carriage down the centre of the stairway, one hand slightly lifting her silk robe, the other laid against the daffodils at her breast. Her face was happy and serene, her steps light, and without hesitation or hurry. Arenta was a little behind her friend. She stepped idly and irresolutely, with one hand slipping along the baluster, and the other restlessly busy with her curls, her ribbons, the lace that partially hid her bosom, and the pearls that made a moonlight radiance on her snowy throat. At the foot of the staircase Cornelia had to wait for her, and they went into the parlour together.

Doctor Moran, Rem Van Ariens, and Lieutenant Hyde were present. The girls had a momentary glance at the latter ere he assumed the manner he thought suitable for youth and beauty. He was talking seriously to the Doctor and playing with an ivory paper knife as he did so, but whatever remark he was making he cut it in two, and stood up, pleased and expectant, to receive Beauty so fresh and so conspicuous.

He was handsomely dressed in a dark-blue velvet coat, silver-laced, a long white satin vest and black satin breeches. His hair was thrown backwards and tied with the customary black ribbon, and his linen and laces were of the finest quality. He met Cornelia as he might have met a princess; and he flashed into Arenta's eyes a glance of admiration which turned her senses upside down, and made her feel, for a moment or two, as if she could hardly breathe.

Upon Arenta's brother he had not produced a pleasant impression. Without intention, he had treated young Van Ariens with that negative politeness which dashes a sensitive man and makes him resentfully conscious that he has been rendered incapable of doing himself justice. And Rem could neither define the sense of humiliation he felt, nor yet ruffle the courteous urbanity of Hyde; though he tried in various ways to introduce some conversation which would afford him the pleasure of contradiction. Equally he failed to consider that his barely veiled antagonism compelled from the Doctor, and even from Cornelia and Arenta, attentions he might not otherwise have received. The Doctor was indeed much annoyed that Rem did not better respect the position of guest; while Mrs. Moran was keenly sensitive to the false note in the evening's harmony, and anxious to atone for it by many little extra courtesies. So Hyde easily became the hero of the hour; he was permitted to teach the girls the charming old-world step of the Pas de Quatre, and afterwards to sing with them merry airs from Figaro, and sentimental airs from Lodoiska, and to make Rem's heart burn with anger at the expression he threw into the famous ballad "My Heart and Lute" which the trio sang twice over with great feeling.

Fortunately, some of Doctor Moran's neighbours called early in the evening. Then whist parties were formed; and while the tables were being arranged Cornelia found an opportunity to reason with Rem. "I never could have believed you would behave so unlike yourself," she said; and Rem answered bluntly—"That Englishman has insulted me ever since he came into the room."

"He is not an Englishman," said Cornelia.

"His father is an Englishman, and the man himself was born in England. The way he looks at me, the way he speaks to me, is insulting."

"I have seen nothing but courtesy to you, Rem."

"You have not the key to his impertinences. To-morrow, I will tell you something about Lieutenant Hyde."

"I shall not permit you to talk evil of him. I have no wish to hear ill reports about my acquaintances, Their behaviour is their own affair; at any rate, it is not mine. Be good-tempered, Rem; you are to be my partner, and we must win in every game."

But though Cornelia was all sweetness and graciousness; though Rem played well, and Lieutenant Hyde played badly; though Rem had the satisfaction of watching Hyde depart in his chair, while he stood with a confident friendship by Cornelia's side, he was not satisfied. There was an air of weariness and constraint in the room, and the little stir of departing visitors did not hide it. Doctor Moran had been at an unusual social tension; he was tired, and not pleased at Rem for keeping him on the watch. Cornelia was silent. Rem then approached his sister and said, "it is time to go home." Arenta looked at her friend; she expected to be asked to remain, and she was offended when Cornelia did not give her the invitation.

On the contrary, Cornelia went with her for her cloak and bonnet, and said not a word as they trod the long stairway but "Oh dear! How warm the evening is!"

"I expected you would ask me to stay with you, Cornelia." Arenta was tying her bonnet strings as she made this remark, and her fingers trembled, and her voice was full of hurt feeling.

"Rem behaved so badly, Arenta."

"I think that is not so. Did I also behave badly?"

"You were charming every moment of the evening; but Rem was on the point of quarrelling with Lieutenant Hyde. You must have seen it. In my father's house, this was not proper."

"I never saw Rem behave badly in my life. Suppose he does quarrel with that dandy Englishman, Rem would not get the worst of it. I have no fear for my brother Rem! No, indeed!"

"Bulk does not stand for much in a sword game."

"Do you mean they might fight a duel?"

"I think it is best for you to go home with Rem. Otherwise, he might, in his present temper, find himself near Becker's; and if a man is quarrelsome he may always get principals and seconds there. You have told me this yourself. In the morning Rem will, I hope, be reasonable."

"I thought you and I would talk things over to-night. I like to talk over a new pleasure."

"Dear Arenta, we shall have so much more time, to-morrow. Come to-morrow."

But Arenta was not pleased. She left her friend with an air of repressed injury, and afterwards made little remarks about Cornelia to her brother, which exactly fitted his sense of wounded pride. Indeed, they stood a few minutes in the Van Ariens' parlour to exchange their opinions still further—

"I think Cornelia was jealous of me, Rem. That, in plain Dutch, is what it all means. Does she imagine that I desire the attentions of a man who is neither an American nor a Dutchman? I do not. I speak the truth always, for I love the truth."

"Cornelia does desire them; I think that—and it makes me wretched."

"Oh, indeed, it is plain to see that she has fallen in love with that black-eyed man of many songs and dances. Well, then, we must admit that he danced to perfection. One may dislike the creature, and yet tell the truth."

"Do you truly believe that Cornelia is in love with him?"

"Rem, there are things a woman observes. Cornelia is changed to-night. She did not wish me to stay and talk about this man Hyde—she preferred thinking about him—such reveries are suspicious. I have felt the symptom. But, however, I may be wrong. Perhaps Cornelia was angry at Hyde, and anxious about you—Do you think that?"

Rem would not admit any such explanation; and, indeed, Arenta only made such suppositions to render more poignant those entirely contrary.

"Ever since she was a little girl, twelve, eleven years old, I have loved her," said Rem; "and she knows it."

"She knows it; that is so. When I was at Bethlehem, I read her all your letters; and many a time you spoke in them of her as your 'little wife.' To be sure, it was a joke; but she understood that you, at least, put your heart in it. Girls do not need to have such things explained. Come, come, we must go to our rooms; for that is our father I hear moving about. In a few minutes he will be angry, and then—"

She did not finish the sentence; there was no necessity; Rem knew what unpleasantness the threat implied, and he slipped off his shoes and stole quietly upstairs. Arenta was not disinclined to a few words if her father wished them; so she did not hurry, though the great Flemish clock on the stair-landing chimed eleven as she entered her room. It was an extraordinarily late hour, but she only smiled, as she struck her pretty fore-fingers together in time with it. She was not disposed to curtail the day; it was her method, always, to take the full flavour of every event that was not disagreeable.

"And, after all," she mused, "the evening was a possibility. It was a door on the latch—I may push it open and go in—who can tell? I saw how amazed he was at my beauty when I first entered the parlour—and he is but a man—and a young man who likes his own way—so much is evident." She was meanwhile unclasping her pearl necklace, and at this point she held it in her hands taking the fourth bead between her fingers, and smiled speculatively.

Then she heard her brother moving about the floor of the room above her, and a shadow darkened her face. She had strong family affections, and she was angry that Rem should be troubled by any man or woman, living:

"I have always thought Cornelia a very saint," she muttered; "but Love is the great revealer. I wonder if she is in love—to tell the truth, she was past finding out. I cannot say that I saw the least sign of it—and between me and myself, Rem was unreasonable; however, I am not pleased that Rem felt himself to be badly used."

It was to this touch of resentment in her drifting thoughts that she performed her last duties. She did not hurry them. "Very soon there will be the noise of chairmen and carriages to disturb me," she thought; "and I may as well think a little, and put my things away."

So she folded each dainty blue morocco slipper in its separate piece of fine paper, and straightened out her ribbons, and wrapped her pale blue robe in its holland covering, and put every comb and pin in its proper place, all the time treading as softly as a mouse. And by and by the street was dark and still, and her room in the most perfect order. These things gave her the comfort of a good conscience; and she said her prayers, and fell calmly asleep, to the flattering thought, "I would not much wonder if, at this moment, Lieutenant Hyde is thinking about me."

In reality, Lieutenant Hyde was at that moment in the Belvedere Club, singing the Marseillaise, and listening to a very inflammatory speech from the French Minister. But a couple of hours later, Arenta's "wonder" would have touched the truth. He was then alone, and very ill satisfied; for, after some restless reflections, he said impatiently—

"I have again made a fool of myself. I have now all kinds of unpleasant feelings; and when I left that good Doctor's house I was well satisfied. His daughter is an angel. I praise myself for finding that out. She made me believe in all goodness; yes, even in patriotism! I, that have seen it sold a dozen times! Oh, how divinely shy and proud she is! I could not get her one step beyond the first civilities; even my eyes failed me to-night—her calm glances killed their fire—and she barely touched my hand, though I offered it with a respectful ardour, she must have understood:"—then he looked admiringly at the long, white hand and thoroughbred wrist which lay idly on the velvet cushion of his armchair; an exquisite ruffle of lace just touched it, and his eyes wandered from the ruffle to the velvet and silver embroidery of his coat; and the delicate laced lawn of his cravat.

"I have the reputation of beauty," he continued; "and I am perfectly dressed, and yet—yet—this little Beauty seemed unconscious of my advantages. But I cannot accept failure in this case. The girl is unparagoned. I am in love with her; sincerely in love. She fills my thoughts, and has done so, ever since I first saw her. It is a pure delight to think of her."

Then he rose, threw off his velvet and lace, and designedly let his thoughts turn to Arenta. "She is pretty beyond all prettiness," he said softly as he moved about, "She dances well, talks from hand to mouth, and she gave me one sweet glance; and I think if she has gone so far—she might go further." At this reflection he smiled again, and lifting a decanter slowly poured into a goblet some amber-coloured sherry; saying—

"I dare not yet drink to the unapproachable Cornelia; but I may at least pour the wine to the blue-eyed goddess, with the pearl necklace, and the golden hair;" and as he lifted the glass, a memory from some past mirthful hour came into his remembrance; and he began to hum a strain of the song it brought to his mind—

"Let the toast pass,
Drink to the lass

I'll warrant, she'll prove an excuse for the glass."

It was remarkable that he did not take Arenta's brother into his speculations at all, and yet Rem Van Ariens was at that very hour chafing restlessly and sleeplessly under insults he conceived himself to have received, in such fashion and under such circumstances as made reprisal impossible. In reality, however, Van Ariens had not been intentionally wounded by Hyde. The situation was the natural result of incipient jealousy and sensitive pride on Rem's part; and of that calm indifference and complaisance on Hyde's part, which appeared tacitly to assert its own superiority and expect its recognition as a matter of course. Indeed, at their introduction, Rem had affected Hyde rather pleasantly; and when the young Dutch gentleman's opposition became evident, Hyde had simply ignored it. For as yet the thought of Rem as a rival had not entered his mind.

But this is the way of Love; its filmiest threads easily spin themselves further; and a man once entangled is bound by that unseen chain which links the soul to its destiny.

CHAPTER III

HYDE AND ARENTA

Seldom is Love ushered into any life with any pomp of circumstance or ceremony; there is no overture to our opera, no prologue to our play, and the most momentous meetings occur as if by mere accident. A friend delayed Cornelia a while on the street; and turning, she met Hyde face to face; a moment more, or less, and the meeting had not been. Ah, but some Power had set that moment for their meeting, and the delay had been intended, and the consequences foreseen!

In a dim kind of way Hyde realized this fact as he sat the next day with an open book before him. He was not reading it; he was thinking of Cornelia—of her pure, fresh beauty; and of that adorable air of reserve, which enhanced, even while it veiled her charms. "For her love I could resign all adventures and prison myself in a law book," he said, "I could forget all other beauties; in a word, I could marry, and live in the country. Oh how exquisite she is! I lose my speech when I think of her!"

Then he closed his book with impatience, and went to Prince's and bought a little rush basket filled with sweet violets. Into their midst he slipped his visiting card, and saw the boy on his way with the flowers to Cornelia ere he was satisfied they would reach her quickly enough. This finished, he began to consider what he should do with his day. Study was impossible; and he could think of nothing that was possible. "It is the most miserable thing," he muttered, "to be in love, unless you can go to the adored one, every hour, and tell her so,"—then turning aimlessly into Pearl Street, he saw Cornelia.

She was dressed only in a little morning gown of Indian chintz, but in such simple toilet had still more distinctively that air of youthful modesty which he had found so charmingly tantalizing. He hasted to her side. He blessed his good angel for sending him such an enchanting surprise. He said the most extravagant things, in the most truthful manner, as he watched the blushes of pleasure come and go on her lovely face, and saw by glimpses, under the veiling eyelids, that tender light that never was on sea or land, but only on a woman's face when her soul is awakening to Love.

Cornelia was going to the "Universal Store" of Gerardus Duyckinck, and Hyde begged to go with her. He said he was used to shopping; that he always went with his mother, and with Lady Christina Griffin, and Mrs. White, and many others; that he had good taste, and could tell the value of laces, and knew how to choose a piece of silk, or match the crewels for her embroidery; and, indeed, pleaded his case so merrily, that there was no refusing his offer. And how it happened lovers can tell, but after the shopping was finished they found themselves walking towards the Battery with the fresh sea wind, and the bright sunshine and the joy of each other's presence all around them.

"Such a miraculous piece of happiness!" the young fellow ejaculated; and his joy was so evident that Cornelia could not bear to spoil it with any reluctances, or with half-way graciousness. She fell into his joyous mood, and as star to star vibrates light, so his soul touched her soul, through some finer element than ordinary life is conscious of. A delightsome gladness was between them, and their words had such heart gaiety, that they seemed to dance as they spoke; while the wind blowing Cornelia's curls, and scarf, and drapery, was like a merry playfellow.

Now Love has always something in it of the sea; and the murmur of the tide against the pier, the hoarse voices of the sailor men, the scent of the salt water, and all the occult unrecognized, but keenly felt life of the ocean, were ministers to their love, and forever and ever blended in the heart and memory of the youth and maid who had set their early dream of each other to its potent witchery. Time went swiftly, and suddenly Cornelia remembered that she was subject to hours and minutes, A little fear came into her heart, and closed it, and she said, with a troubled air, "My mother will be anxious. I had forgotten. I must go home." So they turned northward again, and Cornelia was silent, and the ardour of her lover was a little chilled; but yet never before had Cornelia heard simple conversation which seemed so eloquent, and so full of meanings—only, now and then, a few brief words; but oh! what long, long thoughts, they carried with them!

At the gates of her home they stood a moment, and there Hyde touched her hand, and said, "I have never, in all my life, been so happy. It has been a walk beyond hope, and beyond expression!" And she lifted her face, and the smile on her lips and the light in her eyes answered him. Then the great white door shut her from his sight, and he walked rapidly away, saying to his impetuous steps—

"An enchanting creature! An adorable girl! I have given her my heart; and lost, is lost; and gone, is gone forever. That I am sure of. But, by St. George! every man has his fate, and I rejoice that mine is so sweet and fair! so sweet! so sweet! so fair!"

Cornelia trembled as she opened the parlour door, she feared to look into her mother's face, but it was as serene as usual, and she met her daughter's glance with one of infinite affection and some little expectancy. This was a critical moment, and Cornelia hesitated slightly. Some little false sprite put a ready excuse into her heart, but she banished it at once, and with the courage of one who fears lest they are not truthful enough, she said with a blunt directness which put all subterfuge out of the question—

"Mother, I have been a long time, but I met Lieutenant Hyde, and we walked down to the Battery; and I think I have stayed beyond the hour I ought to have stayed—but the weather was so delightful."

"The weather is very delightful, and Lieutenant Hyde is very polite. Did he speak of the violets he sent you?"

"I suppose he forgot them. Ah, there they are! How beautiful! How fragrant! I will give them to you, mother."

"They are your own, my dear. I would not give them away."

Then Cornelia lifted them, and shyly buried her face in their beauty and sweetness; and afterwards took the card in her hand and read "Lieutenant George Hyde." "But, mother," she said, "Arenta called him Joris."

"Joris is George, my dear."

"Certainly, I had forgotten. Joris is the Dutch, George is the English form. I think I like George better."

"As you have neither right nor occasion to call him by either name, it is of no consequence Take away your flowers and put them in water—the young man is very extravagant, I think. Do you know that it is quite noon, and your father will be home in a little while?"

And there was such kind intent, such a divining sympathy in the simple words, that Cornelia's heart grew warm with pleasure; and she felt that her mother understood, and did not much blame her. At the same time she was glad to escape all questioning, and with the violets pressed to her heart, and her shining eyes dropped to them, she went with some haste to her room. There she kissed the flowers, one by one, as she put them in the refreshing water; and then, forgetting all else, sat down and permitted herself to enter the delicious land of Reverie. She let the thought of Hyde repossess her; and present again and again to her imagination his form, his face, his voice, and those long caressing looks she had seen and felt, without seeming to be aware of them.

A short time after Cornelia came home, Doctor Moran returned from his professional visits. As he entered the room, his wife looked at him with a curious interest. In the first place, the tenor of her thoughts led her to this observation. She wished to assure herself again that the man for whom she had given up everything previously dear to her was worthy of such sacrifice. A momentary glance satisfied her. Nature had left the impress of her nobility on his finely-formed forehead; nothing but truth and kindness looked from his candid eyes; and his manner, if a little dogmatic, had also an unmistakable air of that distinction which comes from long and honourable ancestry and a recognized position. He had also this morning an air of unusual solemnity, and on entering the room, he drew his wife close to his heart and kissed her affectionately, a token of love he was not apt to give without thought, or under every circumstance.

"You are a little earlier to day," she said. "I am glad of it."

"I have had a morning full of feeling. There is no familiarity with Death, however often you meet him."

"And you have met Death this morning, I see that, John?"

"As soon as I went out, I heard of the death of Franklin. We have truly been expecting the news, but who can prepare for the final 'He is gone.' Congress will wear mourning for two months, I hear, and all good citizens who can possibly do so will follow their example. The flags are at half-mast, and there is sorrow everywhere."

"And yet, John, why?" asked Mrs. Moran. "Franklin has quite finished his work; and has also seen the fruit of all his labours. Not many men are so happy. I, for one, shall rejoice with him, and not weep for him."

"You are right, Ava. I must now tell you that Elder Semple died this morning. He has been long sick, but the end came suddenly at last."

"The dear old man! He has been sick and sorrowful, ever since his wife died. Were any of his sons present?"

"None of them. The two eldest have been long away. Neil was obliged to leave New York when the Act forbidding Tory lawyers to practice was passed. But he was not quite alone, his old friend Joris Van Heemskirk was with him to the last moment. The love of these old men for each other was a very beautiful thing."

"He was once rich. Did he lose everything in the war?"

"Very near all. His home was saved by Van Heemskirk, and

he had a little money 'enough to die wi" he said one day to me; and then he continued, 'there's compensations, Doctor, in having naething to leave. My lads will find no bone to quarrel over.' I met a messenger coming for me this morning, and when I went to his bedside, he said, with a pleasant smile, 'I'll be awa' in an hour or twa now, Doctor; and then I'll hae no mair worrying anent rebellion and democrats; I'll be under the dominion o' the King o' kings and His throned Powers and Principalities; and after a' this weary voting, and confiscations, and guillotining, it will be Peace—Peace—Peace:'—and with that word on his lips, the 'flitting' as he called it was accomplished."

"There is nothing to mourn in such a death, John."

"Indeed, no. It was just as he said 'a flitting.' And it was strange that, standing watching what he so fitly called the 'flitting,' I thought of some lines I have not consciously remembered for many years. They reflect only the old Greek spirit, with its calm acceptance of death and its untroubled resignation, but they seemed to me very applicable to the elder's departure:

Not otherwise to the hall of Hades dim
He fares, than if some summer eventide
A Message, not unlooked for, came to him;
Bidding him rise up presently, and ride
Some few hours' journey, to a friendly home."

"There is nothing to fear in such a death."

"Nothing at all. Last week when Cornelia and I passed his house, he was leaning on the garden gate, and he spoke pleasantly to her and told her she was a 'bonnie lassie.' Where is Cornelia?"

"In her room. John, she went to Duyckinck's this morning for me, and George Hyde met her again, and they took a walk together on the Battery. It was near the noon hour when she returned."

"She told you about it?"

"Oh yes, and without inquiry."

"Very good. I must look after that young fellow." But he said the words without much care, and Mrs. Moran was not satisfied.

"Then you do not disapprove the meeting, John?" she asked.

"Yes, I do. I disapprove of any young man meeting my daughter every time she goes out. Cornelia is too young for lovers, and it is not desirable that she should have attentions from young men who have no intentions. I do not want her to be what is called a belle. Certainly not."

"But the young men do not think her too young to be loved. I can see that Rem Van Ariens is very fond of her."

"Rem is a very fine young man. If Cornelia was old enough to marry, I should make no objections to Rem. He has some money. He promises to be a good lawyer. I like the family. It is as pure Dutch as any in the country. There is no objection to Rem Van Ariens."

"And George Hyde?"

"Has too many objectionable qualities to be worth considering."

"Such as?"

Amelia E. Barr

"Well, Ava, I will only name one, and one for which he is not responsible; but yet it would be insuperable, as far as I am concerned. His father is an Englishman of the most pronounced type, and this young man is quite like him. I want no Englishman in my family."

"My family are of English descent."

"Thoroughly Americanized. They are longer in this country than the Washingtons."

"There have been many Dutch marriages among the Morans."

"That is a different thing. The Dutch, as a race, have every desirable quality. The English are natural despots. Rem was quite right last night. I saw and felt, as much as he did, the quiet but sovereign arrogance of young Hyde. His calm assumption of superiority was in reality insufferable. The young man's faults are racial; they are in the blood. Cornelia shall not have anything to do with him. Why do you speak of such disagreeable things, Ava?"

"It is well to look forward, John."

"No. It is time enough to meet annoyances when they arrive. But this is one not even to be thought of—to tell the last truth, Ava, I dislike his father, General Hyde, very much indeed."

"Why?"

"I cannot tell you 'why.' Yes, I will be honest and acknowledge that he always gives me a sense of hostility. He arrogates himself too much. When I was in the army, a good many were angry at General Washington, for making so close a friend of him—but Washington has much of the same exclusive air. I hope it is no treason to say that much, for a good deal of dignity is permissible, even peremptory, when a man fills great positions. As for the Hydes, father and son, I would prefer to hear no more about them. When the youth was my guest, I was civil to him; but Arenta. You know that I have never seen her."

"That is the truth. I had forgotten. Well, then, I went to her with the news; and she rubbed her chin, and called to her man Govert, to get a bow of crape and put it on the front door. 'It is moral, and proper, and respectable, Arenta,' she said, 'and I advise you to do the same.' But then she laughed and added, 'Shall I tell you, niece, what I think of the great men I have met? They are disagreeable, conceited creatures; and ought, all of them, to have died before they were born; and for my part, I am satisfied not to have had the fate to marry one of them. As for Benjamin Franklin,' she continued, 'he was a particularly great man, and I am particularly grateful that I never saw him but once. I formed my opinion of him then; for I only need to see a person once, to form an opinion—and he is dead! Well, then, every one dies at their own time.'"

"My father says Congress goes into mourning for him."

"Does it?" asked Arenta, with indifference. "Aunt was beginning to tell me something about him when he was in France, but I just put a stop to talk like that, and said, 'Now, aunt, for a little of my own affairs.' So I told her about George Berckel, and asked her if she thought I might marry George; and she answered, 'If you are tired of easy days, Arenta, go, and take a husband,' After a while I spoke to her about Lieutenant Hyde, and she said, 'she had seen the little cockrel strutting about Pearl Street.'"

Amelia E. Barr

"That was not a proper thing to say. Lieutenant Hyde carries himself in the most distinguished manner."

"Well, then, that is exactly so; but Aunt Angelica has her own way of saying things. She intended nothing unkind or disrespectful. She told me that she had frequently danced with his father when she was a girl and a beauty; and she added with a laugh, 'I can assure you, Arenta, that in those days he was no saint; although he is now, I hear, the very pink of propriety.'"

"Is not that as it should be, Arenta? We ought surely to grow better as we grow older."

"That is not to be denied, Cornelia. Now I can tell you something worth hearing about General Hyde."

"If it is anything wrong, or unkind, I will not listen to it, Arenta. Have you forgotten that the good Sisters always forbid us to listen to an evil report?"

"Then one must shut one's ears if one lives in New York. But, indeed, it is nothing wrong—only something romantic and delightful, and quite as good as a story book. Shall I tell you?"

"As you wish."

"As you wish."

"Then I would like to hear it."

"Listen! When Madame Hyde was Katherine Van Heemskirk, and younger than you are, she had two lovers; one, Captain Dick Hyde, and the other a young man called Neil Semple; and they fought a duel about her, and nearly cut each other to pieces."

"Arenta!"

"Oh, it is the truth! It is the very truth, I assure you! And while Hyde still lay between life and death, Miss Van Heemskirk married him; and as soon as he was able, he carried her off at midnight to England; and there they lived in a fine old house until the war. Then they came back to New York, and Hyde went into the Continental army and did great things, I suppose, for as we all knew, he was made a general. You should have heard Aunt Angelica tell the story. She remembered the whole affair. It was a delightful story to listen to, as we drank our chocolate. And will you please only try to imagine it of Mrs. General Hyde! A woman so lofty! So calm! So afar off from every impropriety that you always feel it impossible in her presence to commit the least bit of innocent folly. Will you imagine her as Katherine Van Heemskirk in a short, quilted petticoat, with her hair hanging in two braids down her back, running away at midnight with General Hyde!"

"He was her husband. She committed no fault."

"I was thinking of the quilted petticoat, and the two braids; for who now dresses so extravagantly and so magnificently as Madame Hyde? She has an Indian shawl that cost two hundred pounds. Aunt Angelica says John Embree told her 'THAT much at the very least'—and as for the General! is there any man in New York so proud, and so full of dignity—and morality? He is in St. Paul's Chapel every Sunday, and when you see him there, how could you imagine that he had fought half-a-dozen duels, for half-a-dozen beauties?"

"Half-a-dozen duels! Oh, Arenta!"

Amelia E. Barr

"About that number—more or less—before and after the Van Heemskirk incident. Look at him next Sunday, and then try and believe that he was the topmost leader in all the fashionable follies, until he went to the war. People say it is General Washington—"

"General Washington?"

"That has changed him so much. They have been a great deal together, and I do believe the proprieties are catching. If evil is to be taken in bad company, why not good in the presence of all that is moral and respectable? At any rate, who is now more proper than General Hyde? Indeed, as Aunt Angelica says, we must all pay our respects to the Hydes, if we desire our own caps to set straight. Cornelia, shall I tell you why you are working so close to the window this afternoon?"

"You are going to say something I would rather not hear, Arenta."

"Truth is wholesome, if not agreeable; and the truth is, you expect Lieutenant Hyde to pass. But he will not do so. I saw him booted and spurred, on a swift horse, going up the river road. He was bound for Hyde Manor, I am sure. Now, Cornelia, you need not move your frame; for no one will disturb you, and I wish to tell you some of my affairs."

"About your lovers?"

"Yes. I have met a certain French marquis, who is attached to the Count de Moustier's embassy. I met him at intervals all last winter, and to-day, I have a love letter from him—a real love letter—and he desires to ask my father for my hand. I shall now have something to say to Madame Kippon."

"But you would not marry a Frenchman? That is an

impossible thought, Arenta."

"No more so than an Englishman. In fact, Englishmen are not to be thought of at all; while Frenchmen are the fashion. Just consider the drawing-rooms of our great American ladies; they are full of French nobles."

"But they are exiles, for the most part very poor, and devoted to the idea of monarchy."

"Ah, but my Frenchman is different. He is rich, he is in the confidence of the present French government, and he adores republican principles. Indeed he wore at Lady Griffin's, last week, his red cap of Liberty, and looked quite distinguished in it."

"I am astonished that Lady Griffin permitted such a spectacle. I am sure it was a vulgar thing to do. Only the san-culottes, make such exhibition of their private feelings."

"I think it was a very brave thing to do—and Lady Griffin, with her English prejudices and aristocratic notions, had to tolerate it. He is very tall and dark, and he was dressed in scarlet, with a long black satin vest; and you may believe that the scarlet cap on his black curling hair was very imposing."

"Imposing! How could it possibly be that? It is only associated with mobs, and mob law—and guillotining."

"I shall not contradict you—though I could do so easily. I will say, then, that it was very picturesque. He asked me to dance a minuet with him, and when I did not refuse he was beside himself with pleasure and gratitude. And after I had opened the way, several of the best ladies in the town followed. After all, it was a matter of political opinion; and it is against our American ideas to send any man to Jersey for his politics. Mr. Jefferson was in red also."

"I wish to dance with Mr. Jefferson, but I now think of waiting till he gets a new suit."

"I am sure that no one ever made a finer figure in a dance than I, in my white satin and pearls, and the Marquis Athanase de Tounnerre in his scarlet dress and Liberty cap. Every one regarded us. He tells me, to-day, that the emotion I raised in his soul that hour has not been stilled for a moment."

"Have you thought of your father? He would never consent to such a marriage—and what will Rem say?"

"My father will storm, and speak words he should not speak; but I am not afraid of words. Rem is more to be dreaded. He will not talk his anger away. Yes, I should be afraid of Rem."

"But you have not really decided to accept the Marquis Tounnerre?"

"No. I have not quite decided. I like to stand between Yes and No. I like to be entreated to marry, and then again, to be entreated NOT to marry. I like to hesitate between the French and the Dutch. I am not in the least sure on which side I shall finally range myself."

"Then do not decide in a hurry."

"Have I not told you I like to waver, and vacillate, and oscillate, and make scruples? These are things a woman can do, both with privilege and inclination. I think myself to be very clever in such ways."

"I would not care, nor dare, to venture—"

"You are a very baby yet. I am two years older than you. But indeed you are progressing with some rapidity. What about George Hyde?"

"You said he had gone out of town."

"And I am glad of it. He will not now be insinuating himself with violets, and compelling you to take walks with him on the Battery. Oh, Cornelia! you see I am not to be put out of your confidence. Why did you not tell me?"

"You have given me no opportunity; and, as you know all, why should I say any more about it?"

"Cornelia, my dear companion, I fear you are inclined to concealment and to reticence, qualities a young girl should not cultivate—I am now speaking for dear Sister Maria Beroth— and I hope you will carefully consider the advantages you will derive from cultivating a more open disposition."

"You are making a mockery of the good Sisters; and I do not wish to hear you commit such a great fault. Indeed, I would be pleased to return to their peaceful care again."

"And wear the little linen cap and collar, and all the other simplicities? Cornelia! Cornelia! You are as fond as I am of French fashions and fripperies. Let us be honest, if we die for it. And you may as well tell me all your little coquetries with George Hyde; for I shall be sure to find them out. Now I am going home; for I must look after the tea-table. But you will not be sorry, for it will leave you free to think of—"

"Please, Arenta!"

Amelia E. Barr

"Very well. I will have 'considerations.' Good-bye!"

Then the door closed, and Cornelia was left alone. But the atmosphere of the room was charged with Arenta's unrest, and a feeling of disappointment was added to it. She suddenly realized that her lover's absence from the city left a great vacancy. What were all the thousands in its streets, if he was not there? She might now indeed remove her frame from the window; if Hyde was an impossibility, there was no one else she wished to see pass. And her heart told her the report was a true one; she did not doubt for a moment Arenta's supposition, that he had gone to Hyde Manor. But the thought made her lonely. Something, she knew not what, had altered her life. She had a new strange happiness, new hopes, new fears and new wishes; but they were not an unmixed delight; for she was also aware of a vague trouble, a want that nothing in her usual duties satisfied:—in a word, she had crossed the threshold of womanhood and was no longer a girl,

"Singing alone in the morning of life,
In the happy morning of life, and May."

CHAPTER IV

THROWING THINGS INTO CONFUSION

Prudence declares that whenever a person is in that disagreeable situation which compels him to ask "what shall I do?" that the wisest answer is, "nothing." But such answer did not satisfy George Hyde. He was too young, too sure of his own good fortune, too restless and impulsive, to accept Prudence as a councillor. He might have considered, that, hitherto, affairs had happened precisely as he wished them; and that it would be good policy to trust to his future opportunities. But he was so much in earnest, so honestly in love, that he felt his doubts and anxieties could only be relieved by action. Sympathy, at least, he must have; and he knew no man, to whom he would willingly talk of Cornelia. The little jests and innuendoes sure to follow his confidence would be intolerable if associated with a creature so pure and so ingenuous.

"I will go to my mother!" he thought. And this resolution satisfied him so well, that he carried it out at once. But it was after dark when he reached the tall stone portals of Hyde Manor House. The ride, however, had given him back his best self. For when we leave society and come into the presence of Nature, we become children again; and the fictions of thought and action assumed among men drop off

Amelia E. Barr

like a garment. The beauty of the pale green hills, and the flowing river, and the budding trees, and the melody of birds singing as if they never would grow old, were all but charming accessories and horizons to his constant pictures of Cornelia. It was she who gave life and beauty to all he saw; for as a rule, if men notice nature at all, it is ever through some painted window of their own souls. Few indeed are those who hear—

"The Ancient Word,
That walked among the silent trees."

Yet Hyde was keenly conscious of some mystical sympathy between himself and the lovely scenes through which he passed—conscious still more of it when the sun had set and the moon rose—dim and inscrutable—over the lonely way, and filled the narrow glen which was at the entrance to the Manor House full of brooding power.

The great building loomed up dark and silent; there was but one light visible. It was in his mother's usual sitting-room, and as soon as he saw it, he began to whistle. She heard him afar off, and was at the door to give him a welcome.

"Joris, my dear one, we were talking of you!" she cried, as he leaped from the saddle to her arms. "So glad are we! Come in quickly! Such a good surprise! It is our hearts' wish granted! Well, are you? Quite well? Now, then, I am happy. Happy as can be! Look now, Richard!" she called, as she flung the door open, and entered with the handsome, smiling youth at her side.

In his way the father was just as much pleased. He pushed some papers he had been busy with impatiently aside, and stood up with outstretched hand to meet his son.

"Kate, my dear heart," he cried, "let us have something to eat. The boy will be hungry as a hunter after his ride. And George, what brings you home? We were just telling each other—your mother and I—that you were in the height of the city's follies."

"Indeed, sir, there will be few follies for some days. Mr. Franklin is dead, and the city goes into mourning."

"'Tis a fate that all must meet," said the General; "but death and Franklin would look each other in the face as friends— He had a work to do, he did it well, and it is finished. That is all. What other news do you bring?"

"It is said that Mirabeau is arrested somewhere, for something. I did not hear the particulars."

"Probably, for the very least of his crimes. Marat hates him; and Marat represents the fury of the Revolution. The monster wished to erect eight hundred gibbets, and hang Mirabeau first."

"And the deputies are returning to the Provinces, drunk with their own importance. They have abolished titles, and coats of arms, and liveries; and published a list of the names the nobles are to assume—as if people did not know their own names. Mr. Hamilton says 'Revolution in France has gone raving mad, and converted twenty-four millions of people into savages.'"

"I hate the French!" said the General passionately. "It is a natural instinct with me, just as tame animals are born with an antipathy to wild beasts. If I thought I had one drop of French blood in me, I would let it out with a dagger."

George winced a little. He remembered that the Morans were

of French extraction; and he answered—

"After all, father, we must judge people individually. Mere race is not much."

"George Hyde! What are you saying? RACE is everything. It is the strongest and deepest of all human feelings. Nothing conquers its prejudices."

"Except love. I have heard, father, that Love never asks 'of what race art thou?' or even 'whose son, or daughter, art thou?'"

"You have heard many foolish things, George; that is one of them. Men and women marry out of their own nationality, AT THEIR PERIL. I took my life in my hand for your mother's love."

"She was worthy of the peril."

"God knows it."

At this moment Mrs. Hyde entered the room, her fair face alight with love. A servant carrying a tray full of good things to eat, followed her; and it was delightful to watch her eager happiness as she arranged meats, and sweetmeats, in tempting order for the hungry young man. He thoroughly enjoyed this provision for his comfort; and as he ate, he talked to his father of those things interesting to him, answering all questions with that complaisant positiveness of youth which decides everything at once, and without reservation. No one understood this better than General Hyde, but it pleased him to draw out his son's opinions; and it also pleased him to watch the pride of the fond mother, who evidently considered her boy a paragon of youthful judgment.

"And pray," he asked, "what can you tell me about the seat of government? Will New York be chosen?"

"I am sure it will be Philadelphia; and, indeed, I care not. It would, however, amuse you to hear some of the opinions on the matter; for every one hangs his judgment on the peg of his own little interests or likings. Young De Witt says New York wants no government departments; that she is far too busy a city, to endure government idlers hanging around her best streets. Doctor Rush says the government is making our city a sink of political vice. Mr. Wolcott says honesty is the fashion in New York. Some of the clergy think Wall Street as wicked as the most fashionable streets in Tyre and Sodom; and the street-singers—thanks to Mr. Freneau—have each, and all, their little audiences on the subject. As I came up Broadway, a man was shouting a rhyme advising the Philadelphians to 'get ready their dishcloths and brooms, and begin scouring their knockers, and scrubbing their rooms.' Perhaps the most sensible thing on the subject came from one of the New England senators. He thought the seat of government ought to be 'in some wilderness, where there would be no social attractions, where members could go and attend strictly to business.' Upon my word, sir, the opinions are endless in number and variety; but, in truth, Mr. Hamilton and Mr. Morris are arranging the matter. This is without doubt. There is to be some sort of compromise with the Southern senators, who are promised the capital on the Potomac, finally, if they no longer oppose the assumption of the State debts. I hear that Mr. Jefferson has been brought to agree to this understanding. And Mr. Morris doubtless thinks, if the government offices are once opened in Philadelphia, they will remain there."

"And Joris, the ladies? What say they on the subject?" asked Mrs. Hyde.

"Indeed, mother, some of them are lamenting, and some looking forward to the change. All are talking of the social deposition of the beautiful Mrs. Bingham. 'She will have to abate herself a little before Mrs. Washington,' I heard one lady say; while others declare, that her association with our Republican Court will be harmonious and advantageous; especially, as she is beloved in the home of the President."

"OUR REPUBLICAN COURT! The definition is absurd!" said General Hyde, with both scorn and temper. "A court pre-supposes both royalty and nobility!"

"We have both of them intrinsically, father."

"In faith, George! you will find, that intrinsic qualities have no social value. What people require is their external evidence."

"And their external evidence would be extremely offensive here, sir. For my part, I think, the sneaking hankering after titles and ceremonies, among our wealthy men and women is a very great weakness. Every one knows that nothing would please fussy Mr. Adams better than to be a duke, or even a lord—and he is by no means alone in such desires."

"They may be yet realized."

"They will not, sir—not, at least, while Thomas Jefferson lives. He is the bulldog of Democracy, and he would be at the throat of any such pretences as soon as they were suggested."

"Very well, George! I have no objections."

"I knew, sir, that you were a thorough Democrat."

"Do not go too far, George. I love Democracy; but I hate Democrats! Now I am sleepy, and as Mr. Jefferson is on the watch, I may go to sleep comfortably. I will talk to you more on these subjects in the morning. Good-night!" He put his hand on his son's shoulder, and looked with a proud confidence into the bright face, lifted to the touch.

Then George was alone with his mother; but she was full of little household affairs; and he could not bring into them a subject so close, and so sacred to his heart. He listened a little wearily to her plans, and was glad when she recollected the late hour and hurried him away to his chamber—a large, lofty room in the front of the house, on which she had realized all the ideas that her great love, and her really exquisite taste suggested. He entered it with a sense of delight, and readily surrendered himself to its dreamy air of sleep and rest. "I will speak to my mother in the morning," he thought. "To-night, her mind is full of other things."

But in the morning Mrs. Hyde was still more interested in "other things." She had an architect with her, her servants were to order, her house to look after; and George readily felt that his hour was certainly not in the early morning. He had slept a little late, and his mother did not approve of sleep beyond the normal hour. He saw that he had delayed household matters, and made an environment not quite harmonious. So he ate his breakfast rapidly, and went out to the new stables. He expected to find the General there, and he was not disappointed. He had, however, finished his inspection of the horses, and he proposed a walk to the upper end of the Glen, where a great pond was being dug for Mrs. Hyde's swans, and other aquatic birds.

There was much to interest them as they walked: men were busy draining, and building stone walls; ploughing and sowing, and digging, and planting. Yet, in the midst of all this busy life, George detected in his father's manner an air of melancholy. He looked into his son's face with affection, and pointed out to him with an apparent interest, the improvements in progress, but George knew—though he could not have explained why he knew—that his father's heart was not really in these things. Presently he asked, "How goes it with your law books, George?"

"Faith, sir, I must confess, very indifferently. I have no senses that way; and 'tis only your desire that keeps my books open. I would far rather read my Plutarch, or write with my sword."

"Let me tell you, soberly, that it is a matter of personal interest to you. There is now no question of the law as a profession, for since your cousin's death your prospects have entirely changed. But consider, George, that not only this estate, but also the estate of your Grandfather Van Heemskirk must eventually come to you. Much of both has been bought from confiscated properties, and it is not improbable that claimants may arise who will cause you trouble. How necessary, then, that you should know something of the laws affecting land and property in this country."

"My grandfather is in trouble. I forgot to tell you last night, that his friend, Elder Semple, is dead."

"Dead!"

"Yes, sir."

For a few minutes General Hyde remained silent; then he said with much feeling, "Peace to the old Tory! He was once very kind to me and to my family. Ah, George, I have again defrauded myself of a satisfaction! For a long time I have intended to go and see him—it is now too late! But I will return to the city with you and pay him the last respect possible. Who told you this news?"

"I was walking on Broadway with young McAllister, and Doctor Moran stopped us and sent word to Elder McAllister of the death of his friend. I think, indeed, they were relatives,"

"Was Doctor Moran his physician?"

"Yes, sir. A very good physician, I believe; I know, that he is a very courteous and entertaining gentleman."

"And pray, George, how do you come by such an opinion?"

"I had the honour of spending an evening at Doctor Moran's house this week; and if you will believe me, sir, he has a daughter that shames every other beauty. Such bewildering loveliness! Such entrancing freshness and purity I never saw before!"

"In love again, George. Faith, you make me ashamed of my own youth! But this enchanting creature cannot make of her father—anything but what he is."

"This time I am desperately, and really, in love."

"So you were with Mollie Trefuses, with Sarah Talbot, with Eliza Capel, with Matilda Howard—and a galaxy of minor beauties."

"But it has come to this—I wish to marry Miss Moran; and I never wished to marry any other woman."

"You have forgotten—And by Heaven! you must forget Miss Moran. She is not to be thought of as a wife—for one moment."

"Sir, you are not so unjust as to make such a statement without giving me a reason for it."

"Giving you a reason! My reason ought to have sprung up voluntary in your own heart. It is an incredible thing if you are not already familiar with it."

"Simply, sir, I profess my ignorance."

"Look around you. Look east, and west, and north, and south,—all these rich lands were bought with your Uncle William's money. He made himself poor, to make me rich; because, having brought me up as his heir, he thought his marriage late in life had in a manner defrauded me. You know that the death of his two sons has again made me the heir to the Hyde earldom; and that after me, the succession is yours. Tell me now what child is left to your uncle?"

"Only his daughter Annie, a girl of fourteen or fifteen years."

"What will become of her when her father dies?"

"Sir, how can I divine her future?"

"It is your duty to divine her future. Her father has no gold to leave her—he gave it to me—and the land he cannot leave her; yet she has a natural right, beyond either mine or yours."

"I give her my right, cheerfully."

"You cannot give it to her—unless you outlaw yourself from your native country—strip yourself of your citizenship—declare yourself unworthy to be a son of the land that gave you birth. Even if you perpetrated such a civil crime, you would render no service to Annie. Your right would simply lapse to the son of Herbert Hyde—the young man you met at Oxford—"

"Surely, sir, we need not talk of that fellow. I have already told you what a very sycophant he is. He licks the dust before any man of wealth or authority; his tongue hangs down to his shoe-buckles."

"Well then, sir, what is your duty to Annie Hyde?"

"I do not conceive myself to have any special duty to Annie Hyde."

"Upon my honour, you are then perversely stupid! But it is impossible that you do not realize what justice, honour, gratitude and generosity demand from you! When your uncle wrote me that pitiful letter which informed me of the death of his last son, my first thought was that his daughter must be assured her right in the succession. There is one way to compass this. You know what that way is.—Why do you not speak?"

"Because, sir, if I confess your evident opinion to be just, I bind myself to carry it out, because of its justice."

"Is it not just?"

"It might be just to Annie and very unjust to me."

"No, sir. Justice is a thing absolute; it is not altered by circumstances, especially for a circumstance so trivial as a young man's idle fancy."

"'Tis no idle fancy. I love Cornelia Moran."

"You have already loved a score of beauties—and forgotten them."

"I have admired, and forgot. If I had loved, I should not have forgotten. Now, I love."

"Then, sir, be a man, a noble man, and put your personal gratification below justice, honour, and gratitude. This is the first real trial of your life, George, are you going to play the coward in it?"

"If you could only see Miss Moran!"

"I should find it difficult to be civil to her. George, I put before you a duty that no gentleman can by any possibility evade."

"If this arrangement is so important, why was I not told of it, ere this?"

"It is scarcely a year since your Cousin Harry's death. Annie is not fifteen years old. I did not wish to force matters. I intended you to go to England next year, and I hoped that a marriage might come without my advice or my interference. It seemed to me that Annie's position would itself open your heart to her."

"I have no heart to give her."

"Then you must at least give her your hand. I myself proposed this arrangement, and your uncle's pleasure and gratitude were of the most touching kind. Further, if you will have the very truth, then know, that under no circumstances, will I sanction a marriage with Doctor Moran's daughter."

"You cannot possibly object to her, sir. She is perfection itself."

"I object to her in-toto. I detest Doctor Moran, personally. I know not why, nor care wherefore. I detest him still more sincerely as a man of French extraction. I was brought very much in contact with him for three years, and if we had not been in camp, and under arms, I would have challenged him a score of times. He is the most offensive of men. He brought his race prejudices continually to the front. When Lafayette was wounded, with some of his bragging company, nothing would do but Doctor Moran must go with them to the hospital at Bethlehem; yes, and stay there, until the precious marquis was out of danger. I'll swear that he would not have done this for Washington—he would have blustered about the poor fellows lying sick in camp. Moran talks about being an American, and the Frenchman crops out at every corner. But HE is neither here, nor there, in our affairs; what I wish you to remember is, that rank has its duties as well as its privileges; and you would be a poltroon to accept one and ignore the other. What are you going to do?"

"I know not. I must think—"

"I am ashamed of you! In the name of all that is honourable, what is there to think about? Have you told this Miss Moran that you love her?"

"Not in precise words. I have only seen her three or four times."

"Then, sir, you have only YOURSELF to think about. Have I a son with so little proper feeling that he needs to think a moment when the case is between honour and himself? George, it is high time that you set out to travel. In the neighbourhood of your mother, and your grandparents, and your flatterers in the city, you never get beyond the atmosphere of your own whims and fancies. This conversation has come sooner than I wished; but after it, there is nothing worth talking about."

"Sir, you are more cruel and unreasonable than I could believe possible."

"The railings of a losing lover are not worth answering. Give your anger sway, and when you are reasonable again, tell me. A man mad in love has some title to my pity."

"And, sir, if you were any other man but my father, I would say 'Confound your pity!' I am not sensible of deserving it, except as the result of your own unreasonable demands on me—Our conversation is extremely unpleasant, and I desire to put an end to it. Permit me to return to the house."

"With all my heart. But let me advise you to say nothing to your mother, at present, on this subject:" then with an air of dejection he added—"What is past, must go; and whatever is to come is very sure to happen."

"Sir, nothing past, present, or future, can change me. I shall obey the wishes of my heart, and be true to its love."

"Let me tell you, George, that Love is now grown wise. He follows Fortune."

"Good-morning, sir."

"Let it be so. I will see you to-morrow in town. Ten to one, you will be more reasonable then."

He stood in the centre of the roadway watching his son's angry carriage. The poise of his head, and his rapid, uneven steps, were symptoms the anxious father understood very well. "He is in a naked temper, without even civil disguise," he muttered; "and I hope his own company will satisfy him until the first fever is past. Do I not know that to be in love is to be possessed? It is in the head—the heart—the blood—it is indeed an uncontrollable fever! I hope, first and foremost, that he will keep away from his mother in his present unreason."

His mother was, however, George's first desire. He did not believe she would sanction his sacrifice to Annie Hyde. Justice, honour, gratitude! these were fine names of his father's invention to adorn a ceremony which would celebrate his life-long misery, and he rebelled against such an immolation of his youth and happiness. When he reached the house, he found that his mother had gone to the pond to feed her swans; and he decided to ride a little out of his way in order to see her there. Presently he came to a spot where tall, shadowing pines surrounded a large sheet of water, dipping their lowest branches into it. Mrs. Hyde stood among them, and the white, stately birds were crowding to her very feet. He reined in his horse to watch her, and though accustomed to her beauty, he marvelled again at it. Like a sylvan goddess she stood, divinely tall, and divinely fair; her whole presence suffused with a heavenly serenity and happiness! Upon the soft earth the hoofs of his horse had not been audible, but when he came within her sight, it was wonderful to watch the transformation on her countenance. A great love, a great joy, swept away like a gust of wind, the peace on its surface; and a glowing, loving intelligence made her instantly restless. She called him with sweet imperious-ness, "George! Joris! Joris! My dear one!" and he answered her with the one word ever near, and ever dear, to a woman's heart—"MOTHER!"

"I thought you were with your father. Where have you left him?"

"In the wilderness. There is need for me to go to the city. My father will tell you WHY. I come only to see you—to kiss you—"

"Joris, I see that you are angry. Well then, my dear one, what is it? What has your father been saying to you?"

"He will tell you."

"SO! Whatever it is, your part I shall take. Right or wrong, your part I shall take."

"There is nothing wrong, dear mother."

"Money, is it?"

"It is not money. My father is generous to me."

"Then, some woman it is?"

"Kiss me, mother. After all, there is no woman like unto you."

She drew close to him, and he stooped his handsome face to hers, and kissed her many times. Her smile comforted him, for it was full of confidence, as she said—

"Trouble not yourself, Joris. At the last, your father sees through my eyes. Must you go? Well then, the Best of Beings go with you!"

"When are you coming to town, mother?"

"Next week. There is a dinner party at the President's, and your father will not be absent—nor I—nor you?"

"If I am invited, I shall go, just that I may see you enter the room. Let me tell you, that sight always fills my heart with a tumultuous pride and love."

"A great flatterer are you, Joris!" but she lifted her face again, and George kissed it, and then rode rapidly away.

He hardly drew rein until he reached his grandfather's house, a handsome Dutch residence, built of yellow brick, and standing in a garden that was, at this season, a glory of tulips and daffodils, hyacinths and narcissus—the splendid colouring of the beds being wonderfully increased by their borderings of clipped box. An air of sunshiny peace was over the place, and as the upper-half of the side-door stood open he tied his horse and went in. The ticking of the tall house-clock was the only sound he heard at first, but as he stood irresolute, a sweet, thin voice in an adjoining room began to sing a hymn.

"Grandmother! Grandmother!! Grandmother!!!" he called, and before the last appeal was echoed the old lady appeared. She came forward rapidly, her knitting in her hand. She was singularly bright and alert, with rosy cheeks, and snow-white hair under a snow-white cap of clear-starched lace. A snow-white kerchief of lawn was crossed over her breast, and the rest of her dress was so perfectly Dutch that she might have stepped out of one of Tenier's pictures.

"Oh, my Joris!" she cried, "Joris! Joris! I am so happy to see thee. But what, then, is the matter? Thy eyes are full of trouble."

"I will tell you, grandmother." And he sat down by her side and went over the conversation he had had with his father. She never interrupted him, but he knew by the rapid clicking of her knitting needles that she was moved far beyond her usual quietude. When he ceased speaking, she answered—

"To sell thee, Joris, is a great shame, and for nothing to sell thee is still worse. This is what I think: Let half of the income from the earldom go to the poor young lady, but THYSELF into the bargain, is beyond all reason. And if with Cornelia Moran thou art in love, a good thing it is;—so I say."

"Do you know Cornelia, grandmother?"

"Well, then, I have seen her; more than once. A great beauty I think her; and Doctor John has Money—plenty of money— and a very good family are the Morans. I remember his father—a very fine gentleman."

"But my father hates Doctor Moran."

"Very wicked is he to hate any one. Why, then?"

"He gave me only one reason—that his family is French."

"SO! Thy mother was Dutch. Every one cannot be English— a God's mercy they cannot! Now, then, thy grandfather is coming; thy trouble tell to him. Good advice he will give thee."

Senator Van Heemskirk however went first into his garden and gathering great handfuls of white narcissus and golden daffodils, he called a slave woman and bade her carry them to the Semple house, and lay them in, and around, his friend's coffin. One white lily he kept in his hand as he came towards his wife and grandson, with eyes fixed on its beauty.

"Lysbet," he said,—but he clasped George's hand as he spoke—"My Lysbet, if in the Dead Valley of this earth grow such heavenly flowers as this, we will not fear the grave. It is only to sleep on the breast that gives us the lily and the rose, and the wheat, and the corn. Oh, how sweet is this flower! It has the scent of Paradise."

He laid it gently down while he put off his fine broadcloth coat and lace ruffles and assumed the long vest and silk skull cap, which was his home dress; then he put it in a buttonhole of his vest, and seemed to joy himself in its delicate fragrance. With these preliminaries neither Joris nor Lysbet interfered; but when he had lit his long pipe and seated himself comfortably in his chair, Lysbet said—

"Where hast thou been all this afternoon?"

"I have been sealing up my friend's desk and drawers until his sons arrive. Very happy he looks. He is now ONE OF THOSE THAT KNOW."

"Well, then, after the long strife, 'He Rests.'"

"Men have written it. What know they about it? Rest would not be heaven to my friend Alexander Semple. To work, to be up and doing His Will, that would be his delight."

"I wonder, Joris, if in the next life we shall know each other?"

"My Lysbet, in this life do we know each other?"

"I think not. Here has come our dear Joris full of trouble to thee, for his father has said such things as I could not have believed. Joris, tell thy grandfather what they are."

And this time George, being very sure of hearty sympathy, told his tale with great feeling—perhaps even with a little anger. His grandfather listened patiently to the youth's impatience, but he did not answer exactly to his expectations.

"My Joris," he said, "so hard it is to accept what goes against our wishes. If Cornelia Moran you had not met, would your father's desires be so impossible to you? Noble and generous would they not seem—"

"But I have seen Cornelia, and I love her."

"Two or three times you have seen her. How can you be sure that you love her?"

"In the first hour I was sure."

"Of nothing are we quite sure. In too great a hurry are you. Miss Moran may not love you. She may refuse ever to love you. Her mind you have not asked. Beside this, in his family her father may not wish you. A very proud man is Doctor John."

"Grandfather, I may be an earl some day."

"An English earl. Doctor John may not endure to think of his only child living in that far-off country. I, myself, know how this thought can work a father to madness. And, again, your Cousin Annie may not wish to marry you."

"Faith, sir, I had not thought of myself as so very disagreeable."

"No. Vain and self-confident is a young man. See, then, how many things may work this way, that way, and if wise you are you will be quiet and wait for events. One thing, move not in your anger; it is like putting to sea in a tempest. Now I shall just say a word or two on the other side. If your father is so set in his mind about the Hydes, let him do the justice to them he wishes to do; but it is not right that he should make YOU do it for him."

"He says that only I can give Annie justice."

"But that is not good sense. When the present Earl dies, and she is left an orphan, who shall prevent your father from adopting her as his own daughter, and leaving her a daughter's portion of the estate? In such case, she would be in exactly the same position as if her brother had lived and become earl. Is not that so?"

"My dear, dear grandfather, you carry wisdom with you! Now I shall have the pleasure to propose to my father that he do his own justice! O wise, wise grandfather! You have made me happy to a degree!"

"Very well, but say not that *I* gave you such counsel. When your father speaks to me, as he is certain to do, then I will say such and such words to him; but my words in your mouth will be a great offence; and very justly so, for it is hard to carry words, and carry nothing else. Your dear mother—how is she?"

"Well and happy. She builds, and she plants, and the days are too short for her. But my father is not so happy. I can see that he is wearied of everything."

"Not here, is his heart. It is in England. And no longer has he great hopes to keep him young. If of Liberty I now speak to him, he has a smile so hopeless that both sad and angry it makes me. No faith has he left in any man, except Washington; and I think, also, he is disappointed that Washington was not crowned King George the First."

"I can assure you, sir, that others share his disappointment. Mr. Adams would not object to be Duke of New York, and even little Burr would like a lordship."

"I have heard; my ears are not dull, nor my eyes blind. But too much out of the world lives your father; men who do so grow unfit to live in the world. He dreams dreams impossible to us—impossible to France—and then he says 'Liberty is a dream.' Well, well, Life also is a dream—when we awake—"

Then he ceased speaking, and there was silence until Lysbet Van Heemskirk said, softly, "When we awake, WE SHALL BE SATISFIED."

Van Heernskirk smiled at his wife's cheerful assurance, and continued, "It is true, Lysbet, what you say; and even here, in our dreaming, what satisfaction! As for me, I expect not too much. The old order and the new order fight yet for the victory; and what passes now will be worth talking about fifty years hence."

"It is said, grandfather, that the Dutch church is anti-Federal to a man."

"Not true are such sayings. The church will be very like old Van Steenwyck, who boasts of his impartiality, and who votes for the Federals once, and for the anti-Federals once, and the third time does not vote at all. If taken was the vote of the Church, it would be six for the Federals and half-a-dozen for the anti-Federals."

"Mr. Burr—"

"Of Mr. Burr I will not talk. I like not his little dirty politics."

"He is very clever."

"Well, then, you have to praise him for being clever; for being honest you cannot praise him."

"'Tis a monstrous pity that Right can only be on one side; yet sometimes Right and Mr. Burr may happen to be on the same side."

"The right way is too straight for Aaron Burr. If into it he wanders 'tis for a wrong reason."

"My dear grandfather, how your words bite!"

"I wish not to say biting things; but Aaron Burr stands for those politicians who turn patriotism into shopkeeping and their own interest—men who care far more for WHO governs us than for HOW we are governed. And what will be the end of such ways? I will tell you. We shall have a Democracy that will be the reign of those who know the least and talk the loudest."

At this point in the conversation Van Heemskirk was called to the door about some business matter and George was left alone with his grandmother. She was setting the tea-table, and her hands were full of china; but she put the cups quickly down, and going to George's side, said—

"Cornelia Moran spends this evening with her friend Arenta Van Ariens. Well then, would thou like an excuse to call on Arenta?"

"Oh, grandmother! Do you indeed know Arenta? Can you send me there?"

"Since she was one month old I have known Arenta. This morning, she came here to borrow for her Aunt Jacobus my ivory winders. Now then, I did not wish to lend Angelica Jacobus my winders; and I said to Arenta that 'by and by I would look for them.' Not far are they to seek; and for thy pleasure I will get them, and thou canst take them this evening to Arenta."

"O you dear, dear grandmother!" and he stood up, and lifted her rosy face between his hands and kissed her.

"I am so fond of thee," she continued. "I love thee so much; and thy pleasure is my pleasure; and I see no harm—no harm at all—in thy love for the beautiful Cornelia. I think, with thee, she is a girl worth any man's heart; and if thou canst win her, I, for one, will be joyful with thee. Perhaps, though, I am a selfish old woman—it is so easy to be selfish."

"Let me tell you, grandmother, you know not how to be selfish."

"Let me tell thee, Joris, I was thinking of myself, as well as of thee. For while thy grandfather talked of Aaron Burr, this thought came into my mind—if to Annie Hyde my Joris is married, he will live in England, and I shall see him no more in this world. But if to Cornelia Moran he is married, when his father goes to England, then here he will stay; he will live at Hyde Manor, and I shall go to see him, and he will call here to see me;—and then, many good days came into my thoughts. Yes, yes, in every kind thing, in every good thing, somewhere there is hid a little bit of our own will and way. Always, if I look with straight eyes, I can find it." "Get me the winders, grandmother; for now you have given me a reason to hurry."

"But why so quickly must you go?"

"Look at me! It will take me two hours to dress. I have had no dinner—I want to think—you understand, grandmother?"

Then she went into the best parlour, and opening one of the shutters let in sufficient light to find in the drawer of a little

Chinese cabinet some ivory winders of very curious design and workmanship. She folded them in soft tissue paper and handed them to her grandson with a pleasant nod; and the young man slipped them into his waistcoat pocket, and then went hurriedly away.

He had spoken of his dinner, but though somewhat hungry, he made but a light meal. His dress seemed to him the most vitally important thing of the hour; and no girl choosing her first ball gown could have felt more anxious and critical on the subject. His call was to be considered an accidental one; and he could not therefore dress as splendidly as if it were a ceremonious or expected visit. After much hesitation, he selected a coat and breeches of black velvet, a pearl-coloured vest, and cravat and ruffles of fine English bone lace. Yet when his toilet was completed, he was dissatisfied. He felt sure more splendid apparel set off his dark beauty to greater advantage; and yet he was equally sure that more splendid apparel would not—on this occasion—be as suitable.

Doubting and hoping, he reached the Van Ariens' house soon after seven o'clock. It was not quite dark, and Jacob Van Ariens stood on the stoop, smoking his pipe and talking to a man who had the appearance of a workman; and who was, in fact, the foreman of his business quarters in the Swamp.

"Good-evening, sir," said George with smiling politeness. "Is Miss Van Ariens within?"

"Within? Yes. But company she has tonight," said the watchful father, as he stood suspicious and immovable in the entrance.

It did not seem to George as if it would be an easy thing to pass such a porter at the door, but he continued,

"I have come with a message to Miss Van Ariens."

"A very fine messenger!" answered Van Ariens, slightly smiling.

"A fine lady deserves a fine messenger. But, sir, if you will do my errand for me, I am content. 'Tis from Madame Van Heemskirk—"

"SO then? That is good."

"I am George Hyde, her grandson, you know."

"Well then, I did not know. 'Tis near dark, and I see not as well as once I did."

"I have brought from Madame Van Heemskirk some ivory winders for Madame Jacobus."

"Come in, come in, and tell my Arenta the message thyself. I know nothing of such things. Come in, I did not think of thee as my friend Van Heemskirk's grandson. Welcome art thou!" and Van Ariens himself opened the parlour door, saying, "Arenta, here is George Hyde. A message he brings for thy Aunt Angelica."

And while these words were being uttered, George delighted his eyes with the vision of Cornelia, who sat at a small table with some needlework in her hand. Arenta's tatting was over her foot, and she had to remove it in order to rise and meet Hyde. Rem sat idly fingering a pack of playing cards and talking to Cornelia. This situation George took in at a glance; though his sense of sight was quite satisfied when it rested on the lovely girl who dropped her needle as he entered, for he saw the bright flush which overspread her face and throat, and the light of pleasure which so filled her eyes that they seemed to make her whole face luminous.

In a few moments, Arenta's pretty enthusiasms and welcomes dissipated all constraint, and Hyde placed his chair among the happy group and fell easily into his most charming mood. Even Rem could not resist the atmosphere of gaiety and real enjoyment that soon pervaded the room. They sang, they played, they had a game at whist, and everything that happened was in some subtle, secret way, a vehicle for Hyde's love to express itself. Yet it was to Arenta he appeared to be most attentive; and Rem was good-naturedly inclined to permit his sister to be appropriated, if only he was first in the service of Cornelia.

But though Hyde's attentions were so little obvious, Cornelia was satisfied. It would have been a poor lover who could not have said under such circumstances "I love you" a hundred times over; and George Hyde was not a poor lover. He had naturally the ardent confidence and daring which delight women, and he had not passed several seasons in the highest London society without learning all those sweet, occult ways of making known admiration, which the presence of others renders both necessary and possible.

About half-past nine, a negro woman came with Cornelia's cloak and hood. George took them from Arenta's hand and folded the warm circular round Cornelia's slight figure; and then watched her tie her pretty pink hood, managing amid the pleasant stir of leave-taking to whisper some words that sang all night like sweetest music in her heart. It was Rem, however, that gave her his arm and escorted her to her own door; and with this rightful privilege to his guest young Hyde was far too gentlemanly and just to interfere. However, even in this moment of seeming secondary consideration, he heard a few words which gave him a delightful assurance of coming satisfaction. For as the two girls stood in the hall,

Arenta said—

"You will come over in the morning, Cornelia?"

"I cannot," answered Cornelia. "After breakfast, I have to go to Richmond Hill with a message from my mother to Mrs. Adams; and though father will drive me there I shall most likely have to walk home. But I will come to you in the afternoon."

"Very well. Then in the morning I will go to Aunt Angelica's with the winders. I shall then have some news to tell you in the afternoon—that is, if the town makes us any."

And George, hearing these words, could hardly control his delight. For he was one of Mrs. Adams' favourites, and so much at home in her house that he could visit her at any hour of the day without a ceremonious invitation. And it immediately struck him that his mother had often desired to know how Mrs. Adams fed her swans, and also that she had wished for some seeds from her laburnum trees. These things would make a valid excuse for an early call, as Mrs. Adams might naturally suppose he was on his way to Hyde Manor.

He took a merry leave of Arenta, and with his mind full of this plan, went directly to his rooms. The Belvedere Club was this night, impossible to him. After the angelic Cornelia, he could not take into his consciousness the hideous Marat, and the savage orgies of the French Revolution. Such a thought transference would be an impossible profanation. Indeed, he could consider no other thing, but the miraculous fact, that Cornelia was going to Mrs. Adams'; and that it was quite within his power to meet her there.

"'Tis my destiny! 'Tis my happy destiny to love her!" he said softly to himself. "Such an adorable girl! Such a ravishing beauty is not elsewhere on this earth!" And he was not conscious of any exaggeration in such language. Nor was there. He was young, he was rich, he had no business to consider, no sorrow to sober him, no care of any kind to mingle with the rapturous thoughts which his transported imagination and his captivated heart blended with the image of Cornelia.

"I shall tell Mrs. Adams how far gone in love I am," he continued. "She is herself set on that clever little husband of hers; and 'tis said, theirs was a love match, beyond all speculation. I shall say to her, 'Help me, madame, to an opportunity'; and I think she will not refuse. As for my father, I heard him this morning with as much patience as any Christian could do; but I am resolved to marry Cornelia. I will not give her up; not for an earldom! not for a dukedom! not for the crown of England!"

And to these thoughts he flung off, with a kind of passion, his coat and vest. The action was but the affirmation of his resolve, a materialization of his will. To have used an oath in connection with Cornelia would have offended him; but this passionate action asserted with equal emphasis his unalterable resolve. A tender, gallant, courageous spirit possessed him. He was carried away by the feelings it inspired: and nobly so, for alas for that man who professes to be in love and is not carried away by his feelings; in such case, he has no feelings worth speaking of!

Joris Hyde allowed the sweet emotions Cornelia had inspired to have, and to hold, and to occupy his whole being. His heart burned within him; memories of Cornelia closed his eyes, and then filled them with adorable visions of her pure, fresh loveliness; his pulses bounded; his blood ran warm and free as the ethereal ichor of the gods. Sleep was a thousand leagues away; he was so vivid, that the room felt hot; and he flung open the casement and sat in a beatitude of blissful hopes and imaginations.

And after midnight, when dreams fall, the moon came up over Nassau and Cedar Streets and threw poetic glamours over the antique churches, and grassy graveyards, and the pretty houses, covered with vines and budding rosebushes; and this soft shadow of light calmed and charmed him. In it, he could believe all his dreams possible. He leaned forward and watched the silvery disc, struggling in soft, white clouds; parting them, as with hands, when they formed in baffling, airy masses in her way. And the heavenly traveller was not silent; she had a language he understood; for as he watched the sweet, strong miracle, he said softly to himself—

"It is a sign to me! It is a sign! So will I put away every baffling hindrance between Cornelia and myself. Barriers will only be as those vaporous clouds. I shall part them with my strong resolves—I shall—I shall—I—" and he fell asleep with this sense of victory thrilling his whole being. Then the moon rose higher, and soon came in broad white bars through the window and lay on his young, handsome, smiling face, with the same sweet radiance that in the days of the gods glorified the beautiful shepherd, sleeping on the Ephesian plains.

CHAPTER V

TURNING OVER A NEW LEAF

When Hyde awakened, he was in that borderland between dreams and day which we call dawn. And as the ear is the last sense to go to sleep, and the first sense to throw off its lethargy, the voices of men calling "Milk Ho!" and the shrill childish cries of "Sweep Ho!" were the first intruders into that pleasant condition between sleeping and waking, so hard for any of us to leave without a sigh of regret. These sounds were quickly supplemented by the roll of the heavy carts which purveyed the only water suitable for drinking and culinary purposes; and by the sounds of wood-sawing and wood-chopping before the doors of the adjacent houses— sounds quickly blending themselves with the shuffling feet of the slaves cleaning the doorsteps and sidewalks, and chattering, singing, quarrelling the while with their neighbours, or with other early ministers to the city's domestic wants.

These noises had never before made any impression on him. "I am more alive than ever I was in my life," he said; and he laughed gayly, and went to the window. "It is a lovely day; and that is so much in my favour," he added, "for if it were raining, Cornelia would not leave the house." Then a big man, with a voice like a bull of Bashan, went down the

Amelia E. Barr

opposite side of the street, shouting as he went—"Milk Ho!" and Hyde considered him. He had a heavy wooden yoke across his shoulders; and large tin pails, full of milk, hanging from it.

"How English we are!" he exclaimed, with a touch of irony. "We have not thrown off the yoke, by any means—at Mr. Adams', for instance, I could believe myself in England. How exclusive is the pompous little Minister! What respect for office! What adoration for landed gentry! What super-cilious tolerance for tradesmen! Oh, indeed, it confounds me! But why should I trouble myself? I, who have the most adorable mistress in the world to think about! What are the kings, presidents, ministers, knaves of the world to me? Let Destiny shuffle them back and forth. I am indifferent to whichever is trumps."

Then he fell into a reverie about his proposed visit to Mrs. Adams. Last night it had appeared to him an easy and natural thing to do. He was not so sure of his position this morning. Mr. Adams might be present; he was punctilious in the extreme, and a call without an invitation at that early hour might be considered an impertinence—especially if he had no opportunity to enlighten Mrs. Adams about his love for Miss Moran, and so ask her assistance. Then he began to doubt whether his mother was on sufficient terms of intimacy to warrant his speaking about the swans and laburnum seeds—in short, the visit that had seemed so natural and proper when he first conceived it, assumed, on reflection, an aspect of difficulty and almost of impropriety.

But there are times when laissez-aller carries all before it, and Hyde was in just such a mood. "I'll run the chance," he said. "I'll risk it. I'll let things take their course." Then he began to dress, and as doubt of any kind is best ended by action, he gathered confidence as he did so. Fortunately, there was no hesitation this morning in his mind about his dress. He was going to ride to Richmond Hill, and he was quite satisfied with his riding suit. He knew that it was the next thing to a becoming uniform. He knew that he looked well in it; and he remembered with complaisance that it was old enough to be individual; and new enough to be handsome and striking.

And, after all, when a man is in love, to be reasonable is often to be cowardly. But Hyde was no coward; so then, it was not long ere he put all fears and doubts behind him and set his musings to the assertion: "I said to my heart, last night, that I would meet Cornelia at Richmond Hill this morning. I will not go back on my word. Such fluctuability is only fit for failure."

When he was dressed he went to his hotel and breakfasted there; for the "cup of coffee" he had intended to ask of Mrs. Adams appeared, now, a little presumptuous. In the enthusiasm of the previous night, with Cornelia's smiles warming his imagination and her words thrilling his heart, everything had seemed possible and natural; but last night and this morning were different epochs. Last night, he had been better, stronger than himself; this morning, he felt all the limitations of social conveniences and tyrannies. Early as it was, there were many members and senators present— eating, drinking coffee, and talking of Franklin, or of the question of the Senate sitting with closed doors, or of some other of the great little subjects then agitating society. Hyde took no notice of any of these disputes until a man— evidently an Englishman—called Franklin "a beggar-on-horseback-Yankee." Then he put down his knife and fork, and looked steadily at the speaker, saying with the utmost coolness and firmness—

"You are mistaken, sir. The beggar-on-horseback is generally

　　　　　　　Amelia E. Barr

supposed to ride to the devil. Franklin rode to the highest posts of political honour and to the esteem and affection of worthy men in all the civilized world."

"I understand, I understand, sir," was the reply. "The infatuation of a nation for some particular genius or leader is very like that of a man for an ugly woman. When they do get their eyes opened, they wonder what bewitched them."

"Sir, what is unreasonable is irrefutable." With these words he rose, pushed aside his chair with a little temper, and, turning, met Jefferson face to face. The great man smiled, and put his hand affectionately on Hyde's shoulder. He had evidently heard the conversation, for when he had made the usual greetings, he added—

"You spoke well, my young friend. Now, I will give you a piece of advice—when any one abuses a great man in your presence, ask them what kind of people, THEY admire. You will certainly be consoled." With these words he took Hyde's chair; and Hyde, casting his eyes a moment on this tall, loose-limbed man, whose cold blue eyes and red hair emphasized the stern anger of his whole appearance, was well disposed to leave the scurrilous Englishman to his power of reproof. Besides, the badge of mourning which Jefferson wore had reminded him of his own neglect. Probably, it was the want of this badge that had made the stranger believe he was speaking to one who would sympathize with his views.

So he went at once to his tailor's and procured the necessary band of crape for his arm. But these events took time, and though he rode hard afterwards, it was quite half-past nine when he drew rein at the door of Richmond Hill. A slave in a fine livery was lounging there; and he gave him his card. In a few moments the man returned with an invitation to dismount and come into the breakfast-room. Thus far, he had suffered himself to be carried forward by the impulse of his heart; and he still put firmly down any wonder as to what he should say or do.

He was shown into a bright little parlour with open windows. A table, elegantly and plentifully spread, occupied the centre of the room; and sitting at it were the Vice-President and Mrs. Adams; and also their only daughter, the beautiful, but not very intellectual, Mrs. Smith. It was easy to see that the meal was really over, and that the trio had been simply lingering over the table because of some interesting discussion; and it was quite as easy to understand that his entrance had put an end to the conversation. Mrs. Adams met him with genuine, though formal, kindness; Mrs. Smith with courtesy; and the Vice-President rose, bowed handsomely, hoped he was well, and then after a minute's reflection said—

"We were talking about the official title proper for General Washington. What do you think, Lieutenant? Or have you heard General Hyde express any opinion on the subject?"

"Sir, I do not presume to understand the ceremonials of government. My father is of the opinion, that 'The President of the United States' has a Roman and republican simplicity, and that any addition to it would be derogatory and childish."

"My dear young man, the eyes of the world are upon us. To give a title to our leaders and rulers belongs to history. In the Roman republic great conquerors assumed even distinctive titles, as well as national ones."

"Then our Washington is superior to them. Let us be grateful that he has not yet called himself—Americanus. I like Doctor Kunz's idea of Washington best, but I see not how it could be put into a civil title."

Amelia E. Barr

"Doctor Kunz! Doctor Kunz! Oh yes, of the Dutch congregation. Pray what is it?"

"'And there came up a lion out of Judah.' My grandfather is an elder in that church, and he said the verse and the sermon on it lifted the people to their feet."

"That might do very well for one side of a state seal; but it is a proper prefix we need. I don't think we can say 'Your Majesty the President.'"

"I should think not," replied Mrs. Adams with an air of decision.

"Chief Justice McKean thinks 'His Serene Highness the President of the United States' is very suitable. Roger Sherman is of the opinion that neither 'His Highness' nor 'His Excellency' are novel and dignified enough; and General Muhlenberg says Washington himself is in favour of 'High Mightiness,' the title used by the Stadtholder of Holland."

"That would please the Dutch-Americans," said Mrs. Adams—" if a title at all is necessary, which I confess I cannot understand. Is it to be 'High Mightiness' then?" she asked with a little laugh.

"I think not. Muhlenberg, however, has seriously offended the President by making a joke of the proposition; and I must say, it was ill-timed of Muhlenberg, and not what I should have expected of him."

"But what was the joke?"

"Something to the effect that if the office was certain to be held by men as large as Washington, the title of 'High Mightiness' would not be amiss; but that if a little man—say like Aaron Burr—should be elected, the title would be a ridiculous one. The fact is, Muhlenberg is against any title whatever but that of 'President of the United States.'"

"And how will you vote, John?"

"In favour of a title. Certainly, I shall. Your Majesty is a very good prefix. It would draw the attention of England, and show her that we were not afraid to assume 'the majesty' of our conquest."

"And if you wish to please France," continued Mrs. Adams —"which seems the thing in fashion—you might have the prefix 'Citizen.' 'Citizen Washington' is not bad."

"It is execrable, Mrs. Adams; and I am ashamed that you should make it, even as a pleasantry."

"Indeed, my friend, there is no foretelling what may be. The French fever is rising every day. I even may be compelled to drop the offensive 'Mistress' and call myself Citoyenne Adams. And, after all, I do believe that the President regards his citizenship far above his office. What say you, Lieutenant?"

"I think, madame, that fifty, one hundred, one thousand years after this day, it will be of little importance what prefix is put before the name of the President. He will be simply GEORGE WASHINGTON in every heart and on every page."

"That is true," said Mrs. Adams. "Fame uses no prefixes. It is Pompey, Julius Caesar, Pericles, Alfred, Hampden, Oliver Cromwell. Or it is a suffix like Alexander the Great; or Richard Coeur-de-Lion. I have no objection to Washington the Great, or Washington Coeur-de-Lion."

Amelia E. Barr

"Washington will do for love and for fame," continued Hyde. "The next generation may say MR. Madison, or MR. Monroe, or MR. Jay; but they will want neither prefix nor suffix to Washington, Jefferson, Franklin,—and, if you permit me, sir—Adams."

The Vice-president was much pleased. He said "Pooh! Pooh!" and stood up and stepped loftily across the hearth-rug, but the subtle compliment went warm to his heart, and the real worth of the man's nature came straight to the front, as he looked, under its influence, the honest, positive, honourable gentleman that every great occasion found him to be.

"Well, well," he answered; "heartily, and from our souls, we must do our best, and then trust to Truth and Time, our name and our memory. But I must now go to town—our affairs give us no holidays." And then instantly the room was in a fuss and a flurry. No Englishman could have made a more bustling exit; and, indeed, even in his physical aspect, John Adams was a perfect picture of the traditional John Bull. His natural temperament carried out this likeness: high-mettled as a game-cock during the Revolutionary war, he was, in politics, passionate, dogmatic and unconciliating, and in social life ceremonious and showy as any Englishman could be.

After he had gone, Mrs. Adams proposed a walk in the lovely garden; and Hyde hoped then to obtain a few words with her. But Mrs. Smith accompanied them, and introduced immediately a grievance she had evidently been previously discussing. With a provoking petulance she told and re-told some slight which Sir John Temple had offered Mr. Smith: adding always "Lady Temple is very civil to me; but I cannot, and I will not, exchange visits with any lady who does not pay my William an equal civility." Enlarging and enlarging on this text, Hyde found no opportunity to get a word in on his own affairs; and then, suddenly, as they turned into the main avenue, Doctor Moran and Cornelia appeared.

Quite as suddenly, Mrs. Adams divined the motive of Hyde's early visit; she opened her eyes wide, and looked at him with a comprehension so clear and real that Hyde was compelled to answer, and acknowledge her suspicion by a look and movement quite as unequivocal. Yet this instantaneous understanding contained neither promise nor sympathy; and he could not tell whether he had gained a friend or simply made a confession.

Doctor Moran was evidently both astonished and annoyed. He stepped out of his carriage and joined Mrs. Adams but kept Cornelia by his side, so that Hyde was compelled to escort Mrs. Smith. And Cornelia, beyond a very civil "Good-morning, sir," gave him no sign. He could watch her slight, virginal figure, and the bend of her head in answering Mrs. Adams gave him transient glimpses of her fair face; but there was no message in all its changes for him. In fact, in spite of Mrs. Smith's little rill of social complaining, he felt quite "out" of the inner circle of the company's interests, and he was also deeply mortified at Cornelia's apparent indifference.

When the party reached the steps before the house door, though Mrs. Adams certainly invited him to remain, he had come to the conclusion that he was just the one person NOT wanted at that time; yet as he had plenty of self-command he completely hid beneath a gay and charming manner the chagrin and disappointment that were really tormenting him. For one moment he caught Cornelia's eyes, but his glance was too rapid and inquisitive. She was embarrassed, and a little frightened by it; and with a deep blush turned towards Mrs. Smith and said something trivial about the weather and the fine view. He could not understand this attitude. Feelings of tenderness, anger, mortification,—feelings strong and

Amelia E. Barr

threefold crowded his beating heart and vivid brain. He longed to set his restless thoughts to rapid movement—to gallop—to ejaculate—to do any foolish thing that would relieve his sense of vexation and defeat. But until he was out of sight and hearing he rode slowly, with the easy air of a man who was only sensitive to the beauty of his surroundings, and thoroughly enjoying them.

He kept this pace till quite outside the precincts of Richmond Hill, then he struck his horse with a passion that astonished the animal and the next moment shamed himself. He stooped instantly and apologized to the quivering creature; and was as instantly forgiven. Then he began to talk to himself in those elliptical, unfinished sentences, which the inner man understands, and so thoroughly finishes—" If I were not morally sure—It is as plain as can be—How in the name of wonder?—I'll say so much for myself—I am sorry that I went there—A couple of uninteresting women—This for you, sir!—Whistled myself up this morning on a fool's errand—No more! no more to save my life!—Grant me patience—Mrs. Smith giving herself a parcel of airs—Oh, adorable Cornelia!"

Such reflections, blended with pet names and apologies to his horse, brought him in sight of the Van Heemskirk house, and he instantly felt how good his grandmother's sympathy would be. He saw her at the door, leaning over the upper-half and watching his approach.

"I knew it was thee!" she cried; "always, the clatter of thy horse's hoofs says plainly to me, 'Grand-moth-er! grand-moth-er! grand-moth-er!' Now, then, what is the matter with thee? Disappointed, wert thou last night?"

"No—but this morning I have been badly used; and I am angry at it." Then he told her all the circumstances of his visit to Richmond Hill, and she listened patiently, as was her way with all complainers.

"In too great haste art thou," were her first words. "No worse I think of Cornelia, because a little she draws back. To want, and to have thy want, that has been the way with thee all thy life long. Even thy sword and the battlefield were not denied thee; but a woman's love!—that is to be won. Little wouldst thou value it, lightly wouldst thou hold it, if it were thine for the wishing. Thy mother has taught thee to expect too much."

"And my grandmother?"

"That is so. A very foolish old woman is thy grandmother. Too much she loves thee, or she had not sent thee to Arenta's last night with her best ivory winders."

"Oh, Arenta is a very darling! Had she been present this morning, she had taken the starch out of all our fine talk and fine manners. We should have chattered like the swallows about pleasant homely things; and left title-making to graver fools."

"If, now, thou had fallen in love with Arenta, it had been a good thing."

"If I had not seen Cornelia, I might have adored Arenta— but, then, Arenta has already a lover."

"So? And pray who is it?"

"Of all men in the world, the gay, handsome Frenchman, Athanase Tounnerre, a member of the French embassy. How a girl so plainly Dutch can endure the creature confounds me."

"Stop a little. The grandmother of Arenta was French. Very well I remember her—a girl all alive, from head to foot; never still. Thy grandfather used to say, 'In her veins is quick-silver, not blood,' And, too soon, she wore away her life; Arenta's mother was but a baby, when she died."

"Ah! So it is! We are the past, as well as the present. As for myself—"

"Thou art thy father over again; only sweeter, and better—that is the Dutch in thee—the happy, easy-going Dutch—if only thou wert not so lazy."

"That is the English in me—the self-indulgent, masterful English. So then, Arenta, being partly French, back to the French she goes. 'Tis passing strange."

"Of this, art thou sure?"

"I have listened to the man. Every one has. He wears Arenta's name on his sleeve. He drinks her health in all companies. He will talk to any stranger he meets, for an hour at a time, about his 'fair Arenta.' I can but wonder at the fellow. It is inconceivable to me; for though I am passionately taken with Cornelia Moran, I hide her close in my heart. I should want to strike any man who breathed her name. Yet it is said of Athanase de Tounnerre that he paid a visit to every one he knew, in order to tell them of his felicity."

"And her father? To such a marriage what will he say?"

Hyde stretched out his legs and struck them lightly with his riding whip. Then, with a smile, he answered, "He will be proud enough in his heart. Arenta would certainly leave him soon, and the Dutch are very sensible to the charm of a title.

His daughter, the Marquise de Tounnerre, will be a very great woman in his eyes."

"That is the truth. I was glad for thy mother to be a lady, and go to Court, and see the Queen. Yes, indeed! in my heart I was proud of it 'Twas about that very thing poor Janet Semple and I became unfriends."

"Indeed, it is the common failing; and at present, there is no one like the French. I will except the President, and Mr. Adams, and Mr. Hamilton, and say the rest of us are French mad."

"Thy grandfather, and thy grandmother too, thou may except. And as for thy father, with a great hatred he names them."

"My father is English; and the English and French are natural and salutary enemies. I once heard Lord Exmouth say that France was to England all that Carthage was to Rome—the natural outlet for the temper of a people so quarrelsome that they would fight each other if they had not the French to fight."

"Listen! That is thy father's gallop. Far off, I know it. So early in the morning, what is he coming for?"

"He had an intention to go to Mr. Semple's funeral."

"That is good. Thy grandfather is already gone—" and she looked so pointedly down at her black petticoat and bodice, that Hyde answered—

"Yes; I see that you are in mourning. Is it for Mr. Franklin, or for Mr. Semple?"

"Franklin was far off; by my fireside Alexander Semple

Amelia E. Barr

often sat; and at my table often he ate. Good friends were we once—good friends are we now; for all but Love, Death buries."

At this moment General Hyde entered the room. Hurry and excitement were in his face, though they were well controlled. He gave his hand to Madame Van Heemskirk, saying—

"Good-morning, mother! You look well, as you always do:"—then turning to his son and regarding the young man's easy, smiling indifference, he said with some temper, "What the devil, George, are you doing here, so early in the day? I have been through the town seeking you—everywhere— even at that abominable Club, where Frenchmen and vagabonds of all kinds congregate."

"I was at the Vice-President's, sir," answered George, with a comical assumption of the Vice-President's manner.

"You were WHERE?"

"At Richmond Hill. I made an early call on Mrs. Adams."

Then General Hyde laughed heartily. "You swaggering dandy!" he replied. "Did you take a bet at the Belvedere to intrude on His Loftiness? And have you a guinea or two on supping a cup of coffee with him? Upon my honour, you must now be nearly at the end of your follies. Mother, where is the Colonel?"

"He has gone to Elder Semple's house. You know—"

"I know well. For a long time I have purposed to call on the old gentleman, and what I have neglected I am now justly denied. I meant, at least, to pay him the last respect; but even that is to-day impossible. For I must leave for England this afternoon at five o'clock, and I have more to do than I can well accomplish."

George leaped to his feet at these words. Nothing could have been more unexpected; but that is the way with Destiny, her movements are ever unforeseen and inevitable. "Sir," he cried, "what has happened?"

"Your uncle is dying—perhaps dead. I received a letter this morning urging me to take the first packet. The North Star sails this afternoon, and I do not wish to miss her, for she flies English colours, and they are the only ones the Barbary pirates pretend to respect. Now, George, you must come with me to Mr. Hamilton's office; we have much business to arrange there; then, while I pay a farewell visit to the President, you can purchase for me the things I shall require for the voyage."

So far his manner had been peremptory and decided, but, suddenly, a sweet and marvellous change occurred. He went close to Madame Van Heemskirk, and taking both her hands, said in a voice full of those tones that captivate women's hearts—

"Mother! mother! I bid you a loving, grateful farewell! You have ever been to me good, and gentle, and wise—the very best of mothers. God bless you!" Then he kissed her with a solemn tenderness, and Lysbet understood that he believed their parting to be a final one. She sat down, weeping, and Hyde with an authoritative motion of the head, commanding his son's attendance, went hastily out. It was then eleven o'clock, and there was business that kept both men hurrying here and there until almost the last hour. It had been agreed that they were to meet at the City Hotel at four o'clock; and soon after that hour General Hyde joined his son. He looked

　　　　　Amelia E. Barr

weary and sad, and began immediately to charge George concerning his mother.

"We parted with kisses and smiles this morning," he said; "and I am glad of it; if I went back, we should both weep; and a wet parting is not a lucky one. I leave her in your charge, George; and when I send her word to come to England, look well to her comfort. And be sure to come with her. Do you hear me?"

"Yes, sir."

"On no account—even if she wishes it—permit her to come alone. Promise me."

"I promise you, sir. What is there that I would not do for my mother? What is there I would not do to please you, sir?"

"Let me tell you, George, such words are very sweet to me. As to yourself, I do not fear for you. It is above, and below reason, that you should do anything to shame your kindred, living or dead—the living indeed, you might reconcile; the dead are implacable; and their vengeance is to be feared."

"I fear not the dead, and I love the living. The honour of Hyde is safe in my keeping. If you have any advice to give me, sir, pray speak plainly."

"With all my soul. I ask you, then, to play with some moderation. I ask you to avoid any entanglement with women. I ask you to withdraw yourself, as soon as possible, from those blusterers for French liberty—or rather French license, robbery, and assassination—I tell you there is going to be a fierce national fracas on the subject. Stand by the President, and every word he says. Every word is sure to be wise and right."

"Father, I learnt the word 'Liberty' from your lips. I drew my sword under your command for 'Liberty.' I know not how to discard an idea that has grown into my nature as the veining grows into the wood."

"Liberty! Yes; cherish it with your life-blood. But France has polluted the name and outraged the idea. Neither you nor I can wish to be swept into the common sewers, being by birth, nobles and aristocrats. Earl Stanhope, who was heart and soul with the French Revolution while it was a movement for liberty, has just scratched his name with his own hand from the revolutionary Club. And Burke, who was once its most enthusiastic defender, has now written a pamphlet which has given it, in England, a fatal blow. This news came in my letters to-day." Then taking out his watch, he rose, saying, "Come, it is time to go to the ship—MY DEAR GEORGE!"

George could not speak. He clasped his father's hand, and then walked by his side to Coffee House Slip, where the North Star was lying. There was no time to spare, and the General was glad of it; for oh, these last moments! Youth may prolong them, but age has lost youth's rebound, and willingly escapes their disintegrating emotion. Before either realized the fact, the General had crossed the narrow plank; it was quickly withdrawn; the anchor was lifted to the chanty of "Homeward bound boys," and the North Star, with wind and tide in her favour, was facing the great separating ocean.

George turned from the ship in a maze. He felt as if his life had been cut sharply asunder; at any rate, its continuity was broken, and what other changes this change might bring it was impossible to foresee. In any extremity, however, there is generally some duty to do; and the doing of that duty is the first right step onward. Without reasoning on the matter, George followed this plan. He had a letter to deliver to his mother; it was right that it should be delivered as soon as possible; and indeed he felt as if her voice and presence would be the best of all comfort at that hour; so late as it was, he rode out to Hyde Manor. His mother, with a lighted candle in her hand, opened the door for him.

"I thought it was thy father, Joris," she said; "but what? Is there anything wrong? Why art thou alone?"

"There is nothing wrong, dear mother. Come, I will tell you what has happened."

Then she locked the door carefully, and followed her son into the small parlour, where she had been sitting. He gave her his father's letter, and assumed for her sake, the air of one who has brought good tidings. She silently read, and folded it; and George said, "It was the most fortunate thing, the North Star being ready for sea. Father could hardly have had a better boat; and they started with wind and tide in their favour. We shall hear in a few weeks from him. Are you not pleased, mother?"

"It is too late, Joris;—twenty years too late. And I wish not to go to England. Very unhappy was I in that cold, grey country. Very happy am I here."

"But you must have expected this change?"

"Not until your cousin died was there any thought of such a thing. And long before that, we had built and begun to love dearly this home. I wish, then, it had been God's will that your cousin had not died."

"My father—"

"Ah, Joris, your father has always longed in his heart for

England. Like a weaning babe that never could be weaned was he. In many ways, he has lately shown me that he felt himself to be a future English earl. And thou too? Wilt thou become an Englishman? Then this fair home I have made for thee will forget thy voice and thy footstep. Woe is me! I have planted and planned, for whom I know not."

"You have planned and planted for your Joris. I swear to you that I like England as little as you do. I despise the tomfoolery of courts and ceremonies. I count an earl no better than any other honourable gentleman. I desire most of all to marry the woman I love, and live here in the home that reminds me of you wherever I turn. I want your likeness on the great stairway, and in all the rooms; so that those who may never see your face may love you; and say, 'How good she looks! How beautiful she is!'"

"So true art thou! So loving! So dear to me! Even in England I can be happy if I think of thee Here—filling these big rooms with good company; riding, shooting, over thine own land, fishing in thy own waters, telling thy boys and girls how dear grandmother had this pond dug—this hedge planted—these woods filled with game—these streams set with willows—these summerhouses built for pleasure. Oh, I have thought ever as I worked, I shall leave my memory here —and here—and here again—for never, Joris, never, dear Joris, while thou art in this world, must thou forget me!"

"Never! Never, oh never, dear, dear mother!"

And that night they said no more. Both felt there would be plenty of time in the future to consider whatever changes it might have in store for them.

Amelia E. Barr

CHAPTER VI

AUNT ANGELICA

The first changes referred especially to Hyde's life, and were not altogether approved by him. His pretence of reading law had to be abandoned, for he had promised to remain at home with his mother, and it would not therefore be possible for him to dawdle about Pearl Street and Maiden Lane watching for Cornelia. But he had that happy and fortunate temper that trusts to events; and also, he soon began to realize that if circumstances alter cases, they also alter feelings.

For, looking upon Hyde Manor as the future home of himself and his wife—and that wife, happily, Cornelia—he found it very easy to take an almost eager interest in all that concerned its welfare and beauty. "How good! How unselfish he is!" thought his mother. "Never before has he been so ready to listen and so willing to please me." But, really, the work soon became delightful to him. The passion for land and for its improvement—the ruling passion of an Englishman—was not absent in George; it was only latent, and the idea of home, of his own personal home, developed it with amazing rapidity. He was soon able to make excellent suggestions to his mother; for her ideas, beautiful enough in the cultivation of flat surfaces, did not embody the grander possibilities of the higher lands near the river. But George saw every advantage, and with great ability directed his little gang of labourers among the rocks and woody crags of the yet unplanted wilderness.

In spite of their anxiety about the General, in spite of George's longing to see Cornelia, these early summer days, with their glory of sunshine and shade and their miracles of growth, were very happy days; though madame reached her happiness by putting the future quite out of her thoughts, and George reached his by anticipating the future as the fruition of the present. Never since his early boyhood had madame and her son been so near and so dear to each other; for her brother-in-law's probable death and her husband's dangerous journeying released her from social engagements, and permitted her to spend her time in the employments and the companionship she loved best of all.

George, while accepting for himself the same partial seclusion, had more freedom. He rode into town three or four times every week; got the news of the clubs and the streets; loitered about Maiden Lane and the shopping district; and when disappointed and vexed at events went to his Grandmother Van Heemskirk for sympathy. For, as yet, he hesitated about naming Cornelia to his mother. He was sure she was aware of his passion, and her reticence on the subject made him fear she was going to advocate the fulfilment of his father's promise. And he had such a singular delicacy about the girl he loved that he could not endure the thought of bandying her name about in an angry discussion. Added to this fine sense was an adoring love for his mother. She was in anxiety enough, and would be, until she heard of her husband's safety; why, then, should he add his anxiety to hers?

Yet he was not happy about Cornelia. Since that unfortunate morning at Richmond Hill they had never met. If she saw him go up or down Maiden Lane, she made no sign. Several times Arenta's face at her parlour window had given him a passing hope; but Arenta's own love affairs were just then at a very interesting point; and, besides, she regarded the young Lieutenant's admiration for her friend as only one of his many transient enthusiasms.

"If there was anything real in it," she reflected, "Cornelia would have talked about him; and that she has never done." Then she began to remember, with pride, the very sensible behaviour of her own lover. "My Athanase," she reflected, "did not give me an hour's rest until we were engaged. He insisted on talking to father about our marriage settlements and our future—in fact, he made of love a thing possible and practical. A lover like Joris Hyde is not, I think, very fortunate."

She did not understand that the quality of love in its finest revelation desires, after its first sweet inception, a little period of withdrawal—it wonders at its strange happiness—broods over it—is fearful of disturbing emotions so exquisite—prefers the certainty of its delicious suspense to a more definite understanding, and finds a keen strange delight in its own poignant anxieties and hopes. These are the birth pangs of an immortal love—of a love that knows within itself, that it is born for Eternity, and need not to hurry the three-score-and-ten years of time to a consummation.

Of such noble lineage was the love of Cornelia for Joris Hyde. His gracious, beautiful youth, seemed a part of her own youth; his ardent, tender glances had filled her heart with a sweet trouble that she did not understand. It was the most natural thing in the world that she should wish to be apart; that she should desire to brood over feelings so strangely happy; and that in this very brooding they should grow to the perfect stature of a luminous and unquenchable affection.

Joris was moved by a sentiment of the same kind, though in a lesser degree. The masculine desire to obtain, and the delightful consciousness that he possessed, at least, the tremendous advantage of asking for the love he craved, roused him from the sweet torpor to which delicious, dreamy love had inclined him.

"I have thought of Cornelia long enough," he said one delightful summer morning; "with all my soul I now long to see her. And it is not an impossible thing I desire. In short, there is some way to compass it." Then a sudden, invincible persuasion of success came to him; he believed in his own good fortune; he had a conviction that the very stars connived with a true lover to work his will. And under this enthusiasm he galloped into town, took his horse to a stable, and then walked towards Maiden Lane.

In a few moments he saw Arenta Van Ariens. She was in a mist of blue and white, with flowing curls, and fluttering ribbons; and a general air of happiness. He placed himself directly in her path, and doffed his beaver to the ground as she approached.

"Well, then," she cried, with an affected air of astonishment, "who would have thought of seeing you? Your retirement is the talk of the town."

"And pray what does the town say?"

"Some part of it says you have lost your fortune at cards; another part says you have lost your heart and got no compensation for it. 'Tis strange to see the folly of young people of this age," she added, with a little pretended sigh of superior wisdom.

"As if you, also, had not lost your heart!" exclaimed Hyde.

Amelia E. Barr

"No, sir! I have exchanged mine for its full value. Where are you going?"

"With you."

"In a word, no. For I am going to Aunt Angelica's."

"Upon my honour, it is to your Aunt Angelica's I desire to go most of all!"

"Now I understand. You have found out that Cornelia Moran is going there. Are you still harping on that string? And Cornelia never said one word to me. I do not approve of such deceit. In my love affairs I have always been open as the day."

"I assure you that I did NOT know Miss Moran was going there. I had not a thought of Madame Jacobus until we met. To tell the very truth, I came into town to look for you."

"For me? And why, pray?"

"I want to see Miss Moran. If I cannot see her, then I want to hear about her. I thought you, of all people, could tell me the most and the best. I assured myself that you had infinite good temper. Now, pray do not disappoint me."

"Listen! We meet this afternoon at my aunt's, to discuss the dresses and ceremonies proper for a very fine wedding."

"For your own wedding, in fact—Is not that so?"

"Well, then?"

"Well, then, who knows more on that subject than Joris Hyde? Was I not, last year, at Lady Betty Somer's splendid nuptials; and at Fanny Paget's, and the Countess of Carlisle's? Indeed, I maintain that in such a discussion *I* am an absolute necessity. And I wish to know Madame Jacobus. I have long wished to know her. Upon my honour, I think her to be one of the most interesting women in New York!"

"I will advise you a little. Save your compliments until you can say them to my aunt. I never carry a word to any one."

"Then take me with you, and I will repeat them to her face."

"So? Well, then, here we are, at her very door. I know not what she will say—you must make your own excuses, sir."

As she was speaking, they ascended the white steps leading to a very handsome brick house on the west side of Broadway. It had wide iron piazzas and a fine shady garden at the back, sloping down to the river bank; and had altogether, on the outside, the very similitude of a wealthy and fashionable residence. The door was opened by a very dark man, who was not a negro, and who was dressed in a splendid and outlandish manner—a scarlet turban above his straight black hair, and gold-hooped earrings, and a long coat or tunic, heavily embroidered in strange devices.

"He was an Algerine pirate," whispered Arenta. "My Uncle Jacob brought him here—and my aunt trusts him—I would not, not for a moment."

As soon as the front door closed, Joris perceived that he was in an unusual house. The scents and odours of strange countries floated about it. The hall contained many tall jars, full of pungent gums and roots; and upon its walls the weapons of savage nations were crossed in idle and harmless fashion. They went slowly up the highly polished stairway into a large, low parlour, facing the vivid, everyday business

Amelia E. Barr

drama of Broadway; but the room itself was like an Arabian Night's dream, for the Eastern atmosphere was supplemented by divans and sofas covered with rare cashmere shawls, and rugs of Turkestan, and with cushions of all kinds of oriental splendour. Strange tables of wonderful mosaic work held ivory carvings of priceless worth; and porcelain from unknown lands. Gods and goddesses from the yellow Gehenna of China and the utterable idolatry of India, looked out with brute cruelty, or sempiternal smiles from every odd corner; or gazed with a fascinating prescience from the high chimney-piece upon all who entered.

The effect upon Hyde was instantaneous and uncanny. His Saxon-Dutch nature was in instant revolt against influences so foreign and unnatural. Arenta was unconsciously in sympathy with him; for she said with a shrug of her pretty shoulders, as she looked around, "I have always bad dreams after a visit to this room. Do these things have a life of their own? Look at the creature on that corner shelf! What a serene disdain is in his smile! He seems to gaze into the very depths of your soul. I see that there is a curtain to his shrine; and I shall take leave to draw it." With these words she went to the scornful divinity, and shut his offending eyes behind the folds of his gold-embroidered curtain.

Hyde watched her flitting about the strange room, and thought of a little brown wren among the poisonous, vivid splendours of tropical swamp flowers. So out of place the pretty, thoughtless Dutch girl looked among the spoils of far India, and Central America, and of Arabian and African worship and workmanship. But when the door opened, and Madame Jacobus, with soft, gliding footsteps entered, Hyde understood how truly the soul, if given the wherewithal, builds the habitation it likes best. Once possessed of marvellous beauty, and yet extraordinarily interesting, she seemed the very genius of the room and its strange, suggestive belongings. She was unusually tall, and her figure had kept its undulating, stately grace. Her hair, dazzlingly white, was piled high above her ample brow, held in place with jewelled combs and glittering pins. Her face had lost its fine oval and youthful freshness, but who of any feeling or intelligence would not have far preferred the worn countenance, expressing in a thousand sensitive shades and emotions the story of her life and love? And if every other beauty had failed, Angelica's eyes would have atoned for the loss. They were large, softly-black, slow-moving, or again, in a moment, flashing with the fire that lay hidden in the dark pit of the iris.

It was said that her slaves adored her, and that no man who came within her influence had been able to resist her power—no man, perhaps, but Captain Jacobus; and he had not resisted, he had been content to exercise over her a power greater than her own. He had made her his wife; he had lavished on her for ten years the spoils of the four quarters of the world; and his worship of her had only been equalled by her passionate attachment to him. Ten years of love, and then parting and silence—unbroken silence. Yet she still insisted that he was alive, and would certainly come back to her. With this faith in her heart, she had refused to put on any symbol of loss or mourning. She kept his fine house open, his room ready, and herself constantly adorned for his home-coming. Society, which insists on uniformity, did not approve of this unreasonable hope. It expected her to adopt the garments of widowhood for a time, and then make a match in accordance with the great fortune Captain Jacobus had left her. But Angelica Jacobus was a law unto herself; and society was compelled to take her with those apologizing shrugs it gives to whatever is original and individual.

She came in with a smile of welcome. She was always pleased that her fine home should be seen by those strange to it; and perhaps was particularly pleased that General Hyde's son should be her visitor. And as Joris was determined to win her favour, there was an almost instantaneous birth of good-will.

"Let me kiss your hand, madame," said the handsome young fellow, lifting the jewelled fingers in his own. "I have heard that my father had once that honour. Do not put me below him;" and with the words he touched with his warm lips the long white fingers.

Her laugh rang merrily through the dim room, and she answered—"You are Dick Hyde's own son—nothing else. I see that"—and she drew the young man towards the light and looked with a steady pleasure into his smiling face as she asked—

"What brought you here this morning, sir?"

"Madame, I have heard my father speak of you; I have seen you; can you wonder that I desired to know you? This morning I met Miss Van Ariens, and when she said she was coming here, I found myself unable to resist the temptation of coming with her."

"Let me tell you something, aunt. I think Lieutenant Hyde can be of great service to us. He took part in several noble English weddings last year, and he offers his advice in our consultation to-day."

"But where is Cornelia? I thought she would come with you."

"She will be here in a few minutes. I saw her half-an-hour ago."

"What a beautiful girl she has become!" said madame.

"She is an angel," said Hyde.

Angelica laughed. "The man who calls a woman an angel has never had any sisters," she answered; "but, however, she has beauty enough to set young hearts ablaze. I like the girl, and I wonder not that others do the same."

Even as she spoke Cornelia entered. There was a little flush and hurry on her face; but oh, how innocent and joyous it was! Quick-glancing, sweetly smiling, she entered the musky, scented parlour, and in her white robe and white hat stood like a lily in its light and gloom. And when she turned to Hyde an ineffable charm and beauty illumed her countenance. "How glad I am to see you!" she said, and the very ring of gladness was in her voice. "And how strange that we should meet here!"

"That is so," replied Madame Jacobus. "One can never see where the second little bird comes from."

"Am I late, madame? Surely your clock is wrong."

"My clock is never wrong, Cornelia, A Dutch clock will always go just about so. Come, now, sit down, and let us talk of such follies as weddings and wedding gowns."

In this conversation Hyde triumphantly redeemed his promise of assistance. He could describe with a delightful accuracy—or inaccuracy—the lovely toilets and pretty accessories of the high English wedding feasts of the previous year. And in some subtle way he threw into these descriptions such a glamour of romance, such backgrounds of old castles and chiming bells, of noble dames glittering with gems, and village maids scattering roses, of martial

108   Amelia E. Barr

heroes, and rejoicing lovers, all moving in an atmosphere of song and sunshine, that the little party sat listening, entranced, with sympathetic eyes drinking in his wonderful descriptions.

Madame Jacobus was the first to interrupt these pretty reminiscences. "All this is very fine," she said, "but the most of it is no good for us. The satin and the lace and even the gems, we can have; the music can be somehow managed, and we shall not make a bad show as to love and beauty. But castles and lords and military pomp, and old cathedrals hung with battle flags—Such things are not to be had here, and, in plain truth, they are not necessary for the wedding of a simple maid like our Arenta."

"You forget, then, that my Athanase is of almost royal descent," said Arenta. "A very old family are the Tounnerres—older, indeed, than the royal Capets."

"No one is to-day so poor as to envy the royal Capets; and as for an ancient family, Captain Jacobus used to speak of his forefathers as 'the old fellows whom the flood could not wash away.' Jacobus always put his ideas in such clear, forcible words. What I want to know is this—where is the ceremony to be performed?"

"The civil ceremony is to be at the French Embassy," answered Arenta with some pride.

"Is that all there is to it?"

"Aunt! How could you imagine that I should be satisfied with a civil ceremony? My father also insists upon a religious ceremony; and my Athanase told him he was willing to marry me in every church in America. I am not Gertrude Kippon! No, indeed! I insist on everything being done in a moral and respectable manner. My father spoke of Doctor Kunz for the religious part."

"I like not Doctor Kunz," answered madame. "Bishop Provoost and the Episcopal service is the proper thing. Doctor Kunz will be sure to say some sharp words—his tongue is full of them—he stands too stiff—he does not use his hands gracefully—his walk and carriage is not dignified —and he looks at you through spectacles—and I, for one, do not like to be looked at through spectacles. We must decide for the Episcopal church."

"And the little trip after it," continued Arenta. "Lieutenant Hyde says that, in England, it is now the proper thing."

"But in America it is not the proper thing. It is a rude unmannerly way to run off with a bride. We are not red Indians, nor is the Marquis carrying you by force from some hostile tribe. The nuptial trip is a barbarism. I am now weary. Lieutenant, take Miss Moran and show her my garden. I tell you, it is worth walking through; and when you have seen the flowers, Arenta and I will give you a cup of tea."

Arenta would gladly have gone into the garden also, but her aunt detained her. "Can you not see," she asked, "that those two are in love with each other? Give love its hour. They do not want your company."

"And for that very reason I wish to go with them. My brother is in love with Cornelia, and I am for Rem, and not for a stranger—also, my father and Cornelia's father are both for Rem; and, besides, Doctor Moran hates the Hydes. He will not let Cornelia marry the man."

"HE WILL NOT LET! When did Doctor John become omnipotent? Love laughs at fathers, as well as at locksmiths.

And if Doctor John is against young Hyde, then I shall the more cheerfully be for him—a pleasant, handsome youth as ever I saw, is he; and Doctor John—well, he is neither pleasant nor handsome."

"Aunt Angelica! I am astonished at you! Every one will contradict what you say."

"For that reason, I will maintain it. It is not my way to shout with the multitude."

With some hesitation, yet quite carried away by Hyde's personal longing and impulse, Cornelia went into the garden with her lover. It was a green, shady place, full of great maple-trees and flowering vines and shrubs, and patches of green grass. All kinds of sweet old-fashioned flowers grew there, mingling their scent with the strawberries' perfume and the woody odours of the ripening cherries. They were alone in this lovely place; the high privet hedges hid them from the outside world, and the babble and rumble of Broadway came to them only as the murmur of noise in a dream. Speechless with joy, Hyde clasped Cornelia's slender fingers, and they went together down the few broad low steps which led them into the green shadows of the trees. How soft was the grassy turf! How exquisite the westering sunlight, sifting through the maple leaves! They looked into each other's eyes and smiled, but were too happy to speak. For they had suddenly come into that land, which is east of the sun, and west of the moon; that land not laid down on any chart, but which we feel to be our rightful heritage.

Slowly, as they stepped, they came at length to a little summerhouse. It was covered with a thick jessamin vine; and the mysterious, languorous perfume of its starlike flowers filled the narrow resting-place with the very atmosphere of love. They sat down there, and in a few moments the seal was broken and Hyde's heart found out all the sweetest words that love could speak. Cornelia trembled; she blushed, she smiled, she suffered herself to be drawn close to his side; and, at last, in some sweet, untranslatable way, she gave him the assurance of her love. Then they found in delicious silence the eloquence that words were incompetent to translate; time was forgotten, and on earth there was once more an interlude of heavenly harmony in which two souls became one and Paradise was regained.

Arenta's voice, petulant and not pleasant, broke the charm. With a sigh they rose, dropped each other's hand, and went out of their heaven on earth to meet her.

"Tea is waiting," she said, "and Rem is waiting, and my aunt is tired, and you two have forgotten that the clock moves." Then they laughed, and laughter is always fatal to feeling; the magical land of love was suddenly far away, and there was the sound of china, and the heavy tones of Rem's voice—dissatisfied, if not angry—and Arenta's lighter fret; and they stood once more among fetishes and forms so foreign, fabulous and fantastical, that it was difficult to pass from the land of love, and all its pure delights, into their atmosphere.

It would have been harder but for Madame Jacobus. She understood; and she sympathized; and there was a kindly element in her nature which disposed her to side with the lovers. Her smile,—quick and short as a flash of the eyes— revealed to Hyde her intention of favour, and without one spoken word, these two knew themselves to be of the same mind. And, in parting, she held his hand while she talked, saying at last the very words he longed to hear—

"We shall expect you again on Thursday, Lieutenant. Everything is yet undecided, and the work you have begun, it is right that you should finish."

He answered only, "Thank you, madame!" but he accompanied the words with a look which asked so much, and confessed so much, that madame felt herself to be a silent confidante and a not unwilling accomplice. And when she had closed the door on her guests, she acknowledged it. "But then," she whispered, "I always did dearly love a lover; and this promises to be a love affair that will need my help— plenty of good honest hatred for it to combat—and wealth and rank and all sorts of conflicting conditions to get the better of—Well, then, my help is ready. In plain truth, I don't like such perfection as Doctor John; and my nephew Rem is not interesting. He is sulky, and Hyde is good-tempered, just like his father, too; and there never was a more fascinating man than Dick Hyde. HE-HO! I remember!—I remember!— and yet I dare say Dick has forgotten my very name—this is a marriage that will exactly suit me—I don't care who is against it!" Then she said softly to herself—

"REM went to Cornelia as they were about to leave, and he reminded her that, by her permission, he had come to walk home with her."

"CORNELIA turned to Hyde, excused herself, and, cool and silent, took her place by Rem's side."

"HYDE accepted the position with a smile, and a gracious bow, and then joined Arenta."

"ARENTA was far less agreeable than she ought to have been; for both she and her brother had a kind of divination. They knew, in spite of appearances, that Rem had not got the best of Joris Hyde. I am quick in my observations, and I know this is so. Well then, it is a very interesting affair as it stands—and it is like to grow far more interesting. I am not opposed to that. I shall enjoy it. Hyde and Cornelia ought to marry—and they have my good wishes."

As for Hyde, no thought that could mar the sweetness and joy of this fortunate hour came into his mind. Neither Rem's evident hatred, nor Arenta's disapproval, nor yet Cornelia's silence, troubled him. He had within his heart a talisman that made everything propitious. And he was so joyous that the people whom he passed on the street caught happiness from him. Men and women alike turned to look after the youth, for they felt the virtue of his passing presence, and wondered what it might mean. Even the necessary parting from Cornelia was only a phase of this wonderful gladness; for Love never fails of his token, and, though Arenta's sharp eyes could not discover it, Hyde received the silent message that was meant for him, and for him only. That one thought made his heart bound and falter with its exquisite delight— for him only—for him only, was that swift but certain assurance; that instantaneous bright flash of love that held in it all heaven and earth, and left him, as he told himself again and again, the happiest man in all the world.

He was hardly responsible for his actions at this hour; for when a swift gallop brought him to the Van Heemskirk house, he quite unconsciously struck the door some rapid, forceful blows, with his riding whip. His grandfather opened it with an angry face.

"I thought it was thee," he said. "Now, then, in such lordly fashion, whom didst thou summon? dog or slave, was it?"

"Oh, grandfather, I intended no harm. Did I strike so hard? Upon my word, I meant it not."

At this moment Madame Van Heemskirk came quickly forward. She turned a face of disapproval on her husband,

and asked sharply, "Why dost thou complain?"

"I like not my house-door struck so rudely, Lysbet. No man in all America, but Joris Hyde, would dare to do it."

At these words Joris flung himself from his horse and clasped his grandfather's hand. "I did wrong," he said warmly; "but I am beside myself with happiness; and I thought of nothing but telling you. My heart was in such a hurry that my hands forgot how to behave themselves."

"So happy as that, art thou? Good! Come in, and tell us what has happened to thee."

But Lysbet divined the joy in her grandson's face; and she said softly as he seated himself at the open window where his grandfather's chair was placed—

"It is Cornelia?"

"Yes, it is Cornelia. She loves me! The most charming girl the sun ever shone upon loves me. It is incredible! It is amazing! I cannot believe in my good fortune. Will you assure me it is possible? I want to hear some one say so— and who is there but my grandfather and you? I do not like to tell my mother, just yet. What do you say?"

"I say that thou hast chosen a good girl for a wife. God bless thee," answered Lysbet with great emotion.

Van Heemskirk smiled, but was silent; and Hyde stooped forward, gently moved his long pipe away from his lips, and said, "Grandfather, speak, You know Cornelia Moran?"

"I have seen her. With thee I saw her—walking with thee— dancing with thee. A great beauty I thought her. Thy grandmother says she is good. Well, then, the love of a good, beautiful girl, is something to be glad over. Not twice in a lifetime comes such great fortune. But make up thy mind to expect much opposition. Doctor John and thy father were ever unfriends. Thy father has other plans for thee; Cornelia's father has doubtless other plans for her. Few men can stand against Doctor John; he has the word, and the way, to carry all before him. I know not how the little Cornelia can dare to disobey him."

"She has said 'yes' to me; and, before heaven and earth, she will stand by it."

"Say that much. And of thyself, art thou sure?"

"Why art thou throwing cold water on such sweet hopes?" said Lysbet to her husband.

"Because, when love flames beyond duty and honour and all expediences, Lysbet, some one a little cold water ought to throw. And THOU will not do it. No! Rather, would thou add fuel to the flame."

"I know not what you mean, sir," said Hyde, vaguely troubled by his grandfather's words.

"I think thou knowest well what I mean. Thy father has told thee that thy duty and thy honour are pledged to Annie Hyde."

"I never pledged! Never!"

"But, as in thy baptism thy father made vows for thee, so also for thy marriage he made promises. Noble birth has responsibility, as well as privilege. For thyself alone it is not permitted thee to live, from both the past and the future there

Amelia E. Barr

are demands on thee."

"Grandfather, this living for the future is the curse of the English land-owners. They enjoy not the present, for they are busy taking care of the years they will never see. Their sons are in their way; it is their grandsons and their great-grandsons that interest them. Why should my father plan for my marriage? He may be Earl Hyde for twenty years—and I hope he will. For twenty years Cornelia and I can be happy here in America; and twenty years is a great opportunity. Everything can happen in twenty years. Of one thing I am sure—I will marry Cornelia Moran, even if I run away with her to the ends of the earth."

"'Run away with her.' To be sure! That is in the blood;" and the old man looked sternly back to the days when Hyde's father ran away with his own little daughter.

With some anger Lysbet answered his thoughts. "What art thou talking about? What art thou thinking of? Many good men have run away with their wives. This almighty Doctor John ran away with his wife. Did not Ava Willing leave her father's house and her friends and her faith for him? And did not the Quakers read her out of their Meeting for her marriage?—and I blame them not. Doctor John was no match for Ava Willing. More, too, if thou must look back; remember one May night, when thou and I sat by the Collect in the moonlight, and thou gave me this ring. What did thou say to me that night?"

"'Tis years ago, Lysbet, and If I have forgotten—"

"Forgotten! Well, then, men do forget; but they may be thankful that God has so made women that they do NOT forget. The words thou said that night have been singing in my heart for fifty years; and yet, if thou must be told, some of those words were about RUNNING AWAY WITH THEE;—for, at the first, my father liked thee not."

"Lysbet! My sweet Lysbet! I have not forgotten. For thy dear sake I will stand by Joris, though in doing so I am sure I shall make some unfriends."

"Good, my husband. I take leave to say that thou art doing right."

"Well, then," said Hyde, "if my grandmother stand by me, and you also, sir; and also Madame Jacobus—"

"Madame Jacobus!" cried Lysbet.

"Yes, indeed!" answered Hyde. "'Tis to her understanding and kindness I owe my opportunity; and she gave me, also, one look which I cannot pretend to misunderstand—a look of clear sympathy—a look that promised help."

"She is a clever woman," said Van Heemskirk. "If Joris has her good will it is not to be thrown away."

"I like her not," said Lysbet. "With my grandson, with my affairs, why should she meddle? Pray, now, what took thee, Joris, to her house? It is full of idolatries and graven images. Doctor Kunz once wrote to her a letter about them. He said she ought to remember the Second Commandment. And she wrote to him a letter, and told him to trouble himself with his own business. Much anger and shame there might have been out of this, but Angelica Jacobus is rich, and she is generous to the church, and to the poor; and Doctor Kunz said to the elders, 'Let her alone, for there is a savour of righteousness in her;' and when she heard of that, she was pleased with the Doctor, and sent him one hundred dollars for the Indian Mission. But, Joris, she is no good to thee. I hear many queer

Amelia E. Barr

stories of her."

"Downright lies, all of them," replied Hyde. Then he rose, saying, "I must ride onward. My mother will not sleep until she sees me."

"It is nearly dark," said Van Heemskirk, "and to-night thou art in the clouds. The land and the water will be alike to thee. Rest until the morning."

"I fear not the dark. I know the road by night or by day."

"Yet, even so, mind what I tell thee—if thou ride in the dark, be not wiser than thy beast."

Then they walked with him to the door, and watched him leap to his saddle and ride into the twilight trembling over the misty meadows, trickling with dews. And a great melancholy fell over them, and they could not resume the conversation. Joris re-lit his pipe, and Lysbet went softly and thoughtfully about her household duties. It was one of those hours in which Life distills for us her vague melancholy wine; and Joris and Lysbet drank deeply of it.

The moon was in its third day, and the silent crescent has no calmer and sweeter time; yet Joris it inclined to a sad presentiment. "In my heart there is a fear, Lysbet," he said softly. "I think our boy has gone a road he will dearly rue. I foresee disputing, and wounded hearts, and lives made barren by many disappointed hopes."

"Nothing of the kind," answered Lysbet cheerfully. "Our little Joris is so happy to-night, why wilt thou think evil for him? To think evil is to bring evil. Out of foolishness or perchance such a great love has not come. No, indeed! That it comes from heaven I am sure; and to heaven I will leave its good fortune."

"Pleasant are thy hopes, Lysbet; but, too often, vain and foolish."

"Thy reasoning, is it any wiser? No. Often I have found it wrong. One thing the years have said to me, it is this— 'Lysbet put not thy judgment in the place of Providence. If thou trust Providence, thou hast the easy heart of a child of God; if thou trust to thine own judgment, thou hast the troubled heart of an anxious woman.'"

CHAPTER VII

ARENTA'S MARRIAGE

For a few weeks, Hyde's belief that the very stars would connive with a true lover seemed a reliable one. Madame Jacobus, attracted at their first meeting to the youth, soon gave him an astonishing affection. And yet this warm love of an old woman for youth and beauty was a very natural one— a late development of the maternal instinct leading her even to what seemed an abnormal preference. For she put aside her nephew's claims with hardly a thought, and pleased herself day by day in so managing and arranging events that Hyde and Cornelia met, as a matter of course. Arenta was not, however, deceived; she understood every maneuvre, but the success of her own affairs depended very much on her aunt's cooperation and generosity, and so she could not afford, at this time, to interfere for her brother.

"But I shall alter things a little as soon as I am married," she told herself. "I will take care of that. At this time I must see, and hear, and say nothing. I must act politely—for I am always polite—and Athanase also is in favour of politeness—but I take leave to say that Joris Hyde shall not carry so much sail when a few weeks are gone by. So happy he looks! So pleased with himself! So sure of all he says and does! I am angry at him all the time. Well, then, it will be a satisfaction to abate a little the confidence of this cock-sure young man."

Arenta's feelings were in kind and measure shared by several other people; Doctor Moran held them in a far bitterer mood; but he, also,—environed by circumstances he could neither alter nor command,—was compelled to satisfy his disapproval with promises of a future change. For the wedding of Arenta Van Ariens had assumed a great social importance. Arenta herself had talked about the affair until all classes were on the tiptoe of expectation. The wealthy Dutch families, the exclusive American set, the home and foreign diplomatic circles, were alike looking forward to the splendid ceremony, and to the great breakfast at Peter Van Ariens' house, and to the ball which Madame Jacobus was to give in the evening. None of the younger people had ever been in madame's fantastic ballroom, and they were eager for this entry into her wonderful house. For their mothers— seeing things through the mists of Time—had, innocently enough, exaggerated the marvels of the Chinese lanterns, the feather flowers and gorgeously plumed birds, the cases of tropical butterflies and beetles, and the fascination of the pagan deities, until they were ready to listen to any tale about Madame Jacobus and to swallow it like cream.

So Doctor Moran, being physician and family friend to most of the invited guests, had to listen to such reminiscences and anticipations wherever he went. He knew that he could not talk against the great public current, and that in the excited state of social feeling it would be a kind of treason even to hint disapproval of Arenta, or of any of her friends or doings. But he suffered. He was questioned by some, he was enlightened by others; his opinion was asked about dresses and ceremonies, he was constantly congratulated on his daughter's prominence as bridesmaid, and he was sent for professionally, that he might be talked to socially. Yet if he

Amelia E. Barr

ventured to hint dissatisfaction, or to express himself by a scornful "Pooh! Pooh!" he was answered by looks of such astonishment, of such quick-springing womanly suspicions, that he could not doubt the kind of conversation which followed his exit:

"Do you think Doctor Moran VERY clever?"

"Most people think so."

"He is so unsympathetic. Doctor Moore knows everything Madame Jacobus is going to have, and to do. I think doctors ought to be chatty. It is so good for their patients to be cheered up a little."

Doctor Moran divined perfectly this taste for gossip and MEDICINAL sympathy combined, and to administer it was, to him, more nauseous than his own bitterest drugs. So in these days he was not a cheerful man to live with, and Cornelia's beauty and radiant happiness affected him very much as Hyde's pronounced satisfaction affected Arenta. One morning, as he was returning home after a round of disagreeable visits, he saw Cornelia and Hyde coming up Broadway together. They were sauntering side by side in all the lazy happiness of perfect love; and as he looked at them the sorrow of an immense disillusion filled him to the lips. He had believed himself, as yet, to be the first and the dearest in his child's love; but in that moment his eyes were opened, and he felt as if he had been suddenly thrust out from it and the door closed upon him.

He did the wisest thing possible: he went home to his wife. She heard him ride with clattering haste into the stone court, and soon after enter the house from the back, banging every door after him. She knew then that something had angered him—that he was in that temper which makes a woman cry, but which a man can only relieve by noisy or emphatic movement of some kind. A resolute look came into her face and she said to herself, "John has always had his own way—and my way also; but Cornelia's way—the child must surely have something to say about that."

"Where is Cornelia, Ava?" He asked the question with a quick glance round the room, as if he expected to find her present.

"Cornelia is not at home to-day."

"Is she ever at home now?"

"You know that Arenta's wedding—"

"Arenta's wedding! I am tired to death of it: I have heard nothing this morning but Arenta's wedding. Why the deuce! should my house be turned upside down and inside out for Arenta's wedding? Women have been married before Arenta Van Ariens, and women will be married after her. What is all this fuss about?"

"You know—"

"Bless my soul! of course I know. I know one thing at least, that I have just met Cornelia and that young fop George Hyde coming up the street together, as if they two alone were in the world. They never saw me, they could see nothing but themselves."

"Men and women have done such a thing before, John, and they will do it again. Cornelia is a beautiful girl; it is natural that she should have a lover."

"It is very unnatural that she should choose for her lover the son of my worst enemy."

"I am sure you wrong General Hyde. When was he your enemy? How could he be your enemy?"

"When was he my enemy? Ever since the first hour we met. Often he tried to injure me with General Washington; often he accused me of showing partiality to certain officers in the army; only last year he prevented my election to the Senate by using all his influence in favour of Joris Van Heemskirk. If he has not done me more injury and more injustice, 'tis because he has not had the opportunity. And you want me to give Cornelia to his son! Yes, you do, Ava! I see it on your face. You stretch my patience too far. Can I not see—"

"Can an angry man ever see? No, he cannot. You feed your own suspicions, John. You might just as well link Cornelia's name with Rem Van Ariens as with Joris Hyde. She is continually in Rem's company. He is devoted to her. She cannot possibly misunderstand his looks and words, she must perceive that he is her ardent lover. You might have seen them the last three evenings sitting together at that table preparing the invitations for the wedding breakfast and ball; arranging the cards and favours.—So happy! So pleasantly familiar! So confidential! I think Rem Van Ariens has as much of Cornelia's liking as George Hyde; and perhaps neither of them have enough of it to win her hand. All lovers do not grow to husbands."

"Thank God, they do not! But what you say about Rem is only cobweb stuff. She is too friendly, too pleasantly familiar, I would like to see her more shy and silent with him. Every one has already given my daughter to Hyde, and, say what you will, common fame is seldom to blame."

"Dinner is waiting, John, and whether you eat it or not

Destiny will go straight to her mark. Love is destiny; and the heart is its own fate. There are those to whom we are spiritually related, and the tie is kinder than flesh and blood. Can you, or I, count such kindred? No; but souls see each other at a glance. Did I not know thee, John, the very moment that we met?"

She spoke softly, with a voice sweeter than music, and her husband was touched and calmed. He took the hand she stretched out to him and kissed it, and she added—

"Let us be patient. Love has reasons that reason does not understand; and if Cornelia is Hyde's by predestination, as well as by choice, vainly we shall worry and fret; all our opposition will come to nothing. Give Cornelia this interval, and tithe it not; in a few days Arenta will have gone away; and as for Hyde, any hour may summon him to join his father in England; and this summons, as it will include his mother, he can neither evade nor put off. Then Rem will have his opportunity."

"To be patient—to wait—to say nothing—it is to give opportunity too much scope. I must tell that young fellow a little of my mind—"

"You must not make yourself a town's talk, John. Just now New York is all for lovers. If you interfere between Hyde and Cornelia while it is in this temper, every one will cry out, 'Oh, the pity of it!' and you will be bayed into doing some mad thing or other. Do I not know you, dear one?"

"God's precious!" and he took her in his arms, saying, "the man who learns nothing from his wife will never learn anything from anybody. Come, then, and we will eat our meal. I had forgotten Rem, and as you say, Hyde may have to go to England to-morrow; putting-off has broken up many an ill marriage."

"Time and absence against any love affair that is not destiny! And if it be destiny, there is only submission, nothing else. But life has a 'maybe' in everything dear; a maybe that is just as likely to please us as not."

Then Doctor John looked up with a smile. "You are right, Ava," he said cheerfully. "I will take the maybe. Maybes have a deal to do with life. When you come to think of it, there is not a victory of any kind gained, nor a good deed done except on a maybe. So maybe all I fear may pass like a summer cloud. Yet, take my word for it, there is, I think, no maybe in Rem's chances with Cornelia."

"We shall see. I think there is."

Certainly Rem was of this opinion. The past few weeks had been very favourable to him. In them he had been continually associated with Cornelia, and her manner towards him had been so frankly kind and familiar, so confidential and sympathetic, that he could not help but contrast it with their previous intercourse, when she had appeared to withdraw herself from all his approaches and to forbid by her retiring manner even the courtesies to which his long acquaintance with her entitled him.

If he had known more of women he would not have given himself any hope on this change of attitude. It simply meant that Cornelia had arrived at that certainty with regard to her own affections which permitted her a more general latitude. She knew that she loved Hyde, and she knew that Hyde loved her. They had a most complete confidence in each other; and she was not afraid, either for his sake or her own, to give to Rem that friendship which the circumstances warranted. That this friendship could ever grow to love on her part was an impossible thing; and if she thought of Rem's feelings, it was to suppose that he must understand this position as well as she did herself.

Rem, however, was quite aware of his rival, and with the blunt directness of his nature watched with jealous dislike, and often with rude impatience, the familiar intercourse which his aunt's partiality permitted Hyde. He was, indeed, often so rude that a less sweet-tempered, a less just youth than George Hyde would have pointedly resented many offences that he passed by with that "noble not caring" which is often the truest courage.

Still the situation was one of great tension, and it required not only the wise forbearance of Hyde and Cornelia, but the domineering selfishness of Arenta and the suave clever diplomacies of Madame Jacobus to preserve at times the merely decent conventionalities of polite life. To keep the peace until the wedding was over—that was all that Rem promised himself; THEN! He often gave voice to this last word, though he had no distinct idea as to what measures he included in those four letters.

He told himself, however, that it would be well for George Hyde to be in England, and that if he were there, the General might be trusted to look after the marriage of his son. For he knew that an English noble would be of necessity bound by his caste and his connections, and that Hyde would have to face obligations he would not be able to shirk. "Then, then, his opportunity to win Cornelia would come!" And it was at this point the hopeful "maybe" entered into Rem's desires and anticipations.

But wrath covered carries fate. Every one was in some measure conscious of this danger and glad when the wedding day approached. Even Arenta had grown a little weary of the prolonged excitement she had provoked, for everything had gone so well with her that she had taken the public very much into her confidence. There had been frequent little notices in the Gazette and Journal of the approaching day—of the wedding presents, the wedding favours, the wedding guests, and the wedding garments. And, as if to add the last touch of glory to the event, just a week before Arenta's nuptials a French armed frigate came to New York bearing despatches for the Count de Moustier; and the Marquis de Tounnerre was selected to bear back to France the Minister's Message. So the marriage was put forward a few days for this end, and Arenta in the most unexpected way obtained the bridal journey which she desired; and also with it the advantage of entering France in a semi-public and stately manner.

"I am the luckiest girl in the world," she said to Cornelia and her brother when this point had been decided. They were tying up "dream-cake" for the wedding guests in madame's queer, uncanny drawing-room as she spoke, and the words were yet on her lips when madame entered with a sandal wood box in her hands.

"Rem," she said, "go with Cornelia into the dining-room a few minutes. I have something to say to Arenta that concerns no one else."

As soon as they were alone madame opened the box and upon a white velvet cushion lay the string of oriental pearls which Arenta on certain occasions had been permitted to wear. Arenta's eyes flashed with delight. She had longed for them to complete her wedding costume, but having a very strong hope that her aunt would offer her this favour, she had resolved to wait for her generosity until the last hour. Now she was going; to receive the reward of her prudent patience, and she said to herself, "How good it is to be discreet!" With an intense desire and interest she looked at the beautiful beads, but madame's face was troubled and sombre, and she said almost reluctantly—

"Arenta, I am going to make you an offer. This necklace will be yours when I die, at any rate; but I think there is in your heart a wish to have it now. Is this so?"

"Aunt, I should like—oh, indeed I long to wear the beads at my marriage. I shall only be half-dressed without them."

"You shall wear the necklace. And as you are going to what is left of the French Court, I will give it to you now, if the gift will be to your mind."

"There is nothing that could be more to my mind, dear aunt. I would rather have the necklace, than twice its money's worth. Thank you, aunt. You always know what is in a young girl's heart."

"First, listen to what I say. No woman of our family has escaped calamity of some kind, if they owned these beads. My mother lost her husband the year she received them. My Aunt Hildegarde lost her fortune as soon as they were hers. As for myself, on the very day they became mine your Uncle Jacobus sailed away, and he has never come back. Are you not afraid of such fatality?"

"No, I am not. Things just happen that way. What power can a few beads have over human life or happiness? To say so, to think so, is foolishness."

"I know not. Yet I have heard that both pearls and opals have the power to attract to themselves the ill fortune of their wearers. If they happen to be maiden pearls or gems that would be good; but would you wish to inherit the evil fortune of all the women who have possessed before you?"

"Poor pearls! It is they who are the unfortunates."

"Yes, but a time comes when they have taken all of misfortune they can take; then the pearls grow black and die, really die. Yes, indeed! I have seen dead pearls. And if the necklace were of opals, when that time came for them the gems would lose their fire and colour, grow ashy grey, fall apart and become dust, nothing but dust."

"Do you believe such tales, aunt? I do not. And your pearls are yet as white as moonlight. I do not fear them. Give them to me, aunt. I snap my fingers at such fables."

"Give them to you, I will not, Arenta; but you may take them from the box with your own hands."

"I am delighted to take them. I have always longed for them."

"Perhaps then they longed for you, for what is another's yearns for its owner."

Then madame left the room and Arenta lifted the box and carried it nearer to the light. And a little shiver crept through her heart and she closed the lid quickly and said irritably—

"It is my aunt's words. She is always speaking dark and doubtful things. However, the pearls are mine at last!" and she carried them with her downstairs, throwing back her head as if they were round her white throat and—as was her way—spreading herself as she went.

All fine weddings are much alike. It was only in such accidentals as costume that Arenta's differed from the fine weddings of to-day. There was the same crush of gayly attired women, of men in full dress, or military dress, or distinguished by diplomatic insignia:—the same low flutter of silk, and stir of whispered words, and suppressed excitement—the same eager crowd along the streets and around the church to watch the advent of the bride and bridegroom. All of the guests had seen them very often before, yet they too looked at the dazzling girl in white as if they expected an entirely different person. The murmur of pleasure, the indefinable stir of human emotion, the solemn mystical words at the altar that were making two one, the triumphant peal of music when they ceased, and the quick crescendo of rising congratulation—all these things were present then, as now. And then, as now, all these things failed to conceal from sensitive minds that odour of human sacrifice, not to be disguised with the scent of bridal flowers—that immolation of youth and beauty and charming girlhood upon the altar of an unknown and an untried love.

New York was not then too busy making money to take an interest in such a wedding, and Arenta's drive through its pleasant streets was a kind of public invitation. For Jacob Van Ariens was one of a guild of wealthy merchants, and they were at their shop doors to express their sympathy by lifted hats and smiling faces; while the women looked from every window, and the little children followed, their treble voices heralding and acclaiming the beautiful bride. Then came the breakfast and the health-drinking and the speech-making and the rather sadder drive to the wharf at which lay La Belle France. And even Arenta was by this time weary of the excitement, so that it was almost with a sense of relief she stepped across the little carpeted gangway to her deck. Then the anchor was lifted, the cable loosened, and with every sail set La Belle France went dancing down the river on the tide-top to the open sea.

Van Ariens and his son Rem turned silently away. A great and evident depression had suddenly taken the place of their assumed satisfaction. "I am going to the Swamp office," said Rem after a few moments' silence, "there is something to be done there."

"That is well," answered Peter. "To my Cousin Deborah I will give some charges about the silver, and then I will follow you."

Both men were glad to be alone. They had outworn emotion and knew instinctively that some common duty was the best restorer. The same feeling affected, in one way or another, all the watchers of this destiny. Women whose household work was belated, whose children were strayed, who had used up their nervous strength in waiting and feeling, were now cross and inclined to belittle the affair and to be angry at Arenta and themselves for their lost day. And men, young and old, all went back to their ledgers and counters and manufacturing with a sense of lassitude and dejection.

Peter had nearly reached his own house when he met Doctor Moran. The doctor was more irritable than depressed. He looked at his friend and said sharply, "You have a fever, Van Ariens. Go to bed and sleep."

"To work I will go. That is the best thing to do. My house has no comfort in it. Like a milliner's or a mercer's store it has been for many weeks. Well, then, my Cousin Deborah is at work there, and in a little while—a little while—" He suddenly stopped and looked at the doctor with brimming eyes. In that moment he understood that no putting to rights could ever make his home the same. His little saucy, selfish, but dearly loved Arenta would come there no more; and he found not one word that could express the tide of sorrow rising in his heart. Doctor John understood. He remained quiet, silent, clasping Van Ariens' hand until the desolate father with a great effort blurted out—

"She is gone!—and smiling, also, she went."

"It is the curse of Adam," answered Doctor Moran bitterly— "to bring up daughters, to love them, to toil and save and deny ourselves for them, and then to see some strange man, of whom we have no certain knowledge, carry them off captive to his destiny and his desires. 'Tis a thankless portion to be a father—a bitter pleasure."

"Well, then, to be a mother is worse."

"Who can tell that? Women take for compensations things that do not deceive a father. And, also, they have one grand promise to help them bear loss and disappointment—the assurance of the Holy Scripture that they shall have salvation through child-bearing. And I, who have seen so much of family love and life, can tell you that this promise is all many a mother has for her travail and sorrowful love."

"It is enough. Pray God that we miss not of that reward some share," and with a motion of adieu he turned into his house. Very thoughtfully the Doctor went on to William Street where he had a patient,—a young girl of about Arenta's age—very ill. A woman opened the door—a woman weeping bitterly.

"She is gone, Doctor."

"At what hour?"

"The clock was striking three—she went smiling."

Then he bowed his head and turned away.

Amelia E. Barr

There was nothing more that he could do; but he remembered that Arenta had stepped on board the La Belle France as the clock struck three, and that she also had gone smiling to her unknown destiny.

"Two emigrants," he thought, "pilgrims of Love and Death, and both went smiling!" An unwonted tenderness came into his heart; he thought of the bright, lovely bride clinging so trustfully to her husband's arm, and he voiced this gentle feeling to his wife in very sincere wishes for the safety and happiness of the little emigrant for Love. He had a singular reluctance to name her—he knew not why—with the other little maid who also had left smiling at three o'clock, an emigrant for whom Death had opened eternal vistas of delight.

"I do not know," said Mrs. Moran, "how Van Ariens could suffer his daughter to go to a country full of turmoil and bloodshed."

"He was very unhappy to do so, Ava. But when things have gone a certain length they have fatality. The Marquis had promised to become eventually a citizen of this Republic, and Van Ariens had no idea in sanctioning the marriage that his daughter would leave New York. It was even supposed the Marquis would remain here in the Count de Moustier's place, and the sudden turn of events which sent de Tounnerre to France was a severe blow to Van Ariens. But what could he do?"

"He might have delayed the marriage until the return of de Tounnerre."

"Ah, Ava! you are counting without consideration. He could not have detained Arenta against her will, and if he had, a miserable life would have been before both of them—

domestic discomfort, public queries and suspicions, questions, doubts, offending sympathies—all the griefs and vexations that are sure to follow a Fate that is crossed. He did the best thing possible when he let the wilful girl go as pleasantly as he could. Arenta needs a wide horizon."

"Is she in any danger from the state of affairs in Paris?"

"Mr. Jefferson says in no danger whatever. Our Minister is living there in safety. Arenta will have his friendship and protection; and her husband has many friends in the most powerful party. She will have a brilliant visit and be very happy."

"How can she be very happy with the guillotine daily enacting such murders?"

"She need not be present at such murders. And Mr. Jefferson may be right, and we outsiders may make too much of circumstances that France, and France alone, can properly estimate. He says that the God that made iron wished not slaves to exist, and thinks there is a profound and eternal justice in this desolation and retribution of aristocrats who have committed unmentionable oppressions. I know not; good and evil are so interwoven in life that every good, traced up far enough, is found to involve evil. This is the great mystery of life. However, Ava, I am a great believer in sequences; there are few events that break off absolutely. In Arenta's life there will be sequences; let us hope that they will be happy ones. Where is Cornelia?"

"I know not. She is asleep. The ball to-night is to be fairy-land and love-land, an Arabian night's dream and a midsummer night's dream all in one. I told her to rest, for she was weary and nervous with expectation."

Amelia E. Barr

"I dare say. But what is the good of being young if it is not to expect miracles?"

"George Hyde calls for her at eight o'clock. I shall let her sleep until seven, give her some refreshment, and then assist her to dress."

"George Hyde! So you still believe in trusting the cat with the cream?"

"I still believe in Cornelia. Come, now, and drink a cup of tea. To-morrow the Van Ariens' excitement will be over, and we shall have rest."

"I think not. The town is now ready to move to Philadelphia. I hear that Mrs. Adams is preparing to leave Richmond Hill. Washington has already gone, and Congress is to meet in December. Even the Quakers are intending all sorts of social festivities."

"But this will not concern us."

"It may. If George Hyde does not go very soon to England, we shall go to Philadelphia. I wish to rid myself and Cornelia of his airs and graces and wearisome good temper, his singing and reciting and tringham-trangham poetry. This story has been long enough; we will turn over and end it."

"It will be a great trial to Cornelia."

"It may, or it may not—there is Rem—Rem is your own suggestion. However, we have all to sing the hymn of Renunciation at some time; it is well to sing it in youth."

Mrs. Moran did not answer. When answering was likely to provoke anger, she kept silence and talked the matter over with herself. A very wise plan. For where shall we find a friend so intimate, so discreet, so conciliating as self? Who can speak to us so well?—without obscurity, without words, without passion. Yes, indeed: "I will talk to myself" is a very significant phrase.

CHAPTER VIII

TWO PROPOSALS

The ruling idea of any mind assumes the foreground of thought; and after Arenta's marriage the dominant desire of George Hyde was to have his betrothal to Cornelia recognized and assured. He was in haste to light his own nuptial torch, and afraid every day of that summons to England which would delay the event. Hitherto, both had been satisfied with the delicious certainty of their own hearts. To bring Love to discussion and catechism, to talk of Love in connection with house and money matters, to put him into bonds, however light those bonds might be, was indeed a safe and prudent thing for their future happiness; but, so far, the present with its sweet freedom and uncertainty had been more charming to their imagination. Suddenly, however, Hyde felt the danger and stress of this uncertainty and the fear of losing what he appeared to hold so lightly.

"I may have to go away with mother at any time—I may be detained by events I cannot help—and I have not bound Cornelia to me by any personal recognized tie—and Rem Van Ariens will be ever near her. Oh, indeed, this state of affairs will never do! I will write to Cornelia this very moment and tell her I must see her father this evening. I cannot possibly delay it longer. I have been a fool—a careless, happy fool—too long. There is not now a day to lose. I have already wasted more time than was reasonable over the love affairs of other people; now I must look after my own. Safe bind, safe find; I will bind Cornelia to me before I leave her, then I have a good right to find her safe when I return to claim her."

While such thoughts were passing through his mind he had risen hastily from the chair in which he had been musing. He opened his secretary and sitting resolutely down, began a letter to Doctor Moran. He poured out his heart and desires, and then he read what he had written. It would not do at all. It was a love letter and not a business letter. He wrote another, and then another. The first was too long, it left nothing in the inkstand; the last was not to be thought of. When he had finished reading them over, he was in a passion with himself.

"A fool in your teeth twice over, Joris Hyde!" he cried, "yes, sir, three times, and far too good for you! Since you cannot write a decent business letter, write, then, to the adorable Cornelia; the words will be at your finger ends for that letter, and will slip from your pen as if they were dancing:

"MY SWEET CORNELIA:

"I have not seen you for two days, and 'tis a miracle that I have endured it. I can tell you, beloved, that I am much concerned about our affairs, and now that I have begun to talk wisely I may talk a little more without wearying you. You know that I may have to go to England soon, and go I will not until I have asked your father what favour he will show us. On the street, he gets out of my way as if I had the plague. Tell me at what hour I may call and see him in his house. I will then ask him point blank for your hand, and he is so candid that I shall have in a word Yes or No on the matter. Do not keep me waiting longer than seven this very night. I have a fever of anxiety, and I shall not grow better, but worse, until I settle our engagement. Oh, my peerless Cornelia, pearl and flower of womanhood, I speak your speech, I think your thought; you are the noblest thing in my life, and to remember you is to remember the hours when I was the very best and the very happiest. Your image has become part of me, your memory is a perfume which makes sweet my heart. I wish this moment to give you thousands and thousands of kisses. Bid me come to you soon, very soon, sooner than seven, if possible, for your love is my life. Send your answer to my city lodging. I shall follow this letter and be impatiently waiting for it. Oh, Cornelia, am I not ever and entirely yours?

"GEORGE HYDE."

It was not more than eight o'clock in the morning when he wrote this letter, and as soon as possible he despatched a swift messenger with it to Cornelia. He hoped that she would receive it soon after the Doctor had left his home for his usual round of professional visits; then she might possibly write to him at once, and if so, he would get the letter very soon after he reached the city.

Probably Madame Hyde divined something of the importance and tenor of a missive sent in such a hurry of anxious love, so early in the day, but she showed neither annoyance nor curiosity regarding it. In the first place, she knew that opposition would only strengthen whatever resolve her son had made; in the second place, she was conscious of a singular restlessness of her own spirit. She was apprehending change, and she could think of no change but that call to leave her home and her native land which she so much dreaded. If this event happened, then the affairs of Joris would assume an entirely different aspect. He would be obliged to leave everything which now interested him, and he could not live without interests; very well, then, he would be compelled to accept such as a new Fate thrown into his new life. She had a great faith in circumstances. She knew that in the long run every one wrote beneath that potent word, "Your obedient servant." Circumstances would either positively deny all her son's hopes, or they would so powerfully aid them that opposition would be useless; and she mentally bowed herself to an influence so powerful and perhaps so favourable.

"Joris, my dear one," she said, as they rose from the breakfast table; "Joris, I think there is a letter from your father. To the city you must go as soon as you can, for I have had a restless night, full of feeling it has been."

"You should not go to bed to feel, mother. Night is the time for sleep."

"And for dreams, and for many good things to come, that come not in the day. Yes, indeed, the nighttime of the body is the daytime of the soul."

Then Joris smiled and kissing her, said, "I am going at once. If there is a letter I will send a quick rider with it."

"But come thyself."

"That I cannot." "But why, then?"

"To-morrow, I will tell you."

"That is well. Into thy mother's heart drop all thy joys and sorrows. Thine are mine." And she kissed him, and he went away glad and hopeful and full of tender love for the mother who understood him so sympathetically. He stood up in his stirrups to wave her a last adieu, and then he said to himself, "How fortunate I am about women! Could I have a sweeter, lovelier mistress? No! Mother? No! Grandmother? No! Friend? No! Cornelia, mother, grandmother, Madame Jacobus, all of them just what I love and need, sweet souls between me and the angels."

It happened—but doubtless happened because so ordered—that the very hour in which Joris left Hyde Manor, Peter Van Ariens received a letter that made him very anxious. He left his office and went to see his son. "Rem," he said, "there is now an opportunity for thee. Here has come a letter from Boston, and some one must go there; and that too in a great hurry. The house of Blume and Otis is likely to fail, and in it we have some great interests. A lawyer we must have to look after them; go thyself, and it shall be well for both of us."

"I am ready to go—that is, I can be ready in one or two days."

"There are not one or two days to spare. Gerard will take care of thy work here. To-day is the best time of all."

"I cannot go with a happy mind to-day. I will tell you, father. I think now my case with Cornelia will bear putting to the question. As you know, it has been step with step between Joris Hyde and myself in that affair, and if I go away now without securing the ground I have gained, what can hinder Hyde from taking advantage over me? He too must go soon, but he will try and secure his position before he leaves. To do the same thing is my only way. I wish, then, the time to give myself this security."

"That is fair. A man is not a man till he has won a wife. Cornelia Moran is much to my mind. Tell her my home is thine, and she will be a mistress dearly loved and honoured.

And if a thing is to be done, there is no time like the hour that has not struck. Go and see her now. She was in the garden gathering asters when I left home this morning."

"I will write to her. I will tell her what is in my heart—though she knows it well—and ask her for her love and her hand. If she is kind to my offer she will tell me to come and see her to-night, then I can go to Boston with a free heart and look after your money and your business."

"If things be this way, thou art reasonable. A good wife must not be lost for the peril of some gold sovereigns. At once write to the maid; such letters are best done at the first thought, some prudences or some fears may come with the second thoughts."

"I have no fear but Joris Hyde. That Englishman I hate. His calm confidence, his smiling insolent air is intolerable."

"It is the English way. But Cornelia is American—as thou art."

"She thinks much of that, but yet—"

"Be not afraid. The brave either find, or make, a way to success. What is in a girl's heart no man can tell, if she be cold and shy that should not cause thee to doubt. When water is ice, who would suspect what great heat is stored away in it? Write thy letter at once. Put thy heart into thy pen. Not always prudent is this way, but once in a man's life it is wisdom."

"My pen is too small for my heart."

"My opinion is that thou hast wavered too long. It is a great foolishness to let the cherry knock against the lips too often or too long. A pretty pastime, perhaps, to will, and not will, to dare, and not dare; but at last the knock comes that drops the cherry—it may be into some other mouth."

"I fear no one but that rascal, Joris Hyde."

"A rascal he is not, because the same woman he loves as thyself. Such words weaken any cause. No wrong have I seen or known of Lieutenant Hyde."

"I will call him a rascal, and I will give him no other title, though his father leave him an earl."

"Now, then, I shall go. I like not ill words. Write thy letter, but put out of thy mind all bad thoughts first. A love letter from a bitter heart is not lucky. And of all thy wit thou wilt have great need if to a woman thou write."

"Oh, they are intolerable, aching joys! A man who dares to love a woman, or dares to believe in her, dares to be mad."

"Come, come! No evil must thou speak of good women, I swear that I was never out of it yet, when I judged men as they judged women. The art of loving a woman is the art of trusting her—yes, though the heavens fall. Now, then, haste with thy letter. Thou may have 'Yes' to it ere thou sleep to-night."

"And I may have 'No.'"

"To be sure, if thou think 'no.' But, even so, if thou lose the wedding ring, the hand is still left; another ring may be found."

"'No,' would be a deathblow to me."

"It will not. While a man has meat and drink love will not starve him; with world's business and world's pleasure an unkind love he makes shift to forget. Bring to me word of thy good fortune this night, and in the morning there is the Boston business. Longer it can hardly wait."

But the letter to Cornelia which Hyde found to slip off his pen like dancing was a much more difficult matter to Rem. He wrote and destroyed, and wrote again and destroyed, and this so often that he finally resolved to go to Maiden Lane for his inspiration. "I may see Cornelia in the garden, or at the window, and when I see what I desire, surely I shall have the wit to ask for it."

So he thought, and with the thought he locked his desk and went towards his home in Maiden Lane. He met George Hyde sauntering up the street looking unhappy and restless, and he suspected at once that he had been walking past Doctor Moran's house in the hope of seeing Cornelia and had been disappointed. The thought delighted him. He was willing to bear disappointment himself, if by doing so some of Hyde's smiling confidence was changed to that unhappy uneasiness which he detected in his rival's face and manner. The young men bowed to each other but did not speak. In some occult way they divined a more positive antagonism than they had ever before been conscious of.

"I cannot go out of the house," thought Rem, "without meeting that fop. He is in at one door, and out at another; this way, that way, up street, and down street—the devil take the fellow!"

"What a mere sullen creature that Rem Van Ariens is!" thought Hyde, "and with all the good temper in the world I affirm it. I wonder what he is on the street for at this hour! Shall I watch him? No, that would be vile work. I will let him alone; he may as well play the ill-natured fool on the street as in the house—better, indeed, for some one may have a title to tell him so. But I may assure myself of one thing, when I met him he was building castles in the future, for he was looking straight before him; and if he had been thinking of the past, he would have been looking down. I should not wonder if it was Cornelia that filled his dreams. Faith, we have blockheads of all ages; but on that road he will never overtake his thought"—then with a movement of impatience he added,

"Why should I let him into my mind?—for he is the least welcome of all intruders.—Good gracious! how long the minutes are! It is plain to me that Cornelia is not at home, and my letter may not even have touched her hands yet. How shall I endure another hour?—perhaps many hours. Where can she have gone? Not unlikely to Madame Jacobus. Why did I not think of this before? For who can help me to bear suspense better than madame? I will go to her at once."

He hastened his steps and soon arrived at the well-known residence of his friend. He was amazed as soon as the door was opened to find preparations of the most evident kind for some change. The corded trunk in the hall, the displaced furniture, all things he saw were full of the sad hurry of parting. "What is the matter?" he asked in a voice of fear.

"I am going away for a time, Joris, my good friend," answered madame, coming out of a shrouded and darkened parlour as she spoke. She had on her cloak and bonnet, and before Joris could ask her another question a coach drove to the door. "I think it is a piece of good fortune," she continued, "to see you before I go."

"But where are you going?"

"To Charleston."

"But why?"

"I am going because my sister Sabrina is sick—dying; and there is no one so near to her as I am."

"I knew not you had a sister."

"She is the sister of my husband. So, then, she is twice my sister. When Jacobus comes home he will thank me for going to his dear Sabrina. But what brings you here so early? Yesterday I asked for you, and I was told that you were waiting on your good mother."

"My mother felt sure there was a letter from father, and I came at once to get it for her."

"Was there one?"

"There was none."

"It will come in good time. Now, I must go. I have not one moment to lose. Good-bye, dear Joris!"

"For how long, my friend?"

"I know not. Sabrina is incurably ill. I shall stay with her till she departs." She said these words as they went down the steps together, and with eyes full of tears he placed her carefully in the coach and then turned sorrowfully to his own rooms. He could not speak of his own affairs at such a moment, and he realized that there was nothing for him to do but wait as patiently as possible for Cornelia's answer.

In the meantime Rem was writing his proposal. He was not

assisted in the effort by any sight of his mistress. It was evident Cornelia was not in her home, and he looked in vain for any shadow of the sweet face that he was certain would have made his words come easily. Finally, after many trials, he desisted with the following, though it was the least affective of any form he had written:

To MISS MORAN,

Honoured and Beloved Friend:

Twenty times this day I have tried to write a letter worthy to come into your hands and worthy to tell you how beyond all words I love you, But what can I say more than that I love you? This you know. It has been no secret to you since ever you were a little girl. Many years I have sought your love,—pardon me if now I ask you to tell me I have not sought in vain. To-morrow I must leave New York, and I may be away for some time. Pray, then, give me some hope to-night to take with me. Say but one word to make me the proudest and happiest lover in the world. Give me the permission to come and show to your father that I am able to maintain you in every comfort that is your right; and all my life long I will prove to you the devotion that attests my undying affection and gratitude. I am sick with longing for the promise of your love. May I presume to hope so great a blessing? O dearest Cornelia, I am, as you know well, your humble servant,

REMBRANDT VAN ARIENS.

When he had finished this letter, he folded and sealed it, and walked to the window with it in his hand. Then he saw Cornelia returning home from some shopping or social errand, and hastily calling a servant, ordered him to deliver the letter at once to Miss Moran. And as Cornelia lingered a little among the aster beds, the man put it into her own hands. She bowed and smiled as she accepted it, but Rem, watching with his heart in his eyes, could see that it awakened no special interest. She kept it unopened as she wandered among the purple and pink, and gold and white flowers, until Mrs. Moran came to the door to hurry her movements; then she followed her mother hastily into the house, "Do you know how late it is, Cornelia? Dinner is nearly ready. There is a letter on your dressing table that came by Lieutenant Hyde's servant two or three hours ago."

"And Tobias has just brought me a letter from Rem—at least the direction is in Rem's handwriting."

"Some farewell dance I suppose, before our dancers go to gay Philadelphia."

"I dare say it is." She made the supposition as she went up the stairs, and did not for a moment anticipate any more important information. As she entered her room an imposing looking letter met her eyes—a letter written upon the finest paper, squarely folded, and closed with a large seal of scarlet wax carrying the Hyde arms. Poor Rem's message lost instantly whatever interest it possessed; she let it fall from her hand, and lifting Hyde's, opened it with that marvellous womanly impetuosity which love teaches. Then all the sweet intimate ardour and passionate disquietude of her lover took possession of her. In a moment she felt all that he felt; all the ecstasy and tumult of a great affection not sure. For this letter was the "little more" in Hyde's love, and, oh, how much it was!

She pondered it until she was called to dinner. There was then no time to read Rem's letter, but she broke the seal and glanced at its tenor, and an expression of pity and annoyance came into her eyes. Hastily she locked both letters away in a drawer of her desk, and as she did so, smilingly said to herself, "I wonder if papers are sensitive! Shut close together in one little drawer will they like it? I hope they will lie peaceably and not quarrel."

Doctor Moran was not at home, nor was he expected until sundown, so mother and daughter enjoyed together the confidence which Hyde's letter induced. Mrs. Moran thought the young man was right, and promised, to a certain extent, to favour his proposal. "However, Cornelia," she added, "unless your father is perfectly agreeable and satisfied, I would not advise you to make any engagement. Clandestine engagements come to grief in some way or other, and if your marriage with Joris Hyde is prearranged by THOSE who know what is best for your good, then, my dear, it is as sure to take place as the sun is sure to rise to-morrow. It is only waiting for the appointed hour, and you may as well wait in a happy home as in one you make wretched by the fret and complaining which a secret in any life is certain to produce."

Now, it is not often that a girl has to answer in one hour two such epistles as those received by Cornelia. Yet perhaps such an event occurs more frequently than is suspected, for Love—like other things—has its critical moment; and when that moment arrives it finds a voice as surely as the flower ready to bloom opens its petals. And if there be two lovers equally sincere, both are likely to feel at the same moment the same impetus to revelation. Besides which, Fate of any kind seeks the unusual and the unexpected; it desires to startle, and to force events by surprises.

The answering of these letters was naturally Cornelia's first afternoon thought. It troubled her to remember that Joris had already been waiting some hours for a reply, for she had no hesitation as to what that reply should be. To write to Joris was a delightful thing, an unusual pleasure, and she sat down, smiling, to pen the lines which she thought would bring her much happiness, but which were doomed to bring her a great sorrow.

MY JORIS! My dear Friend:

'Tis scarce an hour since I received your letter, but I have read it over four times. And whatever you desire, that also is my desire; and I am deceived as much as you, if you think I do not love you as much as I am loved by you. You know my heart, and from you I shall never hide it; and I think if I were asleep, I should tell you how much I love you; for, indeed, I often dream that I do so. Come, then, this very night as soon as you think convenient. If my father is in a suitable temper it will be well to speak plainly to him, and I am sure that my mother will say in our favour all that is wise.

Our love, with no recognition but our own, has been so strangely sweet that I could be content never to alter that condition; and yet I fear no bond, and am ready to put it all to the trial. For if our love is not such as will uphold an engagement, it will sink of itself; and if it is true as we believe it to be, then it may last eternally. What more is to say I will keep for your ear, for you are enough in my heart to know all my thoughts, and to know better than I can tell you how dearly, how constantly, how entirely I love you.

Yours forever, CORNELIA.

Without a pause, without an erasure this letter had transcribed itself from Cornelia's heart to the small gilt-edged note paper; but she found it a much more difficult thing to answer the request of Rem Van Ariens. She was angry at him for putting her in such a dilemma. She thought that she had made plain as possible to him the fact that she was pleased to be a companion, a friend, a sister, if he so desired, but that love between them was not to be thought of. She had told Arenta this many times, and she had done so because she was certain Arenta would make this position clear to her brother. And under ordinary circumstances Arenta would have been frank and free enough with Rem, but while her own marriage was such an important question she was not inclined to embarrass or shadow its arrange-ments by suggesting things to Rem likely to cause disagreements when she wished all to be harmonious and cheerful. So Arenta had encouraged, rather than dashed, Rem's hopes, for she did not doubt that Cornelia would finally undo very thoroughly what she had done.

"A little love experience will be a good thing for Rem," she said to herself—"it will make a man of him; and I do hope he has more self-respect and courage than to die of her denial."

It is easy, then, to understand how Cornelia, relying on Arenta's usually ready advice and confidences, was sure that Rem had accepted the friendship that was all in her power to give him, and that this belief gave to their intercourse a frank and kindly intimacy that it would not otherwise have obtained. This state of things was desirable and comfortable for Arenta, and Cornelia also had found a great satisfaction in a friendship which she trusted had fully recognized and accepted its limitations. Now, all these pleasant moderate emotions were stirred into uncomfortable agitation by Rem's unlooked-for and unreasonable request. She was hurt and agitated and withal a little sorry for Rem, and she was also in a hurry, for the letter for Joris was waiting, as she wished to send both by the same messenger. Finally she wrote the following words, not noticing at the time, but remembering afterwards, what a singular soul reluctance she experienced; how some uncertain presentiment, vague and dark and drear, stifled her thoughts and tried to make her understand, or at least pause. But alas! the doom that walks side by side with us, never warns; it seems rather to stand sarcastic at our ignorance, and to watch speculatively the cloud of trouble coming—coming on purpose because we foolishly or carelessly call it to us.

MY DEAR AND HONOURED FRIEND:

Your letter has given me very great sorrow. You must have known for many weeks, even months, that marriage between us was impossible. It has always been so, it always will be so. Why could you not be content? We have been so happy! So happy! and now you will end all. But Fortune, though often cruel, cannot call back times that are past, and I shall never forget our friendship. I grieve at your going away; I pray that your absence may bring you some consolation. Do not, I beg you, attempt to call on my father. Without explanations, I tell you very sincerely, such a call will cause me great trouble; for you know well a girl must trust somewhat to others' judgment in her disposal. It gives me more pain than I can say to write in this mood, but necessity permits me no kinder words. I want you to be sure that the wrench, the "No" here is absolute. My dear friend, pity rather than blame me; and I will be so unselfish as to hope you may not think so kindly of me as to be cruel to yourself. Please to consider your letter as never written, it is the greatest kindness you can do me; and, above all, I beg you will not take my father into your confidence. With a sad sense of the pain my words must cause you, I remain for all time your faithful friend and obedient servant,

CORNELIA MORAN.

Then she rang for a lighted candle, and while waiting for its arrival neatly folded her letters. Her white wax and seal were at hand, and she delayed the servant until she had closed and addressed them.

"You will take Lieutenant Hyde's letter first," she said; "and make no delay about it, for it is very important. Mr. Van Ariens' note you can deliver as you return."

As soon as this business was quite out of her hands, she sank with a happy sigh into a large comfortable chair; let her arms drop gently, and closed her eyes to think over what she had done. She was quite satisfied. She was sure that no length of reflection could have made her decide differently. She had Hyde's letter in her bosom, and she pressed her hand against it, and vowed to her heart that he was worthy of her love, and that he only should have it. As for Rem, she had a decided feeling of annoyance, almost of fear, as he entered her mind. She was angry that he had chosen that day to urge his unwelcome suit, and thus thrust his personality into Hyde's special hour.

"He always makes himself unwelcome," she thought, "he ever has the way to come when he was least wanted; but Joris! Oh there is nothing I would alter in him, even at the cost of a wish! JORIS! JORIS!" and she let the dear name sweeten her lips, while the light of love brightened and lengthened her eyes, and spread over her lovely face a blushing glow.

After a while she rose up and adorned herself for her lover's visit. And when she entered the parlor Mrs. Moran looked at her with a little wonder. For she had put on with her loveliest gown a kind of bewildering prettiness. There was no cloud in her eyes, only a glow of soft dark fire. Her soul was in her face, it spoke in her bright glances, her sweet smiles, and her light step; it softened her speech to music, it made her altogether so delightful that her mother thought "Fortune must give her all she wishes, she is so charming."

The tea tray was brought in at five o'clock, but Doctor Moran had not returned, and there was in both women's hearts a little sense of disappointment. Mrs. Moran was wondering at his unusual delay, Cornelia feared he would be too weary and perhaps, too much interested in other matters to permit her lover to speak. "But even so," she thought, "Joris can come again. To-night is not the only opportunity."

It was nearly seven o'clock when the doctor came, and Cornelia was sure her lover would not be much behind that hour; but tea time was ever a good time to her father, he was always amiable and gracious with a cup in his hand, and the hour after it when his pipe kept him company, was his best hour. She told her heart that things had fallen out better than if she had planned them so; and she was so thoughtful for the weary man's comfort, so attentive and so amusing, that he found it easy to respond to the happy atmosphere surrounding him. He had a score of pleasant things to tell about the fashionable exodus to Philadelphia, about the handsome dresses that had been shown him, and the funny household dilemmas that had been told him. And he was much pleased because Harry De Lancey had been a great part of the day with him, and was very eloquent indeed about the young man's good sense and good disposition, and the unnecessary, and almost cruel, confiscation of property his family had suffered, for their Tory principles.

And in the midst of the De Lancey lamentation, seven o'clock struck and Cornelia began to listen for the shutting of the garden gate, and the sound of Hyde's step upon the flagged walk. It did not come as soon as she hoped it would, and the minutes went slowly on until eight struck. Then the doctor was glooming and nodding, and waking up and saying a word or two, and relapsing again into semi-unconsciousness. She felt that the favourable hour had passed, and now the minutes went far too quickly. Why did he net come? With her work in her hand-making laborious stitches by a drawn thread—she sat listening with all her being. The street itself was strangely silent, no one passed, and the fitful talk at the fireside seemed full of fatality; she could feel the influence, though she did not inquire of her heart what it was, of what it might signify.

Half-past eight! She looked up and caught her mother's eyes, and the trouble and question in them, and the needle going through the fine muslin, seemed to go through her heart. At nine the watching became unbearable. She said softly "I must go to bed. I am tired;" but she put away with her usual neatness her work, and her spools of thread, her thimble and her scissors. Her movement in the room roused the doctor thoroughly. He stood up, stretched his arms outward and upward, and said "he believed he had been sleeping, and must ask their pardon for his indifference." And then he walked to the window and looking out added "It is a lovely night but the moon looks like storm. Oh!"—and he turned quickly with the exclamation—"I forgot to tell you that I heard a strange report to-day, nothing less than that General Hyde returned on the Mary Pell this morning, bringing with him a child."

"A child!" said Mrs. Moran.

"A girl, then, a little mite of a creature. Mrs. Davy told me the Captain carried her in his arms to the carriage which took them to Hyde Manor."

"And how should Mrs. Davy know?"

"The Davys live next door to the Pells, and the servants of

one house carried the news to the other house. She said the General sent to his son's lodging to see if he was in town, but he was not. It was then only eight o'clock in the morning." "How unlikely such a story is! Do you believe it?"

"Ask to-morrow. As for me, I neither know nor care. That is the report. Who can tell what the Hydes will do?"

Then Cornelia said a hasty "good-night" and went to her room. She was sick at heart; she trembled, something in her life had lost its foot-hold, and a sudden bewildering terror—she knew not how to explain—took possession of her. For once she forgot her habitual order and neatness; her pretty dress was thrown heedlessly across a chair, and she fell upon her knees weeping, and yet she could not pray.

Still the very posture and the sweet sense of help and strength it implied, brought her the power to take into consideration such unexpected news, and such unexplained neglect on her lover's part, "General Hyde has returned; that much I feel certain of," she thought, "and Joris must have left Hyde Manor about the time his father reached New York. Joris would take the river road, being the shortest, his father would take the highway as the best for the carriage. Consequently, they passed each other and did not know it. Then Joris has been sent for, and it was right and natural that he should go—but oh, he might have written!—ten words would have been enough—It was right he should go—but he might have written!—he might have written!"—and she buried her face in her pillow and wept bitterly. Alas! Alas! Love wounds as cruelly when he fails, as when he strikes; and even when Cornelia had outworn thought and feeling, and fallen into a sorrowful sleep, she was conscious of this failure, and her soul sighed all night long "He might have written!"

CHAPTER IX

MISDIRECTED LETTERS

The night so unhappy to Cornelia was very much more unhappy to Hyde. He had sent his letter to her before eleven in the morning, and if Fortune were kind to him, he expected an answer soon after leaving Madame Jacobus. Her departure from New York depressed him very much. She had been the good genius of his love, but he told himself that it had now "grown to perfection, and could, he hoped, stand in its own strength." Restlessly he watched the hours away, now blaming, now excusing, anon dreaming of his coming bliss, then fidgeting and fearing disappointment from being too forward in its demanding. When noon passed, and one o'clock struck, he rang for some refreshment; for he guessed very accurately the reason of delay.

"Cornelia has been visiting or shopping," he thought; "and if it were visiting, no one would part with her until the last moment; so then if she get home by dinner-time it is as much as I can expect. I may as well eat, and then wait in what patience I can, another hour or two—yes, it will be two hours. I will give her two hours—for she will be obliged to serve others before me. Well, well, patience is my penance."

But in truth he expected the letter to be in advance of three o'clock. "Twenty words will answer me," he thought; "yes, ten words; and she will find or make the time to write them;" and between this hope and the certainty of three o'clock, he worried the minutes away until three struck. Then there was a knock at his door and he went hastily to answer it. Balthazar stood there with the longed-for letter in his hand. He felt first of all that he must be quite alone with it. So he turned the key and then stood a moment to examine the outside. A letter from Cornelia! It was a joy to see his own name written by her hand. He kissed the superscription, and kissed the white seal, and sank into his chair with a sigh of delight to read it.

In a few moments a change beyond all expression came over his face—perplexity, anger, despair cruelly assailed him. It was evident that some irreparable thing had ruined all his hopes. He was for some moments dumb. He felt what he could not express, for a great calamity had opened a chamber of feeling, which required new words to explain it. This trance of grief was followed by passionate imprecations and reproaches, wearing themselves away to an utter amazement and incredulity. He had flung the letter to the floor, but he lifted it again and went over the cruel words, forcing himself to read them slowly and aloud. Every period was like a fresh sentence of death.

"'YOUR LETTER HAS GIVEN ME VERY GREAT SORROW;' let me die if that is not what she says; 'VERY GREAT SORROW. YOU MUST HAVE KNOWN FOR WEEKS, EVEN MONTHS, THAT MARRIAGE BETWEEN US WAS IMPOSSIBLE;' am I perfectly in my senses? 'IT ALWAYS HAS BEEN AND ALWAYS WILL BE;' why, 'tis heart treason of the worst kind! Can I bear it? Can I bear it? Can I bear it? Oh Cornelia! Cornelia! 'WE HAVE BEEN SO HAPPY.' Oh it is piteous, sad. So young, so fair, so false! and she 'GRIEVES AT MY GOING

AWAY,' and bids me on 'NO ACCOUNT CALL ON HER FATHER'—and takes pains to tell me the 'NO IS ABSOLUTE'—and I am not to 'BLAME HER.' Oh this is the vilest treachery! She might as well have played the coquette in speech as writing. It is Rem Van Ariens who is at the bottom of it. May the devil take the fellow! I shall need some heavenly power to keep my hands off him. This is a grief beyond all griefs—I believed she loved me so entirely. Fool! a thousand times fool! Have I not found all women of a piece? Did not Molly Trefuses throw me over for a duke? and Sarah Talbot tell me my love was only calf-love and had to be weaned? and Eliza Capel regret that I was too young to guide a wife, and so marry a cabinet minister old enough for her grandfather? Women are all just so, not a cherry stone to choose between them—I will never wonder again at anything a woman does—Was ever a lover so betrayed? Oh Cornelia! your ink should have frozen in your pen, ere you wrote such words to me."

Thus his passionate grief and anger tortured him until midnight. Then he had a high fever and a distracting headache, and, the physical torment being the most insistent and distressing, he gave way before it. With such agonizing tears as spring from despairing wounded love he threw himself upon his bed, and his craving, suffering heart at length found rest in sleep from the terrible egotism of its sorrow.

Never for one instant did he imagine this sorrow to be a mistaken and quite unnecessary one. Indeed it was almost impossible for him to conceive of a series of events, which though apparently accidental, had a fatality more pronounced than anything that could have been arranged. Not taking Rem Van Ariens seriously into his consideration, and not fearing his rival in any way, it was beyond all his suspicions that Rem should write to Cornelia in the same hour, and for the same purpose as himself. He had no knowledge of Rem's intention to go to Boston, and could not therefore imagine Cornelia "grieving" at any journey but his own impending one to England. And that she should be forced by circumstances to answer both Rem and himself in the same hour, and in the very stress and hurry of her great love and anxiety should misdirect the letters, were likelihoods outside his consciousness.

It was far otherwise with Rem. The moment he opened the letter brought him by Cornelia's messenger, in that very moment he knew that it was NOT his letter. He understood at once the position, and perceived that he held in his hand an instrument, which if affairs went as he desired, was likely to make trouble he could perchance turn to his own advantage. The fate that had favoured him so far would doubtless go further—if he let it alone. These thoughts sprang at once into his reflection, but were barely entertained before nobler ones displaced them. As a Christian gentleman he knew what he ought to do without cavil and without delay, and he rose to follow the benignant justice of his conscience. Into this obedience, however, there entered an hesitation of a second of time, and that infinitesimal period was sufficient for his evil genius.

"Why will you meddle?" it asked. "This is a very dubious matter, and common prudence suggests a little consideration. It will be far wiser to let Hyde take the first step. If the letter he has received is so worded, that he knows it is your letter, it is his place to make the transfer—and he will be sure to do it. Why should you continue the chase? let the favoured one look after his own affairs—being a lawyer, you may well tell yourself, that it is not your interest to move the question."

And he hesitated and then sat down, and as there is wickedness even in hesitating about a wicked act, Rem easily drifted from the negative to the positive of the crime contemplated.

"I had better keep it," he mused, "and see what will come of the keeping. All things are fair in love and war"—a stupid and slanderous assertion, as far as love is concerned, for love that is noble and true, will not justify anything which Christian ethics do not justify.

He suffered in this decision, suffered in his own way quite as much as Hyde did. Cornelia had been his dream from his youth up, and Hyde had been his aversion from the moment he first saw him. The words were not to seek with which he expressed himself, and they were such words as do not bear repeating. But of all revelations, the revelation of grief is the plainest. He saw clearly in that hour that Cornelia had never loved him, that his hopes had always been vain, and he experienced all the bitterness of being slighted and humbled for an enemy.

After a little while he remembered that Hyde might possibly do the thing which he had resolved not to do. Involuntarily he did Hyde this justice, and he said to himself, "if there is anything in the letter intended for me, which determines its ownership, Hyde will bring it. He will understand that I have the answer to his proposal, and demand it from me—and whether I shall feel in a mood to give it to him, will depend on the manner in which the demand is made. If he is in one of his lordly ways he will get no satisfaction from me. I am not apt to give myself, nor anything I have, away; in fact it will be best not to see him—if he holds a letter of mine he may keep it. I know its tenor and I am not eager to know the very words in which my lady says 'No.' HO! HO! HO!" he laughed, "I will go to the Swamp; my scented rival in his perfumed clothing, will hardly wish the smell of the tanning pits to come between him and his gentility."

The thought of Hyde's probable visit and this way of escaping it made him laugh again; but it was a laughter that had that something terrible in it which makes the laughter of the insane and drunken and cruel, worse than the bitterest lamentation. He felt a sudden haste to escape himself, and seizing his hat walked rapidly to his father's office. Peter looked up as he entered, and the question in his eyes hardly needed the simple interrogatary—

"Well then?"

"It is 'No.' I shall go to Boston early in the morning. I wish to go over the business with Blume and Otis, and to possess myself of all particulars."

"I have just heard that General Hyde came back this morning. He is now the Right Honourable the Earl of Hyde, and his son is, as you know, Lord George Hyde. Has this made a difference?"

"It has not. Let us count up what is owing to us. After all there is a certain good in gold."

"That is the truth. I am an old man and I have seen what altitudes the want of gold can abase, and what impossible things it makes possible. In any adversity gold can find friends."

"I shall count every half-penny after Blume and Otis."

"Be not too strict—too far east is west. You may lose all by demanding all."

Then the two men spent several hours in going over their accounts, and during this time no one called on Rem and he received no message. When he returned home he found affairs just as he had left them. "So far good," he thought, "I will let sleeping dogs lie. Why should I set them baying about my affairs? I will not do it"—and with this determination in his heart he fell asleep.

But Rem's sleep was the sleep of pure matter; his soul never knew the expansion and enlightenment and discipline of the oracles that speak in darkness. The winged dreams had no message or comfort for him, and he took no counsel from his pillow. His sleep was the sleep of tired flesh and blood, and heavy as lead. But the waking from such sleep—if there is trouble to meet—is like being awakened with a blow. He leaped to his feet, and the thought of his loss and the shame of it, and the horror of the dishonourable thing he had done, assailed him with a brutal force and swiftness. He was stunned by the suddenness and the inexorable character of his trouble. And he told himself it was "best to run away from what he could not fight." He had no fear of Hyde's interference so early in the morning, and once in Boston all attacks would lose much of their hostile virulence, by the mere influence of distance. He knew these were cowardly thoughts, but when a man knows he is in the wrong, he does not challenge his thoughts, he excuses them. And as soon as he was well on the road to Boston, he even began to assume that Hyde, full of the glory of his new position, would doubtless be well disposed to let all old affairs drop quietly "and if so," he mused, "Cornelia will not be so dainty, and I may get 'Yes' where I got 'No.'"

He was of course arguing from altogether wrong premises, for Hyde at that hour was unconscious of his new dignity, and if he had been aware of it, would have been indifferent to its small honour. He had spent a miserable night, and a sense of almost intolerable desertion and injury awoke with him. His soul had been in desolate places, wandering in immense woods, vaguely apprehended as stretches of time before this life. He had called the lost Cornelia through all their loneliness, and answers faint as the faintest echo, had come back to that sense of spiritual hearing attuned in other worlds than this. But sad as such experience was, the sole effort had strengthened him. He was indeed in better case mentally than physically.

"I must get into the fresh air," he said. "I am faint and weak. I must have movement. I must see my mother. I will tell her everything." Then he went to his mirror, and looked with a grim smile at its reflection. "I have the face of a lover kicked out of doors," he continued scornfully. He took but small pains with his toilet, and calling for some breakfast sat down to eat it. Then for the first time in his life, he was conscious of that soul sickness which turns from all physical comfort; and of that singular obstruction in the throat which is the heart's sob, and which would not suffer him to swallow.

"I am most wretched," he said mournfully; "and no trouble comes alone. Of all the days in all the years, why should Madame Jacobus have to take herself out of town yesterday? It is almost incredible, and she could, and would have helped me. She would have sent for Cornelia. I might have pleaded my cause face to face with her." Then angrily—" Faith! can I yet care for a girl so cruel and so false? I am not to be pitied if I do. I will go to my dear mother. Mother-love is always sure, and always young. Whatever befalls, it keeps constant truth. I will go to my mother."

He rode rapidly through the city and spoke to no one, but when he reached his Grandfather Van Heemskirk's house, he saw him leaning over the half-door smoking his pipe. He drew rein then, and the old gentleman came to his side:

"Why art thou here?" he asked. "Is thy father, or Lady Annie sick?"

Amelia E. Barr

"I know nothing new. There was no letter yesterday."

"Yesterday! Surely thou must know that they are now at home? Yesterday, very early in the morning, they landed."

"My father at home!"

"That is the truth. Where wert thou, not to know this?"

"I came to town yesterday morning. I had a great trouble. I was sick and kept my room."

"And sick thou art now, I can see that," said Madame Van Heemskirk coming forward—"What is the matter with thee, my Joris?"

"Cornelia has refused me. I know not how it is, that no woman will love me. Am I so very disagreeable?"

"Thou art as handsome and as charming as can be; and it is not Cornelia that has said 'no' to thee, it is her father. Now he will be sorry, for thy uncle is dead and thy father is Earl Hyde, and thou thyself art a lord."

"I care not for such things. I am a poor lord, if Cornelia be not my lady." "I wonder they sent not after thee!"

"They would be expecting me every hour. If there had been a letter I should have gone directly back with it, but it was beyond all surmising, that my father should return. Grandfather, will you see Doctor Moran for me? You can speak a word that will prevail."

"I will not, my Joris. If thy father were not here, that would be different. He is the right man to move in the matter. Ever thou art in too much of a hurry. Think now of thy life as a book of uncut leaves, and do not turn a page till thou hast read it to the very last word."

"*I* will see Cornelia for thee," said Madame Van Heernskirk. "*I* will ask the girl what she means. Very often she passes here, sometimes she comes in. I will say to her—why did thou throw my grandson's love away like an old shoe? Art thou not ashamed to be so light of love, for I know well thou said to my Joris, thou loved him. And she will tell me the truth. Yes, indeed, if into my house she comes, out of it she goes not, until I have the why, and the wherefore."

"Do not be unkind to her, grandmother—perhaps it is not her fault—if she had only said a few sorrowful words—Let me show you her letter."

"No," said Van Heernskirk." One thing at a time, Joris. Now it is the time to go and welcome thy father and thy cousin— too long has been the delay already."

"Then good-bye! Grandmother, you will speak or me?" And she smiled and nodded, and stood on her tiptoe while Joris stooped and kissed her—"Fret not thyself at all. I will see Cornelia and speak for thee." And then he kissed her again and rode away.

Very near the great entrance gates of Hyde Manor he met his father and mother walking. Madame, the Right Honourable the Countess of Hyde, was pointing out the many improvements she had made; and the Earl looked pleased and happy. George threw himself off his horse with a loving impetuosity, and his mother questioned him about his manner of spending the previous day. "How could thou help knowing thy father had landed?" she asked." Was not the whole city talking of the circumstance?"

"I was not in the city, mother. I went to the post office and from there to Madame Jacobus. She was just leaving for Charleston, and I went with her to the boat."

"What an incredible thing! Madame Jacobus leaving New York! For what? For why?"

"She has gone to nurse her sister-in-law, who is dying. That is of all things the most likely—for she has a great heart."

"You say that—I know not."

"It is the truth itself. Afterwards I had my lunch and then came on a fever and a distracting headache, and I was compelled to keep my room; and so heard nothing at all until my grandfather told me the good news this morning."

"Madame Kippon was on the dock and saw thy father and cousin land. The news would be a hot coal in her mouth till she told it, and I am amazed she did not call at thy lodging. Now go forward; when thy father and I have been round the land, we will come to thee. Thy cousin Annie is here."

"That confounds me. I could hardly believe it true."

"She is frail, and her physicians thought the sea voyage might give her the vitality she needs. It was at least a chance, and she was determined to take it. Then thy father put all his own desires behind him, and came with her. We will talk more in a little while. I see thy dress is untidy, and I dare say thou art hungry. Go, eat and dress, by that time we shall be home."

But though his mother gave him a final charge "to make haste," he went slowly. The thought of Cornelia had returned to his memory with a sweet, strong insistence that carried all before it. He wondered what she was doing—how she was dressed—what she was thinking—what she was feeling—He wondered if she was suffering—if she thought he was suffering—if she was sorry for him—He made himself as wretched as possible, and then some voice of comfort anteceding all reasoning, told him to be of good cheer; for if Cornelia had ever loved him, she must love him still; and if she had only been amusing herself with his devotion, then what folly to break his heart for a girl who had no heart worth talking about.

Poor Cornelia! She was at that moment the most unhappy woman in New York. She had excused the "ten words" he might have written yesterday. She had found in the unexpected return of his father and cousin reason sufficient for his neglect; but it was now past ten o'clock of another day, and there was yet no word from him. Perhaps then he was coming. She sat at her tambour frame listening till all her senses and emotions seemed to have fled to her ear. And the ear has memory, it watches for an accustomed sound, it will not suffer us to forget the voice, the step of those we love. Many footsteps passed, but none stopped at the gate; none came up the garden path, and no one lifted the knocker. The house itself was painfully still; there was no sound but the faint noise made by Mrs. Moran as she put down her Dobbin or her scissors. The tension became distressing. She longed for her father—for a caller—for any one to break this unbearable pause in life.

Yet she could not give up hope. A score of excuses came into her mind; she was sure he would come in the afternoon. He MUST come. She read and reread his letter. She dressed herself with delightful care and sat down to watch for him. He came not. He sent no word, no token, and as hour after hour slipped away, she was compelled to drop her needle.

"Mother," she said, "I am not well. I must go upstairs." She had been holding despair at bay so many hours she could bear it no longer. For she was so young, and this was the first time she had been yoke-fellow with sorrow. She was amazed at her own suffering. It seemed so impossible. It had come upon her so swiftly, so suddenly, and as yet she was not able to seek any comfort or sympathy from God or man. For to do so, was to admit the impossibility of things yet turning out right; and this conclusion she would not admit; she was angry at a word or a look that suggested such a termination.

The next morning she called Balthazar to her and closely questioned him. It had struck her in the night, that the slave might have lost the letter, and be afraid to confess the accident. But Balthazar's manner and frank speech was beyond suspicion. He told her exactly what clothing Lieutenant Hyde was wearing, how he looked, what words he said, and then with a little hesitation took a silver crown piece from his pocket and added "he gave it to me. When he took the letter in his hand he looked down at it and laughed like he was very happy; and he gave me the money for bringing it to him; that is the truth, sure, Miss Cornelia."

She could not doubt it. There was then nothing to be done but wait in patience for the explanation she was certain would yet come. But on with what leaden motion the hours went by! For a few days she made a pretence of her usual employments, but at the end of a week her embroidery frame stood uncovered, her books were unopened her music silent, and she declared herself unable to take her customary walk. Her mother watched her with unspeakable sympathy, but Cornelia's grief was dumb; it made no audible moan, and preserved an attitude which repelled all discussion. As yet she would not acknowledge a doubt of her lover's faith; his conduct was certainly a mystery, but she told her heart with a passionate iteration that it would positively be cleared up.

Now and then the Doctor, or a visitor, made a remark which might have broken this implicit trust, and probably did facilitate that end; for it was evident from them, that Hyde was in health, and that he was taking his share in the usual routine of daily life:—thus, one day Mrs. Wiley while making a call said—

"I met the new Countess and the Lady Annie Hyde, and I can tell you the new Countess is very much of a Countess. As for the Lady Annie," she added, "she was wrapped to her nose in furs, and you could see nothing of her but two large black eyes, that even at a distance made you feel sad and uncomfortable. However Lord George Hyde appeared to be very much her servant."

"There has been talk of a marriage between them," answered Mrs. Moran, for she was anxious to put her daughter out of all question. "I should think it would be a very proper marriage."

"Oh, indeed, 'proper marriages' seldom come off. Love marriages are the fashion at present."

"Are they not the most proper of all?"

"On the contrary, is there anything more indiscreet? Of a thousand couples who marry for love, hardly one will convince us that the thing can be done, and not repented of afterwards."

"I think you are mistaken," said Mrs. Moran coldly." Love should always seek its match, and that is love—or nothing."

"Oh indeed! It is you are mistaken," continued Mrs. Wiley." As the times go, Cupid has grown to cupidity, and seeks his match in money or station, or such things."

"Money, or station, or such things find their match in money, or station, or such things.—They are not love."

"Well then the three may go together in this case. But the girl has an uncanny, unworldlike face. Captain Wiley says he has seen mermaids with the same long look in their eyes. Do you know that Rem Van Ariens has gone to Boston?"

"We have heard so;"—and then the Doctor entered, and after the usual formalities said, "I have just met Earl Hyde and his Countess parading themselves in the fine carriage he brought with him, 'Tis a thousand pities the President did not wait in New York to see the sight."

"Was Lady Annie with them?" asked Mrs. Wiley, "we were just talking about her."

"Yes, but one forgets that she is there—or anywhere. She seems as if she were an accident."

"And the young lord?"

"The young lord affects the democratic."

Such conversations were not uncommon, and Mrs. Moran could not with any prudence put a sudden stop to them. They kept Cornelia full of wondering irritation, and gradually drove the doubt into her soul—the doubt of her lover's sincerity which was the one thing she could not fight against. It loosened all the props of life; she ceased to struggle and to hope. The world went on, but Cornelia's heart stood still; and at the end of the third week things came to this—her father looked at her keenly one morning and sent her instantly to bed. At the last the breakdown had come in a night, but it had found all ready for it.

"She has typhoid, or I am much mistaken," he said to the anxious mother. "Why have you said nothing to me? How has it come about? I have heard no complaining. To have let things go thus far without help is dreadful—it is almost murder."

"John! John! What could I do? She could not bear me to ask after her health. She said always that she was not sick. She would not hear of my speaking to you. I thought it was only sorrow and heart-ache."

"Only sorrow and heart-ache. Is not that enough to call typhoid or any other death? What is the trouble? Oh I need not ask, I know it is that young Hyde. I feel it. I saw this trouble coming; now let me know the whole truth."

He listened to it with angry amazement. He said he ought to have been told at the time—he threw aside all excuses—for being a man how could he understand why women put off, and hope, and suffer? He was sure the rascal ought to have been brought to explanation the very first day:—and then he broke down and wept his wife's tears, and echoed all her piteous moan for her daughter's wronged love and breaking heart.

"What is left us now, is to try and save her dear life," said the miserable father." Suffering we cannot spare her. She must pass alone through the Valley of the Shadow; but it may be she will lose this sorrow in its dreadful paths. I have known this to happen often; for THERE the soul has to strip itself of all encumbrances, and fight for life, and life only."

This was the battle waged in Doctor Moran's house for many awful weeks. The girl lay at Death's door, and her father and mother watched every breath she drew. One day, while she was in extremity, the Doctor went himself to the apothecary's for medicine. This medicine was his last hope and he desired to prepare it himself. As be came out of the store with it in his hand, Hyde looked at him with a steady imploration. He had evidently been waiting his exit.

"Sir!" he said, "I have heard a report that I cannot, I dare not believe."

"Believe the worst—and stand aside, sir. I have neither patience nor words for you."

"I beseech you, sir—"

"Touch me not! Out of my sight! Broadway is not wide enough for us two, unless you take the other side."

"Your daughter? Oh sir, have some pity!"

"My daughter is dying."

"Then sir, let me tell you, that your behaviour has been so brutal to her, and to me, that the Almighty shows both kindness and intelligence in taking her away:"—and with these words uttered in a blazing passion of indignation and pity, the young lord crossed to the other side of the street, leaving the Doctor confounded by his words and manner.

"There is something strange here," he said to himself; "the fellow may be as bad as bad can be, but he neither looked nor spoke as if he had wronged Cornelia. If she lives I must get to the bottom of this affair. I should not wonder if it is the work of Dick Hyde—earl or general—as detestable a man as ever crossed my path."

With this admission and wonder, the thought of Hyde passed from his mind; for at that hour the issue he had to consider was one of life or death. And although it was beyond all hope or expectation, Cornelia came back to life; came back very slowly, but yet with a solemn calm and a certain air of conscious dignity, as of one victorious over death and the grave. But she was perilously delicate, and the Doctor began to consider the dangers of her convalescence.

"Ava," he said one evening when Cornelia had been downstairs awhile—"it will not do for the child to run the risk of meeting that man. I see him on the street frequently. The apothecary says he comes to his store to ask after her recovery nearly every day. He has not given her up, I am sure of that. He spoke to me once about her, and was outrageously impudent. There is something strange in the affair, but how can I move in it?"

"It is impossible. Can you quarrel with a man because he has deceived Cornelia? How cruel that would be to the child! You must bear and I must bear. Anything must be borne, rather than set the town wondering and talking."

"It is a terrible position. I see not how I can endure it."

"Put Cornelia before everything."

"The best plan is to remove Cornelia out of danger. Why not take her to visit your brother Joseph? He has long desired you to do so."

"Go to Philadelphia NOW! Joseph tells me Congress is in session, and the city gone mad over its new dignity. Nothing but balls and dinners are thought of; even the Quakers are to be seen in the finest modes and materials at entertainments; and Cornelia will hardly escape the fever of fashion and social gaiety. She has many acquaintances there."

"I do not wish her to escape it. A change of human beings is as necessary as a change of air, or diet. She has had too much of George Hyde, and Madame Jacobus, and Rem Van Ariens."

"I hear that Rem is greatly taken with Boston, and thinks of opening an office there."

"Very prudent of Rem. What chance has he in New York with Hamilton and Burr, to carry off all the big prey? Make your arrangements as soon as possible to leave New York."

"You are sure that you are right in choosing Philadelphia?"

"Yes—while Hyde is in New York. Write to your brother to-day; and as soon as Cornelia is a little stronger, I will go with you to Philadelphia."

"And stay with us?"

"That is not to be expected. I have too much to do here,"

CHAPTER X

LIFE TIED IN A KNOT

One morning soon after the New Year, Hyde was returning to the Manor House from New York. It was a day to oppress thought, and tighten the heart, and kill all hope and energy. There was a monotonous rain and a sky like that of a past age—solemn and leaden—and the mud of the roads was unspeakable. He was compelled to ride slowly and to feel in its full force, as it were, the hostility of Nature. As he reached his home the rain ceased, and a thick mist, with noiseless entrance, pervaded all the environment; but no life, or sound of life, broke the melancholy sense of his utter desolation.

He took the road by the lake because it was the nearest road to the stables, where he wished to alight; but the sight of the livid water, and of the herons standing motionless under the huge cedars by its frozen edges, brought to speech and expression that stifled grief, which Nature this morning had intensified, not relieved.

"Those unearthly birds!" he said petulantly, "they look as if they had escaped the deluge by some mistake. Oh if I could forget! If I could only forget! And now she has gone! She has gone! I shall never see her again! "Grief feels it a kind of luxury to repeat some supreme cry of misery, and this lamentation for his lost love had this poignant satisfaction. He felt New York to be empty and void and dreary, and the Manor House with its physical cheer and comfort, and its store of affection, could not lift the stone from his heart.

In spite of the chilling mist the Earl had gone to see a neighbour about some land and local affairs, and his mother —oblivious of the coronet of a countess—was helping her housekeeper to make out the list of all household property at the beginning of the year 1792. She seemed a little annoyed at his intrusion, and recommended to him a change of apparel. Then he smiled at his forlorn, draggled condition, and went to his room.

Now it is a fact that in extreme dejection something good to eat, and something nice to wear, will often restore the inner man to his normal complacency; and when Hyde's valet had seen to his master's refreshment in every possible way, Hyde was at least reconciled to the idea of living a little longer. The mud-stained garments had disappeared, and as he walked up and down the luxurious room, brightened by the blazing oak logs, he caught reflections of his handsome person in the mirror, and he began to be comforted. For it is not in normal youth to disdain the smaller joys of life; and Hyde was thinking as his servant dressed him in satin and velvet, that at least there was Annie. Annie was always glad to see him, and he had a great respect for Annie's opinions. Indeed during the past few weeks they had been brought into daily companionship, they had become very good friends. So then the absence of the Earl and the preoccupation of his mother was not beyond comfort, if Annie was able to receive him. In spite of his grief for Cornelia's removal from New York, he was not insensible to the pleasure of Annie's approval. He liked to show himself to her when he knew he could appear to advantage; and there was nothing more in this desire, than that healthy wish for approbation that is natural to self-respecting youth.

He heard her singing as he approached the drawing-room, and he opened the door noiselessly and went in. If she was conscious of his entrance she made no sign of it, and Hyde did not seem to expect it. He glanced at her as he might have glanced at a priest by the altar, and went softly to the fireside and sat down. At this moment she had a solemn, saintly beauty; her small pale face was luminous with spiritual joy, her eyes glowing with rapture, and her hands moving among the ivory keys of the piano made enchanting melody to her inspired longing

> Jerusalem the golden,
> With milk and honey blest,
> Beneath thy contemplation
> Sink heart and voice oppressed.
> O one, O only mansion,
> O paradise of joy!
> Where tears are ever banished
> And smiles have no alloy.
> O sweet and blessed country!
> Shall I ever see thy face?
> O sweet and blessed country!
> Shall I ever win thy grace?

and as these eager impassioned words rose heavenward, it seemed to Hyde that her innocent, longing soul was half-way out of her frail little body. He did not in any way disturb her. She ceased when the hymn was finished and sat still a few moments, realizing, as far as she could, the glory which doth not yet appear. As her eyes dropped, the light faded from her face; she smiled at Hyde, a smile that seemed to light all the space between them. Then he stood up and she came towards him. No wonder that strangers spoke of her as a child; she had the size and face and figure of a child, and her look of extreme youth was much accentuated by the simple black gown she wore, and by her carriage, for she leaned slightly forward as she walked, her feet appearing to take no hold upon the floor; a movement springing INTERIORLY from the soul eagerness which dominated her. Hyde placed her in a chair before the fire, and then drew his own chair to her side.

"Cousin," she said, "I am most glad to see you. Everybody has some work to do to-day."

"And you, Annie?"

"In this world I have no work to do," she answered. "My soul is here for a purchase; when I have made it I shall go home again." And Hyde looked at her with such curious interest that she added—"I am buying Patience."

"O indeed, that is a commodity not in the market."

"I assure you it is. I buy it daily. Once I used to wonder what for I had come to earth. I had no strength, no beauty, nothing at all to buy Earth's good things with. Three years ago I found out that I had come to buy for my soul, the grace of Patience. Do you remember what an imperious, restless, hard-to-please, hard-to-serve girl I was? Now it is different. If people do not come on the instant I call them, I rock my soul to rest, and say to it 'anon, anon, be quiet, soul.' If I suffer much pain—and that is very often—I say Soul, it is His Will, you must not cry out against it. If I do not get my own way, I say, Soul, His Way is best; and thus, day by day, I am buying Patience."

"But it is not possible this can content you. You must have some other hope and desire, Annie?"

"Perhaps I once had—and to-day is a good time to speak of it to you, because now it troubles me no longer. You know what my father desired, and what your father promised, for us both?"

"Yes. Did you desire it, Annie?"

"I do not desire it now. You were ever against it?"

"Oh Annie!—"

"It makes no matter, George. I shall never marry you."

"Do you dislike me so much?"

"I am very fond of you. You are of my race and my kindred, and I love every soul of the Hydes that has ever tarried on this earth."

"Well then?"

"I shall marry no one. I will show you the better way. Few can walk in it, but Doctor Roslyn says, he thinks it may be my part—my happy part—to do so:" and as she spoke she took from the little pocket at her side a small copy of the gospels, and it opened of its own account at the twentieth chapter of St. Luke. "See!" she said, "and read it for yourself, George—"

"The children of this world marry and are given in marriage. But they which shall be accounted worthy to obtain that world, and the resurrection from the dead, neither marry, nor are given in marriage.

"Neither can they die any more; for they are equal unto the angels, and are the children of God, being the children of the resurrection." [Footnote: St. Luke, chap. xx. 34-36.]

"To die no more! To be like unto the angels! To be the children of God! This is the end and aim of my desires, to be among 'the children of God!'"

"Dear Annie, I cannot understand this."

"Not yet. It is not your time. My soul, I think, is ages older than yours. It takes ages of schooling to get into that class that may leave Earth forever, and be as the angels. Even now I know, I am sure that you are fretting and miserable for the love of some woman. For whose love, George? Tell me."

Then Hyde plunged with headlong precipitancy into the story of his love for Cornelia, and of the inexplicably cruel way in which it had been brought to a close. "And yesterday," he continued with a sob in his voice—"yesterday I heard that her father had taken her to Philadelphia. I shall see her no more. He will marry her to Rem Van Arenas, or to one of her Quaker cousins, and the taste is taken out of my life, and I am only a walking misery."

"I do not believe it is Cornelia's fault."

"Here is her letter. Read it." Then Annie look the letter and after reading it said, "If she be all you say, I will vow she wrote this in her sleep. I should like to see her. Why do you think wrong of her? What is love without faith in the one you love? Do you know first and finally what true love is? It is THINKING kindly and nobly. For if we GIVE all we have, and DO all we can do, and yet THINK unkindly, it profits us nothing. Doctor Roslyn told me so. You remember him?"

"Your teacher?"

"My teacher, my friend, my father after the spirit. He told me that our thoughts moulded our fate, because thought and life are one. So then, if you really love Cornelia, you must think good of her, and then good will come."

"If thought and life are one, Annie, if doing good, and giving good, are nothing to thinking good, and we are to be judged by our quality of thinking, there will be a greater score against all of us, than we can imagine. I, for one, should not like to be brought face to face with what I think, and have thought about people; it would be an accounting beyond my power to settle."

"There is no accounting. If all the priests in Christendom tell you so, believe them not. Do you think God keeps a score against you? Do you think the future is some torture chamber, or condemned cell? Oh, how you wrong God!"

"But we are taught, Annie, that the future must correct the past."

"True, but the future, like the present, is a school—only a school. And the Great Master is so compassionate, so ready to help, so ready to enlighten, so sure to make out of our foolishness some wise thing. If we learn the lesson we came here to learn, He will say to us 'Well done'—and then we shall go higher."

"If we do not learn it?"

"Ah then, we are turned back to try it over again! I should not like to be turned back—would you ?"

"But He will punish us for failure."

"Our earthly fathers are often impatient with us; His

compassions fail not. Oh this good God!" she cried in an ecstasy—"Oh that I knew where I might find Him! Oh that I could come into His presence!" and her eyes dilated, and were full of an incomparable joy, as if they were gazing upon some glorious vision, and glad with the gladness of the angels.

Hyde looked at her with an intense interest. He wondered if this angelic little creature had ever known the frailties and temptations of mortal life, and she answered his thought as if he had spoken it aloud.

"Yes, cousin, I have known all temptations, and come through all tribulations. My soul has wandered and lost its way, and been brought back many and many a time, and bought every grace with much suffering. But God is always present to help, while quest followed quest, and lesson followed lesson, and goal succeeded goal; ever leaving some evil behind, and carrying forward some of those gains which are eternal."

"If Adam had not fallen!" sighed George, "things might have been so different."

"But the angels fell before Adam," she answered. "I wonder if Adam knew about the fallen angels? Did he know about death before he saw Abel dead? He was all day in the garden of Eden after eating of the fruit of sin and death, and yet he did not put out his hand to take of the Tree of Life. Did he know that he was already immortal? Was he—and are we—fallen angels, working our way back to our first estate through many trials and much suffering? Doctor Roslyn talked to me of these things till I thought I felt wings stirring within me. Wings! Wings! Wings to fly away and be at rest. Wings! they have been the dream of every race and every age. Are they a memory of our past greatness, for they haunt us, and draw us on and on, and higher and higher?—but why do you look so troubled and reluctant?"

Before Hyde could answer, the Earl came into the room and the young man was glad to see his father. A conversation so unusual, so suggestive and cleaving made him unhappy. It took him up the high places that indeed gave him a startling outlook of life, but he was not comfortable at such altitude. He rose with something of this strange air about him, and the Earl understood what the trend of the conversation had been. For Annie had talked much to him on such subjects, and he had been sensibly moved and impressed by the wisdom which the little maid had learned from her venerable teacher. He lifted her head in passing, and kissed her brow with that reverent affection we feel for those who bring out what is noblest and best in our character, and who lead us higher than our daily walk.

"My dear George," he said, "I am delighted to see you. I was afraid you would stay in the city this dreadful weather. Is there any news?"

"A great deal, sir. I have brought you English and French papers."

"I will read them at my leisure. Give me the English news first. What is it in substance?"

"The conquest of Mysore and Madras. Seringapatam has fallen; and Tippoo has ceded to England one half his dominions and three millions of pounds. The French have not now a foothold left in India, and 'Citizen Tippoo' can no longer help the agents of the French Republic. Faith, sir! Cornwallis has given England in the east, a compensation for what she lost in the west."

"To make nations of free men, is the destiny of our race," replied the Earl.

"Perhaps so; for it seems the new colony planted at Sydney Cove, Australia, is doing wonderfully; and that would mean an English empire in the south."

"Yet, I have just read a proclamation of the French Assembly, calling on the people of France 'TO ANNIHILATE AT ONCE, the white, clay-footed colossus of English power and diplomacy.' Anything else?"

"Mr. Fox and Mr. Burke are quarrelling as usual, and Mr. Pitt is making the excesses of France the excuse for keeping back reform in England. It is the old story. I did not care to read it. The French papers tell their side of it. They call Burke a madman, and Pitt a monster, and the Moniteur accuses them of having misrepresented the great French nation, and says, 'they will soon be laid prostrate before the statue of Liberty, from which they shall only rise to mount the scaffold, etc., etc.'"

"What bombastic nonsense!"

"Minister Morris is in the midst of horrors unmentionable. The other foreign ministers have left France, and the French government is deserted by all the world; yet Mr. Morris remains at his post, though he was lately arrested in the street, and his house searched by armed men."

"But this is an insult to the American nation! Why does he endure it? He ought to return home."

"Because he will not abandon his duty in the hour of peril and difficulty. Neither has the President given him permission to do so. How could he desert American citizens unlawfully imprisoned, American vessels unlawfully seized by French privateers, and American captains detained in French ports on all kinds of pretences. I think Minister Morris is precisely where he should be, saving the lives of American citizens; many of whom are trembling to-day in the shadow of the guillotine."

"It is to be hoped that Jefferson is now convinced of the execrable nature of these brutal revolutionists."

"I can assure you, sir, he is not. He still excuses all their abominations and says Minister Morris is a high-flying monarchy man, and not to be taken without great allowance. I hear that Madame Kippon's daughter, whom Mr. Morris rescued at the last hour, has arrived in New York; and yesterday I met Mr. Van Ariens, who is exceedingly anxious concerning his daughter, the Marquise de Tounnerre." "Is she in danger? I thought her husband was a leader in the new National Assembly."

"He is among the Girondists. They are giving themselves airs and making fine speeches at present—but—"

"But what?"

"Their day will be short."

"What of the king?"

"The royal family are all prisoners in the Temple Tower. I do not dare to read the particulars; but not a single protest against their barbarity is made. Frenchmen who silently saw the Abbaye, the Force, and the Carmes turned into human shambles three months ago, now hold their peace while murders no less horrible are being slowly done in the Temple."

"They are inconceivable monsters. Poor little Arenta! What will she do?"

"I am not very uneasy for her; she has wit enough to save her life if put to such extremes; her father is much to be pitied; and it is incredible, though true, that the great majority of our people are still singing the MARSEILLAISE, though every letter of it is washed in blood and tears."

"I am troubled about that pretty little Marquise."

"She is clever and full of resource. I have had only one letter from her since her marriage, and it was written to the word 'glories!' She seemed to be living in a blaze of triumph and very happy. But change is the order of the day in France."

"Say of the hour, and you are nearer the truth."

"If Arenta is in trouble she will cry out, and call for help on every hand. I never knew her to make a mistake where her own interests were concerned. I told her father yesterday that it would be very difficult to corner Arenta, and comforted him beyond my hope."

During this conversation Annie was in a reverie which it in no way touched. She had the faculty of shutting her ears to sounds she did not wish to take into her consciousness, and the French Revolution did not exist for her. She was thinking all the time of her Cousin George, and of the singular abruptness with which his love life had been cut short; and it was this train of thought which led her—when the murmur of voices ceased for a moment—to say impulsively:

"Uncle, it is my desire to go to Philadelphia," The Earl looked at her with incredulity. "What nonsense, Annie!" he exclaimed. "The thing is impossible."

"Why impossible?"

"For you, I mean. You would be very ill before the journey was half-finished. The roads, as George will tell you, are nearly impassable; and the weather after this fog may be intensely cold. For you a journey to Philadelphia would be an arduous undertaking, and one without any reasonable motive."

"Oh, indeed! Do you call George Washington an unreasonable motive? I wish to see him. Imagine me within one hundred miles of this supreme hero, and turning back to England without kissing his hand. I should be laughed at—I should deserve to be laughed at."

"Yes, if the journey were an easier one."

"To be sure, the roads and the cold will be trials; but then my uncle, you can give them to me, as God gives trials to His Beloved. He breaks them up into small portions, and puts a night's sleep between the portions. Can you not also do this?"

"You little Methodist!" answered the Earl, with a tender gleam in his eyes. "I see that I shall have to give you your own way. Will you go with us, George?"

"It will be a relief. New York is in the dumps. Little Burr having beaten the Schuyler faction, thinks himself omnipotent; and this quarrel between Mr. Jay and Governor Clinton keeps every one else on the edge of ill-humour. All the dancing part of the town are gone to Philadelphia; I have scarcely a partner left; and there is no conversation now in New York that is not political. Burr, Schuyler, Jay, Clinton! even the clergy have gone horse and foot into these disputes."

Amelia E. Barr

"Burr has a kind of cleverness; one must admit that."

"He is under the curse of knowing everything."

"Nevertheless his opinions will not alter the axis of the earth. It is however a dangerous thing to live in a community where politics are the staple of talk, quarrels spring full armed from a word in such an atmosphere."

"I have accommodated my politics, sir, to my own satisfaction; and I make shift to answer people according to their idols. I vow, I am so weary of the words 'honour and honesty' that they beat a tattoo on my brain."

"When you are as old as I am, George, you will understand that these words are the coin, with which men buy office. The corruption of courtiers is a general article of faith, but the impudence of patriots going to market with their honesty, beats courtly corruption to nothing. However, let us go to Philadelphia and see the play. That is what Annie desires."

"I desire to see Washington. I wish to see the greatest of Americans."

"Let me tell you, Annie," said the Earl, "that there never was a man in America less American in character and habits, than Washington."

"For all that," interrupted George, "there will never come a man after him, that will be able to rob Washington of the first place in the hearts of the American nation."

"Nor at this day can we judge him as he deserves," added the Earl;" for he is cramped and hustled by the crowd of nobodies around him."

"I shall look at him, and I shall know him," said Annie. "George tells me that he is good and handsome to look at."

"On horseback," continued the Earl, "there is none like him; he is the ideally perfect cavalier—graceful, dignified, commanding. Indeed so superb a man comes not twice in a generation. At Monmouth, where I commanded a division, I remember him flying along the lines, cheering the men and restoring by his tremendous enthusiasm the fortunes of the fight to our standard. The grandest of men! You are right, Annie, it would be a stupidity to go back to England without seeing him."

This was the initial conversation which after some opposition, and a little temper from madame the Countess, resulted in the Hyde family visiting Philadelphia. It was a great trial to the Countess to leave her own well ordered, comfortable home for apartments in an hotel; and she was never done asserting it to be a great imprudence, as far as Annie was concerned. But the girl was immovable, and as she was supported by her uncle and cousin, the Countess was compelled to acquiesce. But really she was so ready to find her pleasure in the pleasure of those she loved, that this acquiescence was not an unmitigated trial. She suspected the motive for her son's eager desire for Philadelphia, and as she had abandoned without much regret the hope of his marriage with Annie Hyde, she was far from being disinclined to Cornelia. She had accustomed herself to the idea of Cornelia as mistress of the beautiful home she had made. She was an American, and madame loved her country and wished her daughter-in-law to be of American lineage. She was aware that some trouble had come between the lovers, and she trusted that this visit might be the ground of a reconciliation. Without question, or plan, or even strong desire, she felt the wisdom of making opportunities, and then leaving the improvement of them to circumstances.

Amelia E. Barr

So about the beginning of February the Hydes were settled in Philadelphia more comfortably than could have been expected. A handsome house, handsomely furnished, had been found; and madame had brought with her the servants necessary to care for it, and for the family's comfort. And she was glad, when the weariness of the journey was over, to see how naturally and pleasantly her husband and son took their places in the gay world around them. She watched the latter constantly, being sure she would be able to read on his face, and by his manner and temper, whether affairs relating to Cornelia were favourable.

In a week she had come to the conclusion that he was disappointed; which indeed was very much the case. He could hear nothing of Cornelia. He had never once got a glimpse of her lovely countenance, and no scrutiny had revealed to him the place of her abode. Every house inhabited by a person of the name of Willing, had been the object of his observation; but no form that by any possibility could be mistaken for hers, had passed in or out of their doors. He became ashamed of haunting particular streets, and fancied the ladies of certain houses watched him; and that the maids and menservants chattered and speculated about his motives.

Every day when he went out Annie gave him an assuring smile, every day when he returned, she opened her eyes on him with the question in them she did not care to formulate; and every day she received in an answer an almost imperceptible negative shake of the head, that slight as it was, said despairingly, "I have not seen her."

A month passed in this unfruitful searching misery, and Hyde was almost hopeless. The journey appeared to be altogether a failure; and he said to Annie, "I am to be blamed for my selfishness in permitting you to come here. I see that you have tired yourself to death for nothing at all."

She gave her head a resolute little shake and answered, "Wait and see. Something is coming. You have no patience."

"I assure you, Annie, I ought to have. I have been buying it every day since we came to this detestable place."

"The place is not to blame. Do you know that I am going to Mrs. Washington's reception to-morrow evening? I shall see the President. He may even speak to me; for my uncle says he appears there, only as a private gentleman. Cousin, you are to be my cavalier if it please you; and my uncle and aunt will attend us."

"I am devotedly at your service, Annie; and I will at least point out to you some of the dazzling beauties of our court— the splendid Mrs. Bingham, the Miss Allens, and Miss Chews, and the brilliant Sally McKean."

"And the lovely Cornelia Moran?"

"She will not be there."

"My aunt says I must wear a white gown, and I shah do you all the justice it is in my power to do."

"I am always proud of you, Annie. There is no one like you."

"Do not say that, George!" The few words were almost a cry; and she closed her eyes, and clasped her small hands tightly.

"What have I said, Annie?"

"Nothing—nothing—only do not flatter me."

"It is the very truth."

"Let it pass?—it is nothing." She was silent afterwards, like a person in pain; all her childlike gaiety gone; and Hyde having a full share of a man's stupidity about matters of pure feeling, did not for one moment suspect why his praise should give her pain. He thought her objection must come from some religious scruple.

The next evening however he had every reason to feel proud of his cousin. She was really an exquisite little creature; angels would have given her all she wished, she was so charming. The touch of phantasy and flame in her nature illumined her face, and no one could look at her without feeling that a fervent and transparent soul gazed from eyes, so lambent with soft spiritual fire. This impression was enhanced by her childlike gown of white crape over soft white silk; it suggested her sweet fretless life, and also something unknown and unseen in her very simplicity.

Hyde, who was dressed in the very finest mode, was proud to take her on his arm; and the Earl watched them with a fond and faithful hope that all would soon fall out as he desired it. He could not indeed imagine a man remaining unimpressed by a beauty so captivating to the highest senses. "It will be as we wish," he said to his Countess as they watched them entering the waiting coach; and she answered with that smile of admission, which has always its reserved opinion.

Mrs. Washington's parlours were crowded when they entered them, but the splendid throng gave the highest expression of their approval possible, by that involuntary silence which indicates a pleased astonishment. The Earl at once presented his niece to Mrs. Washington, and afterwards to the President, who as a guest of Mrs. Washington was walking about the rooms talking to the ladies present. Resplendent in purple and white satin and the finest of laces, the august man captivated Lady Annie at the first glance. She curtsied with inimitable grace, and would have kissed the hand he held out to her, had he permitted the homage. For a few minutes he remained in conversation with the party, then he went forward, and Hyde turning with his beautiful charge, met Cornelia face to face.

They looked at each other as two disembodied souls might meet and look after death—reproaching, questioning, entreating, longing. Hyde flushed and paled, and could not for his very life make the slightest effort at recognition or speech. Not a word would come. He knew not what word to say. Cornelia who had seen his entry was more prepared. She gave him one long look of tender reproach as she passed, but she made no movement of recognition. If she had said one syllable—if she had paused one moment—if she had shown in any way the least desire for a renewal of their acquaintance, Hyde was sure his heart would have instantly responded. As it was, they had met and parted in a moment, and every circumstance had been against him. For it was the most natural thing in life, that he should, after his cousin's interview with Washington, stoop to her words with delight and interest; and it was equally natural for Cornelia to put the construction on his attentions which every one else did. Then being angry at her apparent indifference, he made these attentions still more prominent; and Cornelia heard on every hand the confirmation of her own suspicions: "They are to be married at Easter. What a delightful little creature!"

"They have loved each other all their lives."

"The Earl is delighted with the marriage."

"He is the most devoted of lovers."

And there was not a word of dissent from this opinion until pretty Sally McKean said, "A fig for your prophecies! George Hyde has loved and galloped away a score of times. I would not pay any more attention to his proposals and promises, than I would pay to the wind that blows where it listeth; here to-day, and somewhere else to-morrow."

To all these speculations Cornelia forced herself to listen with a calm unalterable; and Hyde and Annie watched her from a distance. "So that is the marvellous beauty!" said Annie.

"Is she not marvellously beautiful?" asked Hyde.

"Yes. I will say that much. But why did she look at you with so much of reproach? What have you done to her?"

"That is it. What have I done? Or left undone?"

"Who is the gentleman with her?"

"I know not. She has many relatives here; wealthy Quakers, and some of them doubtless of the new order, who do not disdain the frivolity of fine clothing."

"Indeed, I assure you the Quakers were ever nice in their taste for silks and velvets and laces. The man is handsome enough even to be her escort. And to judge by appearances he is her devoted servant. Will you regard them, cousin?"

"I do. Alas, I see nothing else! She is more lovely then ever."

"She is wonderfully dressed. That gown of pale blue and silver would make any woman look like an angel?-but indeed she is lovely beyond comparison. There are none like her in this room. It will be a thousand pities if you lose her."

"I shall be inconsolable."

"You may have another opportunity even tonight. I see that my aunt is approaching with a young lady, if you do not wish to make a new acquaintance, go and try to meet Cornelia again."

"Thank you, Annie. You can tell me what I have missed afterwards."

He wandered through the parlours speaking to one and another but ever on the watch for Cornelia. He saw her no more that night. She had withdrawn as soon as possible after meeting Hyde, and he was so miserably disappointed, so angry at the unpropitious circumstances which had dominated their casual meeting, that he hardly spoke to anyone as they returned home; and was indeed so little interested in other affairs that he forgot until the next day to ask Annie whose acquaintance he had rather palpably refused.

"You cannot guess who it was," said Annie in answer to his query;" so I will make a favour of telling you. Do you remember the Rev. Mr. Darner, rector of Downhill Market?"

"Very well. He preached very tiresome sermons."

"The young lady was his daughter Mary."

"'Tis a miracle! What is Mary Darner doing in America?"

"She is on a visit to her cousin, who is married to the Governor of Massachusetts. He is here on some state matter, and as Miss Damer also wished to see Washington, he brought her with him."

"Mary Damer! We went nutting together one autumn. She came often to Hyde Court when I was a lad."

"And she promises to come often to see me when I return to England. I wonder what we have been brought together for. There must be a reason for a meeting so unlikely—Can it be Cornelia?"

"'Tis the most improbable of suppositions. I do not suppose she ever saw Cornelia."

"She had not even heard of her—and yet my mind will connect them."

"You have no reason to do so; and it is beyond all likelihood. I am sorry I went away from Mary."

"She took no notice of your desertion."

"That is, as maybe. I was a mere lad when I saw her last. Is she passable?"

"She is extremely handsome. My aunt heard that she is to marry a Boston gentleman of good promise and estate. I dare say it is true."

It was so true that even while they were speaking of the matter Mary was writing these words to her betrothed :" Yesterday I met the Hydes. You know my father has the living of Downhill Market from them, and I had a constraint on me to be agreeable. The young Lord got out of my way. Did he imagine I had designs on him? I look for a better man. What fate brought us together in Philadelphia, I know not. I may see a great deal of them in the coming summer, and then I may find out. At present I will dismiss the Hydes. I have met pleasanter company."

Annie dismissed the subject with the same sort of impatience. It seemed to no one a matter of any importance, and even Annie that day had none of the penetrative insight which belongs to

"that finer atmosphere,
Where footfalls of appointed things,
Reverberant of days to be,
Are heard in forecast echoings,
Like wave beats from a viewless sea."

As for Hyde, he was shaken, confused, lifted off his feet, as it were; but after another day had passed, he had come to one steady resolution—HE WOULD SPEAL TO CORNELIA WHEN NEXT HE MET HER, NO MATTER WHERE IT WAS, OR WHO WAS WITH HER. And that passionate stress of spirit which induced this resolve, led him also to go out and seek for this opportunity.

For nearly a week he kept this conscious, constant watch. Its insisting sorrowful longing was like a cry from Love's watch towers, but it did not reach the beloved one; or else she did not answer it. One bright morning he resolved to walk through the great dry goods stores—Whiteside's, Guest's, and the famous Mrs. Holland's, where the beauties of the "gay Quakers" bought their choicest fabrics in foreign chintzes, lawns, and Indian muslins. All along Front, Arch, and Walnut Streets, the pavements were lumbered with boxes and bales of fine imported goods, and he was getting impatient of the bustle and pushing, when he saw Anthony Clymer approaching him. The young man was driving a new and very spirited team, and as he with some difficulty held them, he called to Hyde to come and drive with him. Hyde was just in the weary mood that welcomed change, and he leaped to his friend's side, and felt a sudden exhilaration in the rapid motion of the buoyant, active animals. After an

Amelia E. Barr

hour's driving they came to a famous hostelry, and Clymer said, "Let us give ourselves lunch, and the horses bait and a rest, then we will make them show their mettle home again."

The proposal met with a hearty response, and the young men had a luxurious meal and more good wine than they ought to have taken. But Hyde had at last found some one who could talk of Cornelia; rave of her face and figure, and vow she was the topmost beauty in Philadelphia. He listened, and finally asked where she dwelt, and learned that she was staying with Mr. Theodore Willing, a wealthy gentleman of the strictest Quaker principles, but whose son was one of the "feeble men or wet Quakers" who wore powder and ruffles and dressed like a person of fashion.

"He dangles around the bewitching Miss Moran, and gives no other man a chance," said Clymer spitefully. "It is the talk from east to west, and 'tis said, he is so enamoured of the beauty, that he will have her, if he buy her."

"Do you talk in your sleep? Or do you tell your dreams for truth?" asked Hyde angrily. "'Tis not to be believed that a girl so lovely can be bought by mere pounds sterling. A woman's heart lies not so near her hand—God's mercy for it! or any fool might seize it."

"What are you raging at? She is not your mistress."

"Let us talk of horses—or politics—or the last play—or anything but women. They breed quarrels, if you do but name them."

"Content. I will tell you a good story about Tom Herring,"

The story was evidently a good one, for Hyde laughed at the recital with a noisy merriment very unusual to him. The champ and gallop of the horses, and Clymer's vociferous enjoyment of his own wit, blended with it; and for a moment or two Hyde was under a physical exhilaration as intoxicating as the foam of the champagne they had been drinking. In the height of this meretricious gaiety, a carriage, driving at a rather rapid rate turned into the road; and Cornelia suddenly raised her eyes to the festive young men, and then dropped them with an abrupt, even angry expression.

Hyde became silent and speechless, and Clymer was quickly infected by the very force and potency of his companion's agitation and distressed surprise. He heard him mutter, "Oh this is intolerable!" and then, it was, as if a cold sense of dislike had sprung up between them.—Both were glad to escape the other's company, and Hyde fled to the privacy of his own room, that he might hide there the almost unbearable chagrin and misery this unfortunate meeting had caused him.

"Where shall I run to avoid myself?" he cried as he paced the floor in an agony of shame. "She will never respect me again. She ought not. I am the most wretched of lovers. Such a tom-fool to betray me as Anthony Clymer! A man like a piece of glass, that I have seen through a dozen times!" Then he threw himself into a chair and covered his face with his hands, and wept tears full of anger and shameful distress.

For some days sorrow, and confusion, and distraction bound his senses; he refused all company, would neither eat, nor sleep, nor talk, and he looked as white and wan as a spectre. A stupid weight, a dismal sullen stillness succeeded the storm of shame and grief; and he felt himself to be the most forlorn of human beings. If it had been only possible to undo things done! he would have bought the privilege with years. At length, however, the first misery of that wretched meeting passed away, and then he resolved to forget.

Amelia E. Barr

"It is all past!" he said despairingly. "She is lost to me forever! Her memory breaks my heart! I will not remember any longer! I will forfeit all to forgetfulness. Alas, alas, Cornelia! Though you would not believe me, it was the perfectest love that I gave you!"

Cornelia's sorrow, though quite as profound, was different in character. Her sex and various other considerations taught her more restraint; but she also felt the situation to be altogether unendurable, and after a few moments of bitterly eloquent silence, she said—

"Mother, let us go home. I can bear this place no longer. Let us go home to-morrow. Twice this past week I have been made to suffer more than you can imagine. The man is apparently worthless—but I love him."

"You say 'apparently' Cornelia?"

"Oh, how can I tell? There may be excuses—compulsions—I do not know what. I am only sure of one thing, that I love and suffer."

For despite all reason, despite even the evidence of her own eyes, Cornelia kept a reserve. And in that pitiful last meeting, there had been a flash from Hyde's eyes, that said to her— she knew not what of unconquerable love and wrong and sorrow—a flash swifter than lightning and equally potential. It had stirred into tumult and revolt all the platitudes with which she had tried to quiet her restless heart; made her doubtful, pitiful and uncertain of all things, even while her lover's reckless gaiety seemed to confirm her worst suspicions. And she felt unable to face constantly this distressing dubious questioning, so that it was with almost irritable entreaty she said, "Let us go home, mother."

"I have desired to do so for two weeks, Cornelia," answered Mrs. Moran. "I think our visit has already been too long."

"My Cousin Silas has now begun to make love to me; and his mother and sisters like it no better than I do. I hate this town with its rampant, affected fashion and frivolities! It is all a pretence! The people are naturally saints, and they are absurd and detestable, scheming to make the most of both worlds—going to meeting and quoting texts—and then playing that they are men and women of fashion. Mother, let us go home at once. Lucinda can pack our trunks to-day, and we will leave in the morning."

"Can we go without an escort?"

"Oh yes, we can. Lucinda will wait on us—she too is longing for New York—and who can drive us more carefully than Cato? And my dear mother, if Silas wants to escort us, do not permit him. Please be very positive. I am at the end of my patience. I am like to cry out! I am so unhappy, mother!"

"My dear, we will go home to-morrow. We can make the journey in short stages. Do not break down now, Cornelia. It is only a little longer."

"I shall not break down—if we go home." And as the struggle to resist sorrow proves the capacity to resist it, Cornelia kept her promise. As they reached New York her cheerfulness increased, and when they turned into Maiden Lane, she clapped her hands for very joy. And oh, how delightful was the pleasant sunny street, the familiar houses, the brisk wind blowing, the alert cheerful looking men and women that greeted each other in passing with lively words, and bright smiles! O how delightful the fresh brown garden, in which the crocuses were just beginning to peep, the bright looking home, the dear father running with glad surprise to greet them, the handsome, pleasant rooms, the refreshing tea, the thousand small nameless joys that belong to the little darling word "HOME."

She ran upstairs to her own dear room, laid her head on her pillow, sat down in her favourite chair, opened her desk, let in all the sunshine she could, and then fell with holy gratitude on her knees and thanked God for her sweet home, and for the full cup of mercies He had given her to drink in it.

When she went downstairs the mail had just come in, and the Doctor sat before a desk covered with newspapers and letters. "Cornelia," he cried in a voice full of interest, "here is a letter for you—a long letter. It is from Paris."

"It is from Arenta!" she exclaimed, as she examined the large sheets closed with a great splash of red wax, bearing the de Tounnerre crest. It had indeed come from Paris, the city of dreadful slaughter, yet Cornelia opened it with a smiling excitement, as she said again:—

"It is from Arenta!"

CHAPTER XI

WE HAVE DONE WITH TEARS AND TREASONS

"Here is a letter from Arenta!" repeated the Doctor to his wife, who was just entering the room, "Come, Ava, and listen to what she has to say. I have no doubt it will be interesting." Then Cornelia read aloud the following words:

MY DEAR FRIEND CORNELIA:

If to-day I could walk down Maiden Lane, if to-day I could see you and talk to you, I should imagine myself in heaven. For as to this city, I think that in hell the name of "Paris" must have spread itself far and wide. Indeed I often wonder if I am yet on the earth, or if I have gone away in my sleep to the country of the devil and his angels. Even as I am writing to you, my pen is shaking with terror, for I hear the tumbrel come jolting along, and I know that it is loaded with innocent men and women who are going to the guillotine; and I know also that it is accompanied by a mob of dreadful creatures—mostly women—for I hear them singing—no, screaming—in a kind of rage,

"Ca ira les aristocrates a la lanterne!"

Do you remember our learning in those happy days at Bethlehem of the slaughter of Christians by Nero? Very well; right here in the Paris of Marat and Robespierre, you may hear constantly the same brutal cry that filled the Rome of the Caesars—"DEATH TO THE CHRISTIANS!" Famine, anarchy, murder, are everywhere; and I live from moment to moment, trembling if a step comes near me. For Athanase is imprudence itself. His opinions will be the death of him. He will not desert the Girondists, though Mr. Morris tells him their doom is certain. Marat is against them, and the Jacobins—who are deliriously wicked—are against them, and the mob of the Faubourgs is against them; and this mob is always of one mind, always on the spot, and always hungry and ready for anarchy and blood. Besides which, they are already accused of having sold themselves to Mr. Pitt. Very often I have heard my dear father talking of universal suffrage as the bulwark of liberty; well then, we have now, and here, an universal suffrage that is neither a fraud nor a fiction; and as Athanase says, "it is expressing itself every minute, in the crimes of the Holy Guillotine."

And yet Paris makes a pretence of being gay and of enjoying itself. We go to the theatre and the opera, and we dance, as it were, red, wet-shod to the hideous strains of the Carmagnole. It is indeed a dance of death. The other night we were at a reception given by Madame Talma to the victorious General Dumouriez. All the Brissot party were there. Your father will remember Brissot de Warville very well. He was greatly petted by Mrs. Jay and the aristocracy of New York and Philadelphia. Jefferson made a friend of him, and even Washington talked with him about his book on our country. Then he passed himself off as a noble, but he is really the son of an innkeeper. I had so often heard of him, that I regarded with interest his pale face and grave, melancholy manner.

He was accompanied by Camille Desmoulins, and by Danton; the latter a man almost terrible in his ugliness. David, the painter of Socrates, was there; he had his hair frizzed, and was dressed splendidly; and with him was Chenier, more tragic looking than any of his plays. The salons were filled with flowers and beautiful women; among them the majestic Madame Vestris, and the lovely Mademoiselle Candeille, who was singing a song when there arose a sudden indescribable noise, growing louder and louder, and then the cry of MARAT! MARAT! and the "Friend of the People" entered. Now I shall spare a few minutes to tell you, that no one has made frightful enough his large bony face, his thin lips and his livid complexion. He wore an old carmagnole, a dirty handkerchief twisted about his neck, leather breeches, shoes without stockings, and a piece of red cotton round his head, from which there hung a few locks of greasy hair. A nervous twitching keeps him constantly moving, and he has the leprosy:—this is well known. He walked straight to Dumouriez, who said disdainfully, "Ah! are you the man they call Marat?" Marat immediately demanded from him an account of military measures he had taken. They had some sharp conversation which I did not hear, and Marat finally went away uttering the most insulting threats, and leaving every one in a state of mortal terror. The next day the newsboys were shouting "the discovery of a great plot by Marat, the Friend of the People! Great meeting of Aristocrats at Talmas, etc."

This is the kind of pleasure we have; as to religion, there is no longer any religion. Everywhere the Almighty is spoken of as the "soi-disant God." The monarchy is abolished, and yet so ignorant are the leaders of the people, that when Brissot mentioned the word Republic in Petion's house, Robespierre said with a grin, "Republic! Republic! what's a republic?" Spying, and fear, and death penetrate

Amelia E. Barr

into the most private houses; above all, fear, constant fear of every one with whom you come in contact. This feeling is so universal, that some one has conjugated it thus—I am afraid—Thou art afraid—He is afraid—We are afraid—You are afraid—They are afraid—For as death has been officially declared "an endless sleep" any crime is possible; the mob have no fear of hell, and as for the guillotine, it is their opera and their perpetual comedy. Very soon these things must bring on France the chastisement of the Lord; and I shall not be sorry for it.

I have told you the truth about our condition, because I have just had a letter from my father, and he talks of leaving his business in Claus Bergen's care, and coming here to look after me. You must convince him, that he could do me no good whatever, and that he might do me much harm. He is outspoken as a Zealander, and what is in his head and his heart, would come to his lips; also, if it should come to flight, he would embarrass me very much. Tell him not to fear; Arenta says, not to fear. I may indeed have to take a seat in "the terrible armchair" [Footnote: The chair in which the accused sat before the Revolutionary Tribunal and from which they usually went to the guillotine.] but I shall not go to the guillotine; I know that. While Minister Morris is here I have a friend that can do all that can be done. I have had a few letters from Rem, but they do not satisfy me. He is in love, AND NOT WITH YOU. Will you please inform me what that means? Say to Aunt Angelica that I am astonished at her silence; and ask our good Domine to pray that I may soon return to a country where God reigns. Never again do I wish to spend one minute in a place where there is no God; for whatever they may call that place, its real name is hell. Write me a long letter and tell me all the news of New York, and with my respectful remembrance to your dear father and mother, I am always your loving friend,

ARENTA, MARQUISE DE TOUNNERRE.

"Poor Arenta!" said the Doctor when Cornelia had finished the wretched epistle. "She is however showing the mettle of the race from which she sprang. The spirit of the men who fought Alva is in her, and I think she will be a match for Marat, if it comes to that. Suppose you go and see Van Ariens, and give him all the comfort you can. Are you too weary?"

"I should like to see him, I am not tired now. Home is such a good doctor."

"I think you will find him in his house. He comes from his office very early these days."

Cornelia crossed the street and was going to knock at the door, when Van Ariens hastily opened it. His broad face shone with pleasure, and when Cornelia told him her errand, he was in a hurry of loving anxiety to hear what his child had written.

"I understand," he said, when he had heard the letter. "She is frightened, the poor little one! but she will smile and say 'it is nothing.' That is her way. However, I yet think I must go to her."

"Do not," urged Cornelia. "France is now at war with Holland, and you would be recognized as a Dutchman."

"That is so. My tongue would tell tales on me; and to go— even to heaven—by the guillotine, is not what a good man would wish. No indeed!"

"And you may see by Arenta's letter, that she does not fear the guillotine. Come over to-night and talk to my father and mother, and I will tell you what I saw in Philadelphia."

"Well then, I will come."

"Is Madame Jacobus back in New York yet?"

"She is in London."

"But why in London?"

"That, I know not. Two reasons I can suppose, but which is right, or if either be right, that is beyond my certainty."

"Is her sister-in-law dead?"

"She is dead. Her husband was an Englishman; perhaps then it is about some property in England she has gone. If it is not that, of nothing else can I think but Captain Jacobus. But my sister Angelica had ever two ways—nothing at all she would say about her money or her business; but constantly, to every one, she would talk of her husband. I think then it is money or property that has taken her to England. For if it had been Jacobus, to the whole town she would have told it." Then he took both Cornelia's hands in his, and looking at her earnestly said—

"Poor Rem! Impossible is it?"

"Quite impossible, sir," she answered.

"When he got thy letter refusing his love and offer, he went to Boston. I think he will not come back to me. I am very sorry," he said simply, and he let her hands drop.

"I am sorry also—for your sake. I hear however that Rem is doing well in Boston."

"Better than his hopes. Very good fortune has come to him."

"And you, sir?"

"I am not doing much at present—but Smith and Warren do less. In an hour or two to your house I will come. There is plenty to talk about."

The next day Cornelia walked down Broadway to Madame Jacobus' house. It was closed and desolate looking, and she sighed as she compared its old bright spotless comfort, with its present empty forlornness. The change typified the change in her heart and love, but ere she could entertain the thought, her eyes fell upon the trees in the garden, full of the pale crinkled leaves of spring, and she saw the early flowers breaking through the dark earth, and the early shrubs bursting into white and golden blooms. In some way they had a message for her; and she went home with hope budding in her heart. Soon after Mrs. Moran heard her singing at her work,

"The far east glows,
The morning wind blows fresh and free;
Should not the hour that wakes the rose
Awaken thee?
No longer sleep—
Oh listen now!
I wait and weep,
But where art thou?"

From one to another song she went, simple melodies all of them, delightful little warblings of love, which except for their gladness and loyalty, had nothing in them to charm.

She was a deserted maiden. Her lover had palpably and with extreme cruelty deceived her; but she had grieved, and forgiven. And love brings its reward, even if unrequited. Those who love, and have loved, are the better for the revelation; for love for love's sake enriches and blesses the lover to the very end of life. She did not forget, for love has everlasting remembrance; and she did not wish to forget, for a great affection is a great happiness, and the whole soul can find shelter in it.

Neither were her days monotonous or unhappy. All the real pleasures of life lie in narrow compass; and she found herself very often a little hurried for want of time. She had not, it is true, the resources of the woman of to-day—no literary, musical, social, or sporting clubs existed for Cornelia; but she had duties and devices that made every moment pleasant or profitable. Many hours daily were given to fine needle-work—calm quiet hours full of thought as well as work; she had her music to practice, new books and papers to read, calls to make, mantua makers and milliners to interview, dinners and dances and tea-parties to attend, shopping to look after, delicate bits of darning and mending to exercise her skill on, creams and pasties and cakes to prepare, visitors to welcome and entertain, and many other duties which sprang up—as extras do—unexpectedly, and yet which opened the door for very pleasant surprises and events.

Besides which, there was her father. After her return from school she had always driven with him to some extent; but his claim on her now was often a little exacting. He said the fresh spring winds were good for her, and that she stayed in the house too much, and there was no evading the dictum that came with both parental and medical authority. Perhaps this demand upon her time would not have been made if the Hydes had been in New York; but Doctor Moran by frequent inquiries satisfied himself that they were yet in Philadelphia; and for his daughter's satisfaction he frequently said as they drove up Maiden Lane, "We will take the Greenwich Road, there is no fear of our meeting any one we do not wish to see." She understood the allusion, and was satisfied to escape meetings that promised her nothing but pain.

In the month of May there occurred one of those wet spells which are so irritating "growing weather" of course, but very tiresome to those who felt the joy of spring escaping them. Week after week it was too damp, or the winds were too sharp, or the roads too heavy for quick driving, and thus the month of all months went out of the calendar with few red letter days to brighten it. Then June came in royally, and Cornelia was glad of the sunshine and the breeze and the rapid canter; and for a week or two she was much out with her father. But he was now ever on the watch, and she judged from the circumstance that the Hydes were back in New York. Besides which, he did not any longer give her the assurance of not meeting any one they did not wish to see.

One exquisite day as they went up Maiden Lane the Doctor said—" My friend General Hewitt sails for England to-day, and we will go and wish him a good voyage." So to the pier they went, and the Doctor left his carriage, and taking Cornelia on his arm walked down to where the English packet was lying. They were a little too late to go on board, for the shoremen were taking away the gang-plank, and the sailors preparing to lift the anchor; but the General stood leaning over the side of the vessel, and exchanged some last words with his friend.

While Cornelia listened, she became suddenly conscious of the powerful magnetism of some human eye, and obeying its irresistible attraction she saw George Hyde steadily regarding her. He stood by the side of his father, as handsome as on that May morning when he had first looked love into her heart. She was enthralled again by his glance, and never for one moment thought of resisting the appeal it

Amelia E. Barr

made to her. With a conscious tenderness she waved him an
adieu whose spirit he could not but feel. In the same moment
he lifted his hat and stood bareheaded looking at her with a
pathetic inquiry, which made her inwardly cry out, "Oh,
what does he mean?" The packet was moving—the wind
filled the blowing sails—the hoarse crying of the sailormen
blended with the "good-byes" of the passengers—and the
Earl, aware of the sad and silent parting within his sight—
moved away as Cornelia again waved a mute farewell to her
lost lover. Then the Doctor touched her—

"Why do you do that?" he asked angrily.

"Because I must do it, father; I cannot help it. I desire to
do it."

"I am in a hurry; let us go home."

Filling her eyes with the beauty of the splendid looking
youth still standing bareheaded watching her, seeing even
such trivial things as his long cloak thrown backward over
his shoulder, his white hand holding his lifted hat, and the
wind-tossed curls of his handsome head, she turned away
with a sigh. The Doctor drove rapidly to Maiden Lane and
did not on the way speak a word; and Cornelia was glad of it.
That image of her lover standing on the moving ship
watching her with his heart in his eyes, filled her whole
consciousness. Never would it be possible for her to forget it,
or to put any other image in its place. She thanked her good
angel for giving her such a comforting memory; it seemed as
if the sting had been taken out of her sorrow. Henceforward
she was resolved to love without a doubt. She would believe
in Joris, no matter what she had seen, or what she had heard.
There were places in life to which alas! truth could not come;
and this might be one of them. Though all the world blamed
her lover, she would excuse him. Her heart might ache, her

eyes might weep, but in that aching heart and in those weeping eyes, his splendid image would live in that radiant dimness which makes the unseen face, often more real than the present one.

Doctor Moran divined something of this resolute temper, and it made him silent. He felt that his daughter had come to a place where she had put reason firmly aside, and given her whole assent to the assurances of her intuition. He had no arguments for an antagonism of this kind. What could he say to a soul that presaged a something, and then believed it? His instinctive sagacity told him that silence was now the part of wisdom. But though he took her silently home he was conscious of a great relief. His watch was over.

Now a woman's intuition is like a leopard's spring, it seizes the truth—if it seize it at all—at the first bound; and it was by this unaccountable mental agility Cornelia had arrived at the conviction of her lover's fidelity. At any rate, she felt confident, that if circumstances had compelled him to be false to her, the wrong had been sincerely mourned; and she was able to forgive the offence that was blotted out with tears. She reflected also, that now he was so far away, it would be possible for her to call upon Madame Van Heemskirk, and also upon Madame Jacobus as soon as she returned; but if Hyde had remained in New York, these houses would necessarily be closed to her, for he was a constant visitor at both.

She resolved therefore to call upon Madame Van Heemskirk the following week. She expected the old lady might treat her a little formally, perhaps even with some coldness, but she thought it worth while to test her kindness. Joris had once told her that his grandfather and grandmother both approved their love, and they must know of his desertion, and also of the reason for it. Yet there was in her heart such a reluctance to take any step that had the appearance of seeking her lost lover, that she put off this visit day after day, finding in the weather or in some household duty always a fair excuse for doing so, until one morning the Doctor said at breakfast:

"Councillor De Vrees died yesterday, and there is to be a great funeral. Every Dutchman in town will be there, and many others beside, He has left an immense fortune."

"Who told you this?" asked Mrs. Moran.

"I met Van Heemskirk and his wife going there. Madame De Vrees is their daughter. Now you will see great changes take place."

"What do you mean, John?"

"Madame De Vrees has long wanted to build a mansion equal to their wealth, but the Councillor would never leave the house he built at their marriage. Madame will now build, and her children take their places among the great ones of the city. De Vrees was an oddity; very few people will be sorry to lose him. He had no good quality but money, and he was the most unhappy of men about its future disposal. I never understood until I knew him, how wretched a thing it is to be merely rich."

This conversation again put off Cornelia's visit, and she virtually abandoned the idea. Then one morning Mrs. Moran said, "Cornelia, I wish you to go to William Irvin's for some hosiery and Kendal cottons. It is a new store down the Lane at number ninety, and I hear his cloths are strangely cheap. Go and examine them for me."

"Very well, mother. I will also look in at Fisher's;" and it was at Fisher's that she saw Madame Van Heemskirk. She was talking to Mr. Henry Fisher as they advanced from the back of the store, and Cornelia had time to observe that madame was in deep mourning, and that she had grown older looking since she had last seen her. As they came forward madame raised her eyes and saw Cornelia, and then hastily leaving the merchant, she approached her.

"Good-morning, madame," said Cornelia, with a cheerful smile.

"Good-morning, miss. Step aside once with me. A few words I have to say to you;" and as she spoke she drew Cornelia a little apart from the crowd at the counter, and looking at her sternly, said—

"One question only—why then did you treat my grandson so badly? A shameful thing it is to be a flirt."

"I am not a flirt, madame. And I did not treat your grandson badly. No, indeed!"

"Yes, indeed! He told me so himself."

"He told you so?"

"He told me so. Surely he did."

"That I treated him badly?"

"Pray then what else? You let a young man love you—you let him tell you so—you tell him 'yes, I love you' and then when he says marry me, you say, 'no.' Such ways I call bad, very bad! Not worthy of my Joris are you, and so then, I am glad you said 'no.'"

Amelia E. Barr

"I do not understand you."

"Neither did you understand my Joris—a great mistake he made—and he did not understand you; and I do not understand such ways of the girls of this day. They are shameless, and I am ashamed for you."
"Madame, you are very rude."

"And very false are you."

"I am not false."

"My Joris told me so. Truth itself is Joris. He would not lie. He would not deceive."

"If your grandson told you I had deceived him, and refused to marry him,—let it be so. I have no wish to contradict your grandson."

"That you cannot do. I am ashamed—"

"Madame, I wish you good morning;" and with these words Cornelia left the store. Her cheeks were burning; the old lady's angry voice was in her ears, she felt the eyes of every one in the store upon her, and she was indignant and mortified at a meeting so inopportune. Her heart had also received a new stab; and she had not at the moment any philosophy to meet it. Joris had evidently told his grandmother exactly what the old lady affirmed. She had not a doubt of that, but why? Why had he lied about her? Was there no other way out of his entanglement with her? She walked home in a hurry, and as soon as possible shut herself in her room to consider this fresh wrong and injustice.

She could arrive at only one conclusion—Annie's most unexpected appearance had happened immediately after his proposal to herself. He was pressed for time, his grand-parents would be especially likely to embarrass him concerning her claims, and of course the quickest and surest way to prevent questioning on the matter, was to tell them that she had refused him. That fact would close their mouths in sympathy for his disappointment, and there would be no further circumstances to clear up. It was the only explanation of madame's attitude that was possible, and she was compelled to accept it, much as it humiliated her. And then after it had been accepted and sorrowed over, there came back to her those deeper assurances, those soul assertions, which she could not either examine or define, but which she felt compelled to receive—He loves me! I feel it! It is not his fault! I must not think wrong of him.

There was still Madame Jacobus to hope for. She was so shrewd and so kindly, that Cornelia felt certain of her sympathy and wise advice. But month after month passed away and madame's house remained empty and forlorn-looking. Now and then there came short fateful letters from Arenta, and Van Ariens—utterly miserable—visited them frequently that he might be comforted with their assurances of his child's ability to manage the very worst circumstances in which she could be placed.

And so the long summer days passed and the winter approached again; but before that time Cornelia had at least attained to the wisest of all the virtues—that calm, hushed contentment, which is only another name for happiness—that contentment which accepts the fact that there is a chain of causes linked to effects by an invincible necessity; and that whatever is, could not have wisely been but so. And if this was fatalism, it was at least a brighter thing than the languid pessimism, which would have led her life among quicksands, to end it in wreck.

One day at the close of October she put down her needle-work with a little impatience. "I am tired of sewing, mother," she said, "and I will walk down to the Battery and get a breath of the sea. I shall not stay long."

On her way to the Battery she was thinking of Hyde, and of their frequent walks together there; and for once she passed the house of Madame Jacobus without a glance at its long-closed windows. It was growing dark as she returned, and ere she quite reached it she was aware of a glow of fire light and candle light from the windows. She quickened her steps, and saw a servant well known to her standing at the open door directing two men who were carrying in trunks and packages. She immediately accosted him.

"Has madame returned at last, Ameer?" she asked joyfully.

"Madame has returned home," he answered. "She is weary—she is not alone—she will not receive to-night."

"Surely not. I did not think of such a thing. Tell her only that I am glad, and will call as soon as she can see me."

The man's manner—usually so friendly—was shy and peculiar, and Cornelia felt saddened and disappointed. "And yet why?" she asked herself. "Madame has but reached home —I did not wish to intrude upon her—Ameer need not have thought so—however I am glad she is back again"—and she walked rapidly home to the thoughts which this unexpected arrival induced. They were hopeful thoughts, leaning—however she directed them—towards her absent lover. She felt sure madame would see clearly to the very bottom of what she could not understand. She went into her mother's presence full of renewed expectations, and met her smile with one of unusual brightness.

"Madame Jacobus is at home," said Mrs. Moran, before Cornelia could speak. "She sent for your father just after you left the house, and I suppose that he is still there."

"Is she sick?"

"I do not know. I fear so, for the visit is a long one."

It continued so much longer that the two ladies took their tea alone, nor could they talk of any other subject than madame, and her most unexpected call for Doctor Moran's services." It was always the Dutch Doctor Gansvoort she had before," said Mrs. Moran; "and she was ever ready to scoff at all others, as pretenders.—I do wonder what keeps your father so long?"

It was near ten o'clock when Doctor Moran returned, and his face was sombre and thoughtful—the face of a man who had been listening for hours to grave matters, and who had not been able to throw off their physical reflection.

"Have you had tea, John?" asked Mrs. Moran.

"No. Give me a good strong cup, Ava. I am tired with listening and feeling."

She poured it out quickly, and after he had taken the refreshing drink, Cornelia asked—

"Is madame very ill?"

"She is wonderfully well. It is her husband."

"Captain Jacobus?"

"Who else? She has brought him home, and I doubt if she

has done wisely."

"What has happened, John? Surely you will tell us!"

"There is nothing to conceal. I have heard the whole story—a very pitiful story—but yet like enough to end well, Madame told me that the day after her sister-in-law's burial, James Lauder, a Scotchman who had often sailed with Captain Jacobus, came down to Charleston to see her. He had sought her in New York, and been directed by her lawyer to Charleston. He declared that having had occasion to go to Guy's Hospital in London to visit a sick comrade, he saw there Captain Jacobus. He would not admit any doubt of his identity, but said the Captain had forgotten his name, and everything in connection with his past life; and was hanging about the premises by favour of the physicians, holding their horses, and doing various little services for them."

"Oh how well I can imagine madame's hurry and distress," said Cornelia.

"She hardly knew how to reach London quickly enough. She said thought would have been too slow for her. But Lauder's tale proved to be true. Her first action was to take possession of the demented man, and surround him with every comfort. He appeared quite indifferent to her care, and she obtained no shadow of recognition from him. She then brought to his case all the medical skill money could procure, and in the consultation which followed, the physicians decided to perform the operation of trepanning."

"But why? Had he been injured, John?"

"Very badly. The hospital books showed that he had been brought there by two sailors, who said he had been struck in a gale by a falling mast. The wound healed, but left him mentally a wreck. The physicians decided that the brain was suffering from pressure, and that trepanning would relieve, if it did not cure."

"Then why was it not done at first?"

"Whose interest was it to inquire? No money was left with the injured man. The sailors who took him to the hospital gave false names, and address, and he received only such treatment as a pauper patient was likely to receive. But he made friends, and was supported about the place. Imagine now what a trial was before madame! It was a difficult matter to perform the operation, for the patient could not be made to understand its necessity; and he was very hard to manage. Then picture to yourselves, the terrible strain of nursing which followed; though madame says it was soon brightened and lightened by her husband's recognition of her. After that event all weariness was rest, and suffering ease; and as soon as he was able to travel both were determined to return at once to their own home. He is yet however a sick man, and may never quite recover a slight paralysis of the lower limbs."

"Does he remember how he was hurt?"

"He declares his men mutinied, because instead of returning to New York, he had taken on a cargo for the East India Company; and that the blow was given him either by his first, or second mate. He thinks they sailed his ship out of the Thames, for her papers were all made out, and she was ready to drop down the river with the next tide. He vows he will get well and find his ship and the rascals that stole her; and I should not wonder if he does. He has will enough for anything. Madame desires to see you, Cornelia. Can you go there with me in the morning?"

"I shall be glad to go. Madame is like no one else."

"She is not like herself at present. I think you may be a little disappointed in her. She has but one thought, one care, one end and aim in life—her husband."

The Doctor had judged correctly. Cornelia was disappointed from the first moment. She was taken to the dim uncanny drawing-room by Ameer, and left among its ill-omened gods, and odd treasure-trove for nearly half an hour before madame came to her. The rudely graven faces, so marvellously instinct with life, made her miserable; she fancied a thousand mockeries and scorns in them; and no thought of Hyde, or Arenta, or of the happy hours spent in that ill-boding room, could charm away its sinister influence.

When madame at length came to her, she appeared like the very genius of the place. The experiences of the past year had left traces which no after experience would be able to obliterate. She looked ten years older. Her wonderful dark eyes, glowing with a soft tender fire alone remained untouched by the withering hand of anxious love. They were as vital as ever they had been, and when Cornelia said so, she answered, "That is because my soul dwells in them, and my soul is always young. I have had a year, Cornelia, to crumble the body to dust; but my soul made light of it for love's sake. Did your father tell you how much Captain Jacobus had suffered?"

"Yes, madame."

But in spite of this assurance, madame went over the whole story in detail, and Cornelia could not help but remember that Mr. Van Ariens had said "about her husband she will talk constantly, and to the whole town." For however far the conversation diverged for a moment, madame always brought it sharply back to the one subject that interested her. Even Arenta's peculiarly dangerous position could not detain her thoughts and interest for many minutes.

"I am sorry for Arenta," she said; "no greater hell can there be, than to live in constant fear. But she has the gift of a clever tongue, and every one has not the like talent; and also if a woman with the decency of her sex may be a scholar, Arenta has learning enough to compass the fools who might injure her."

"Marat and Robespierre are both against her husband, and she may share his fate."

"Marat and Robespierre!" she cried. "Both of the creatures have a devil. I wish them to go to the guillotine together, and I would bury them together with their faces downwards. Let them pass out of your memory. Poor Jacobus was in a worse case than Arenta. Till I be key-cold dead, I shall never forget my first sight of him in that dreadful place—" and then she described again her overwhelming emotions when she perceived he was alike apathetic to his pauper condition, and to her love and presence. There never came a moment during the whole visit when it was possible to speak of Hyde. Madame seemed to have quite forgotten her liking for the handsome youth; it had been swallowed up in her adoring affection for her restored husband.

Cornelia would not force the memory upon her. Some day she might remember; but for a little while madame had more than enough of fresh material for her conversation. Every one who had known Captain Jacobus or herself, called with congratulations for their happy return; and when Cornelia made a nearly daily visit with her father, madame had these calls to talk over with her.

Amelia E. Barr

One morning, however, the long-looked-for topic was introduced. "I had a visit from Madame Van Heemskirk yesterday afternoon," she said; "and the dear old Senator came with her to see Captain Jacobus. While they talked, madame told me that you had refused that handsome young fellow, her grandson. What could you mean by such a stupidity, Miss Moran?"

Her voice had just that tone of indifference, mingled with sarcastic disapproval, that hurt and offended Cornelia. She felt that it was not worth while to explain herself, for madame had evidently accepted the offended grandmother's opinion; and the memory of the young Lord was lively enough to make her sympathize with his supposed wrong.

"I never considered you to be a flirt," she continued, "and I am astonished. If, now, it had been Arenta, I could have understood it. I told Madame Van Heemskirk that I had not the least doubt Doctor Moran dictated the refusal."

"Oh, indeed," answered Cornelia, with a good deal of spirit and some anger, "you shall not blame my father. He knew nothing whatever of Lord Hyde's offer, until I had been subjected to such insult and wrong as drove me to the grave's mouth. Only the mercy of God, and my father's skill, brought me back to life."

"Yes, I think your father to be wonderfully skilful. He has done Jacobus a great deal of good, and he now gives him hope of a perfect recovery. Doctor Moran is a fine physician; Jacobus says so."

Cornelia remained silent. If madame did not feel interest sufficient in her affairs to ask for the particulars of one so nearly fatal to her, she determined not to force the subject on her. Then Jacobus rang his bell, and madame flew to his room to see whether his want had received proper attention. Cornelia sat still a few moments, her heart swelling, her eyes filling with the sense of that injustice, harder to bear than any other form of wrong. She was going away, when madame returned to her, and something in her eyes went to the heart of the older woman. She turned her back, with a kind but peremptory word, and taking her hand, said—

"I have been thoughtless, Cornelia, selfish, I dare say; but I do not wish to be so. Tell me, my dear, what has happened. Did you quarrel with George Hyde? And pray what was it about?"

"We never had one word of any kind, but words of affection. He wrote and asked me if he could come and see my father about our marriage, on a certain night. I answered his letter with all the love that was in my heart for him, and told him to come and see my father that very night. He never came. He never sent me the least explanation. He never wrote to me, or spoke to me again."

"Oh, but this is a different story! His grandmother told me that you refused him."

"That is not the truth. Lady Annie Hyde came most unexpectedly that very day, and I suppose the easiest way to stop all inquiries about Miss Moran, was to say 'she refused me.'"

"And after Lady Annie's arrival, what happened?"

"I was absolutely deserted. That is the truth. I may as well admit it. Perhaps you think it impossible for a young man so good-natured to behave in a manner so cruel and dishonourable; but I assure you it is the truth."

Amelia E. Barr

"My dear, I have lived to see it almost impossible to think worse of people than they are; and if you can bear to hear more on this subject, I will tell it to you myself."

"I can always bear the truth. If I have lost my heart, I have not lost my head; nor will I surrender to useless grief the happiness which I can yet make for others, and for myself."

"If what you have told me be so—and I believe it is—then I say Lord George Hyde is an intolerable scoundrel."

"I would rather not hear him spoken of in that way."

"I ask your pardon, but I must give myself a little Christian liberty of railing. The man is false clean through. He was evidently engaged to Lady Annie when he first sought your love, and therefore as soon as she came here, he deserted you. I will tell you plainly that I saw him last summer very frequently, and he was always with her—always listening with ears and heart to what she said—always watching her with all his soul in his eyes—ever on the lookout to see that not a breath of wind ruffled her soft wraps, or blew too strongly on her little white face."

"That was his way, madame. I have seen him devoting himself to you in the same manner; yes, and to Madame Griffin, and Miss White, and a score of other ladies—old and young. You know how good-natured he was. When did you hear him say a wrong word of any one? even of Rem Van Ariens who was often intolerably rude."

"Very well! I would rather have a man 'intolerably rude' like my nephew Rem, than one like Lord Hyde who speaks well of everybody. Upon my word, I think that is the worst kind of slander!"

"I think not."

"It is; for it takes away the reputation of good men, by making all men alike. But this, that, or the other, I saw Lord Hyde in devoted attendance on Lady Annie. Give him up totally. He is in his kingdom when he has a pretty woman to make a fool of. As for marriage, these young men who have the world, or the better part of it, they marry where Cupidity, not Cupid leads them. Give him up entirely."

"I have done so," answered Cornelia. And then she felt a sudden anger at herself, so much so, that as she walked home, she kept assuring her heart with an almost passionate insistence, "I have not given him up! I will not give him up! I believe in him yet."

Madame's advice might be wise, but there are counsels of perfection that cannot be followed; because they are utterly at variance with that intuitive knowledge, which the soul has of old; and which it will not surrender; and whose wisdom it is interiorly sure of. And after this confidence Cornelia did not go so often to madame's. Something jarred between them. We know that a single drop taken from a glass of water changes the water level swift as thought, and the same law is certain in all human relations. Madame was not quite the same; something had been taken away; the level of their friendship was changed; and when Doctor Moran could not but perceive this fact, he said—

"Go less frequently to madame's, Cornelia. You do not enjoy your visits; dissolve a friendship that begins to be incomplete. It is the best plan."

Amelia E. Barr

CHAPTER XII

A HEART THAT WAITS

Late summer on the Norfolk Broads! And where on earth can the lover of boats find a more charming resort? How alluring are the mysterious entrances to these Broads! where a boat seems to make an insane dive into a hopeless cul de sac of a ditch, and then suddenly emerges on a wide expanse of water, teeming with pike and bream and eels; and fringed with a border of plashy ground, full of reeds and willows and flowering flags; and alive with water fowl.

Now close to the Manor of Hyde, the country home of Earl Hyde in Norfolk, there was one of these delightful Broads— flat as a billiard table, and hidden by the tall reeds which bordered it. But Annie Hyde lying at the open window of her room in the Manor House could see its silvery waters, and the black-sailed wherry floating on them, and the young man sitting at the prow fishing, and idling, among the lilies and languors of these hot summer days. Her hands were folded, her lips moved, she was asking of some intelligence among the angels, grace and favour for one who was dearer to her than her own life or happiness.

An aged man sat silently by her, a man of noble beauty, whose soul was in every part of his body, expressive and impressive—a fiery particle not always at its window, but when there, infecting and going through observers, whether they would or not. He was dressed altogether in black, and had fine small hands, a thin austere face and clean sensitive lips which seemed to say, "He hath made us kings and priests"—a man of celestial race, valuing things at their eternal, not at their temporal worth.

There had been silence for some time between them, and he did not appear disposed to break it; but Annie longed for him to do so, because she had a mystical appetite for sacred things, and was never so happy and so much at rest as when he was talking to her of them. For she loved God, and had been led to the love of God by a kind of thirst for God.

"Dear father," she said finally, "I have been thinking of the past years, in which you have taught me so much."

"It is better to look forward, Annie," he answered. "The traveller to Eternity must not continually turn back to count his steps; for if God be leading him, no matter how dangerous or lonely the road, 'He will pluck thy feet out of the net.'"

"Even in the valley of death?"

"'BE NOT AFRAID! NOTHING OF THEE WILL DIE!'" Take these sweet compassionate words of Jesus, as He wept by the dying bed of Joseph, His father, into thy heart. Blessed are the homesick, Annie! for they shall get home."

"All my life I have loved God, and His love has been over me."

"Date not God's love from thy nativity; look far, far back of it—to the everlasting love."

"After death, I SHALL KNOW."

"Death!" he repeated, "Death that deceitful word. What is it? A dream, that wakes us at the end of the night. This is the great saying that men forget—Death is Life!"

"Yet life ceases."

"It does not, Annie. Death, is like the setting of the sun. The sun never sets; life never ceases. Certain phenomena occur which deceive us, because human vision is so feeble—we think the sun sets, and it never ceases shining; we think our friends die, and they never cease living."

As he spoke these words Mary Damer entered, and she laid her hand on his shoulder and said, "My dear Doctor Roslyn, after death what then? we are not all good—what then?"

He looked at her wistfully and answered, "I will give you one thought, Mary, to ponder—the blessedness of heaven, is it not an eternity older than the misery of hell? Let your soul fearlessly follow where this fact leads it; for there is no limit to God's mercy. Do you think it is His way to worry a wandering sheep eternally? Jesus Christ thought better of His father. He told us that the Great Shepherd of souls followed such sheep into the wilderness, and brought them home in His arms, or on His shoulder, and then called on the angels of heaven to rejoice because they were found. Find out what that parable means, Mary. He whose name is 'Love' can teach you."

Then he rose and went away, and Mary sat down in his place, and Annie gradually came back to the material plane of everyday life and duty. Indeed Mary brought this element in a very decided form with her; for she had a letter in her hand from an old lover, and she was much excited by its advent, and eager to discuss the particulars with Annie.

"It is from Captain Seabright, who is now in Pondicherry," she explained. "He loves me, Annie. He loved me long ago, and went to India to make money; now he says he has enough and to spare; and he asks me if I have forgotten."

"There is Mr. Van Ariens to consider. You have promised to marry him, Mary. It is not hard to find the right way on this road, I think."

"Of course. I would scorn to do a dishonourable or unhandsome thing. But is it not very strange Willie Seabright should write to me at this time? How contradictory life is! I had also a letter from Mr. Van Ariens by the same mail, and I shall answer them both this evening." Then she laughed a little, and added, "I must take care and not make the mistake an American girl made, under much the same circumstances."

"What was it?" inquired Annie languidly.

"She misdirected her letters and thus sent 'No' to the man whom of all others, she wished to marry."

As Mary spoke a soft brightness seemed to pervade Annie's brain cells, and she could hardly restrain the exclamation of sudden enlightenment that rose to her lips. She raised herself slightly, and in so doing, her eyes fell upon the tall figure of Hyde standing clearly out in the intense, white sunshine of the Broads; and perhaps her soul may have whispered to his soul, for he turned his face to the house, and lifted the little red fishing cap from his head. The action stimulated to the utmost Annie's intuitive powers.

"Mary," she said, "what a strange incident! Did you know

Amelia E. Barr

the girl?"

"I saw her once in Philadelphia. Mr. Van Ariens told me about her. She is the friend of his sister the Marquise de Tounnerre."

"How did Mr. Van Ariens know of such an event?"

"I suppose the Marquise told him of it."

"I am interested. Is she pretty? Who, and what is her father? Did she lose her lover through the mistake?"

"You are more interested in this American girl, than in me. I think you might ask a little concerning my love affair with Captain Seabright."

"I always ask you about Mr. Van Ariens. A girl cannot have two lovers,"

"But if one is gone away?"

"Then he has gone away; and that is the end of him. He must not trouble the one who has come to stay, eh, Mary?"

"You are right, Annie. But one's first lover has always a charm above reason; and Willie Seabright was once very dear to me."

"I am sorry for that unfortunate American girl."

"So am I. She is a great beauty. Her name is Cornelia Moran; and her father is a famous physician in New York."

"And this beauty had two lovers?"

"Yes; an Englishman of noble birth; and an American. They both loved her, and she loved the Englishman. They must have both asked her hand on the same day, and she must have answered both letters in the same hour; and the letter she intended for the man she loved, went to the man she did not love. Presumably, the man she loved got the refusal she intended for the other, for he never sought her society again; and Mr. Van Ariens told me she nearly died in consequence. I know not as to this part of the story; when I saw her in Philadelphia, she had no more of fragility than gave delicacy to all her charms."

"And what became of the two lovers, Mary?"

"The Englishman went back to England; and the American found another girl more kind to him."

"I wonder what made Mr. Van Ariens tell you this story?"

"He talked much of his sister, and this young lady was her chief friend and confidante."

"When did it happen?"

"A few days after his sister's marriage."

"Then the Marquise could not know of it; and so she could not have told her brother. However in the world could he have found out the mistake? Do you think the girl herself found it out?"

"That is inconceivable," answered Mary. "She would have written to her lover and explained the affair."

"Certainly. It is a very singular incident. I want to think it over—how—did—Mr. Van Ariens—find—it—out, I wonder!"

Amelia E. Barr

"Perhaps the rejected lover confided in him."

"But why did not the rejected lover send the letter he received—and which he must have known he had no right to retain—to Miss Moran, or to the Englishman for whom it was intended? A man who could keep a letter like that, must have some envious sneaking devil in his body. A bad man, Mary, a bad man—the air must be unclean in any room he comes into."

"Why Annie! How angry you are. Let us drop the subject. I really do want to tell you something about Willie Seabright."

"What did Mr. Van Ariens say about the matter? What did he think? Why did he tell you?"

"We were talking of the Marquise. The story came up quite naturally. I think Mr. Van Ariens felt very sorry for Miss Moran. Of course he did. Will you listen to Captain Seabright's letter? I had no idea it could affect me so much."

"But you loved him once?"

"Very dearly."

"Well then, Mary, I think no one has a double in love or friendship. If the loved one dies, or goes away, his place remains empty forever. We have lost feelings that he, and he only, could call up."

At this point in the conversation Hyde entered, brown and wind-blown, the scent of the sedgy water and the flowery woods about him.

"Your servant, ladies," he said gayly, "I have bream enough for a dozen families, Mary; and I have sent a string to the rectory."

"Poor little fish!" answered Annie. "They could not cry out, or plead with you, or beg for their lives, and because they were dumb and opened not their mouths, they were wounded and strangled to death."

"Don't say such things, Annie. How can I enjoy my sport if you do?"

"I don't think you ought to enjoy sport which is murder. You have your wherry to sail, is not that sport enough? I have heard you say nothing that floats on fresh water, can beat a Norfolk wherry."

"I vow it is the truth. With her fine lines and strong sails she can lie closer to the wind than any other craft. She is safe, and fast, and handy to manage. Three feet of water will do her, though she be sixty tons burden; and I will sail her where nothing but a row boat can follow me."

"Is not that sport enough?"

"I must have something to get. I would have brought you armfuls of flowers, but you do not like me to cut them."

"I like my flowers alive, George. You must be dull indeed if you make no difference between the scent of growing flowers, and cut ones. Tomorrow Mary is going to Ranforth, you must go with her, and you may bring me some peaches from the Hall, if you please to do so."

Then Hyde and Mary had a game of battledore, and she watched them tossing the gayly painted corks, until amid their light laughter and merry talk she fell asleep. And when she awakened it was sunset, and there was no one in her room but her maid. She had slept long, but in spite of its refreshment, she had a sense of something uneasy. Then she recalled the story Mary Damer had told her, and because she comprehended the truth, she was instantly at rest. The whole secret was clear as daylight to her. She knew now every turn of an event so full of sorrow. She was positive Rem Van Ariens was himself the thief of her cousin's love and happiness, and the bringer of grief—almost of death—to Cornelia. All the facts she did not have, but facts are little; intuition is everything. She said to herself, "I shall not be long here, and before I go away, I must put right love's wrong."

She considered then what she ought to do, and gradually the plan that pleased her best, grew distinctly just, and even-handed in her mind. She would write to Cornelia. Her word would be indisputable. Then she would dismiss the subject from her conversations with Mary, until Cornelia's answer arrived; nor until that time would she say a word of her suspicions to Hyde. In pursuance of these resolutions the following letter to Cornelia left Hyde Manor for New York the next mail:

To Miss CORNELIA MORAN:

Because you are very dear to one of my dear kindred, and because I feel that you are worthy of his great love, I also love you. Will you trust me now? There has been a sad mistake. I believe I can put it right. You must recollect the day on which George Hyde wrote asking you to fix an hour when he could call on Doctor Moran about your marriage. Did any other lover ask you on that day to marry him? Was that other lover Mr. Van Ariens? Did you write to both about the same time? If so, you mis-directed your letters; and the one intended for Lord Hyde went to Mr. Van Ariens; and the one intended for Mr.

Van Ariens, went to Lord Hyde. Now you will understand many things. I found out this mistake through the young lady Mr. Van Ariens is intending to marry. Can you send to me, for Lord Hyde, a copy of the letter you intended for him. When I receive it, you may content your heart. I may never see you again, but I would like you to remember me by this act of loving kindness; and I wish you all the joy in your love, that I could wish myself. The shadows will soon flee away, and when your wedding bells ring, I shall know; and rejoice with you, and with my dear cousin. Delay not to answer this, why should you delay your happiness? I send you as love gifts my thoughts, desires, prayers, all that is best in me, al! that I give to one high in my esteem, and whom I wish to place high in my affection, This to your hand and heart, with all sincerity,

ANNIE HYDE.

When she had signed her name she was full of content, her face was transfigured with the joy she foresaw for others, and she thought not of her own gain, though it was great— even the riches of that divine self-culture, that comes only through self-sacrifice. She calculated her letter would reach Cornelia about the end of September, and she thought how pleasantly the hope it brought, would brighten her life. And without permitting Hyde to suspect any change in his love affair, she very often led the conversation to Cornelia, and to the circumstances of her life. Hyde was always willing to talk on this subject, and thus she learned so much about Arenta, and Madame Jacobus, and Rem Van Ariens, that the people became her familiars. Arenta particularly interested her, and she spoke and thought continually of the gay little Dutch girl among the human tigers of Paris. And the thought of her ended ever in a silent prayer for her safety. "I must ask some strong angel to go and help her," she said to Hyde, "a city full of blood, must be a city full of evil spirits, and she will need the wings of angels round her—like a pavilion—so when she comes into my mind I say 'angels of deliverance go to her.' And I think she must be in a great strait now, or I should not feel so constrained to pray for her."

"And you believe such prayer avails for deliverance, Annie?"

"I am sure it avails. When we invoke earnestly and sincerely the help of any higher and stronger intelligence than ourselves, the angels are with us. They come when the heart calls them; for they are appointed to be ministers unto those who shall inherit eternal life." And Hyde listened silently, yet the words fell into his deepest consciousness, and after many years brought him strength and consolation when he needed it. Thus it is, that a good woman is a priestess standing by the altar of the heart, thus it is, that the very noblest education any man ever gets is what some woman—mother, wife, sister, friend—gives him.

Certainly the letter sent to Cornelia sped on its way all the more rapidly and joyfully for the good wishes and unselfish prayers accompanying it. The very ship might have known it was the bearer of good tidings; for if there had been one of the mighty angels whose charge is on the great deep at the helm of the Good Intent she could not have gone more swiftly and surely to her haven. One morning, nearly a week in advance of Annie's calculation, the wonderful letter was put into Cornelia's hand. She was passing through the hall on her way to her room, when Balthazar brought in the mail, and she took the little white messenger without any feeling but one of curiosity concerning it. The handwriting was strange, it was an English letter, what could it mean?

Let any one who has loved and been parted from the beloved by some misunderstanding, try to realize what it meant to Cornelia. She read it through in an indescribable hurry and emotion, and then in the most natural and womanly way, began to cry. No one could have loved her the less for that sincere overflow of emotions she could not separate or define, and which indeed she never tried to understand. It was only one wonderful thought she could entertain—IT WAS NOT THE FAULT OF JORIS. This was the assurance that turned her joyful tears into gladder smiles, and that made her step light as a bird on the wing, as she ran down the stairs to find her mother; for her happiness was not perfect till she shared it with the heart that had borne her sorrow, and carried her grief through many weary months, with her.

Oh, how glad were these two women! They were almost too glad to speak. Sitting still was impossible to Cornelia, but as she stepped swiftly to-and-fro across the parlour floor, she stopped frequently at her mother's chair and kissed her. She kissed Annie's letter just as frequently. It was such a gracious, noble letter. It was such a delight to know that friendship so unselfish was waiting for her. It was altogether such a marvellous thing that had come to her, that she could not behave as a superior woman ought to have done. But then she was not a superior woman, she was only lovable and loving, and therefore restless and inconsequent.

In the first hours of her recovered gladness she did not even remember Rem's great fault, nor yet her own carelessness. These things were only accidentals, not worthy to be taken into account while the great sweet hope that had come to her, flooded like a springtide every nook and corner of her heart. In such a mood how easy it was to answer Annie's letter. She recollected every word she had written to Hyde that fateful day, and she wrote them again with a tenfold joy. She told Annie every particular, and she forgot to say a word of reproach concerning the dishonourable retention of her letter by Rem." It is altogether my own fault," she confessed.

Even when this letter was on its way to Annie she was under such excitement that her whole body appeared to think and to feel; her beautiful hair had an unusual freedom, as if some happy wind blew it into exquisite unrestraint; her eyes shone like stars; her garments fluttered; her steps were like dancing; and every now and then, a bar or two of love music warbled in her throat. And oh with what joy the mother watched the return of happiness to her dear child! With her own milk she had fed her. In her own bosom she had carried and tended her. Night and day for nearly twenty years, like a bird, she had feverishly, prayfully, tenderly hovered over her; so there was great joy in the Doctor's home and though he would say little, his heart grew lighter in his wife's and daughter's cheerfulness; for the women in any house make the moral and mental atmosphere of that house just as decidedly, as the sunshine or rain affect the natural atmosphere outside of it.

Now it is very noticeable that when unusual events begin to happen in any life, there is a succession of such events, and not unfrequently they arrive in similar ways. At any rate about ten days after the receipt of Annie's letter, Cornelia was almost equally amazed by the receipt of another letter. It came one day about noon, and a slave of Van Ariens brought it—a piece of paper twisted carelessly but containing these few pregnant words:

Cornelia, dear, come to me. Bring me something to wear. I have just arrived, saved by the skin of my teeth, and I have not a decent garment of any kind to put on. ARENTA.

A thunderbolt from a clear sky could hardly have caused such surprise, but Cornelia did not wait to talk about the wonder. She loaded a maid with clothing of every description, and ran across the street to her friend. Arerita saw her coming, and met her with a cry of joy, and as Van

Ariens was sick and trembling with the sight of his daughter, and the tale of her sufferings, Cornelia persuaded him to go to sleep, and leave Arenta to her care. Poor Arenta, she was ill with the privations she had suffered, she was half-starved, and nearly without clothing, but she did not complain much until she had been fed, and bathed, and "dressed" as she said "like a New York woman ought to be."

"You know what trunks and trunks full of beautiful things I took away with me, Cornelia," she complained; "Well I have not a rag left. I have nothing left at all."

"Your husband, Arenta?"

"He was guillotined."

"Oh, my dear Arenta!"

"Guillotined. I told him to be quiet. I begged him to go over to Marat, but no! his nobility obliged him to stand by his order and his king. So for them, he died. Poor Athanase! He expected me to follow him, but I could not make up my mind to the knife. Oh how terrible it was!" Then she began to sob bitterly, and Cornelia let her talk of her sufferings until she fell into a sleep—a sleep easy to see, still haunted by the furies and terrors through which she had passed.

For a week Cornelia remained with her friend, and Madame Jacobus joined them as often as possible, and gradually the half-distraught woman recovered something of her natural spirits and resolution. In this week she talked out all her frightful experiences in the great prison of La Force, and was completely overwhelmed at their remembrance. But the trouble which has been removed, soon grows far off; and Arenta quickly took her place in her home, and resumed her old life. Of course with many differences. She could not be the same Arenta, she had outlived many of her illusions. She took but little interest for a while in the life around her; her thoughts and conversation were still in Paris, and this was evident from the fact, that during the whole week of Cornelia's stay with her, she never once named Cornelia's love, or life, or prospects. Rem she did talk about, but chiefly because he was going to marry an English girl, an intention she angrily deplored.

"I am sure," she said, "Rem might have learned a lesson from my sad fortune. What does he want to marry a foreigner for? He ought to have prevented me from doing so, instead of following my foolish example."

"No one could have prevented you, Arenta. You would not listen even to your father."

"Oh indeed, it was my fate. We must all submit to fate. Why did you refuse Rem?"

"He was not my fate, Arenta."

"Well then, neither is George Hyde your fate. Aunt Jacobus has told me some things about him. She says he is to marry his cousin. You ought to marry Rem."

As she said these words Van Ariens, accompanied by Joris Van Heemskirk entered the room, and Cornelia was glad to escape. She knew that Arenta would again relate all her experiences, and she disliked to mingle them with her renewed dreams of love and her lover.

"She will talk and talk," said Cornelia to her mother, "and then there will be tea and chocolate and more talk, and I have heard all I wish to hear about that dreadful city, and the demons who walk in blood."

"Arenta has made a great sensation, Cornelia," answered Mrs. Moran. "She has received half the town. Gertrude Kippon stole quietly home and has hardly been seen, or heard tell of."

"But mother, Arenta has far more genius than Gertrude. She has made of her misfortunes a great drama, and wherever you go, it is of the Marquise de Tounnerre people are talking. Senator Van Heemskirk came in with her father as I left."

"I hope he treated you more civilly than madame did."

"He was delightful. I courtesied to him, and he lifted my hand and kissed it, and said, 'I grew lovelier every day,' and I kissed his cheek and said, 'I wished always to be lovely in his sight.' Then I came home, because I would not, just yet, speak of George to him."

"Arenta would hardly have given you any opportunity. I wonder at what hour she will release Joris Van Heemskirk!"

"It will be later than it ought to be."

Indeed it was so late that Madame Van Heemskirk had locked up her house for the night, and was troubled at her husband's delay—even a little cross:

"An old man like you, Joris," she said in a tone of vexation—" sitting till nine o'clock with the last runaway from Paris; a cold you have already, and all for a girl that threw her senses behind her, to marry a Frenchman."

"Much she has suffered, Lysbet."

"Much she ought to suffer. And I believe not in Arenta Van Ariens' suffering. In some way, by hook or crook, by word or deed, she would out of any trouble work her way."

"I will sit a little by the fire, Lysbet. Sit down by me. My mind is full of her story."

"That is it. And sleep you will not, and tomorrow sick you will be; and anxious and tired I shall be; and who for? The Marquise de Tounnerre! Well then, Joris, in thy old age it is late for thee to bow down to the Marquise de Tounnerre!"

"To God Almighty only I bow down, Lysbet, and as for titles what care of them has Jons Van Heemskirk? Think you, when God calls me He will say 'Councillor' or 'Senator'? No, He will say 'Jons Van Heemskirk!' and I shall answer to that name. But you know well, Lysbet, this bloody trial of liberty in Paris touches all the world beside."

"Forgive me, Joris! A shame it is to be cross with thee, nor am I cross even with that poor Arenta. A child, a very child she is."

"But bitter fears and suffering she has come through. Her husband was guillotined last May, and from her home she was taken—no time to write to a friend—no time to save anything she had, except a string of pearls, which round her waist for many weeks, she had worn. From prison to prison she was sent, until at last she was ordered before the Revolutionary Tribunal. From that tribunal to the guillotine is only a step, and she would surely have taken it but for—"

"Minister Morris?"

"No. Twenty miles outside the city, Minister Morris now lives; and no time was there to send him word of her strait. Hungry and sick upon the floor of her prison she was sitting, when her name was called, for bead after bead of her pearl necklace had gone to her jailor, only for a little black bread and a cup of milk twice a day; and this morning for twenty-four hours she had been without food or milk."

"The poor little one! What did she do?"

"This is what she did, and blame her I will not. When in that terrible iron armchair before those bloody judges, she says she forgot then to be afraid. She looked at Fouquier-Tinville the public prosecutor, and at the fifteen jurymen, and flinched not. She had no dress to help her beauty, but she declares she never felt more beautiful, and well I can believe it. They asked her name, and my Lysbet, think of this child's answer! 'I am called Arenta JEFFERSON de Tounnerre,' she said; and at the name of 'Jefferson' there were exclamations, and one of the jurymen rose to his feet and asked excitedly, 'What is it you mean? Jefferson! The great Jefferson! The great Thomas Jefferson! The great American who loves France and Liberty?' 'It is the same,' she answered, and then she sat silent, asking no favour, so wise was she, and Fouquier-Tinville looked at the President and said—'among my friends I count this great American!' and a juryman added, 'when I was very poor and hungry he fed and helped me,' and he bowed to Arenta as he spoke. And after that Fouquier-Tinville asked who would certify to her claim, and she answered boldly, 'Minister Morris.' When questioned further she answered, 'I adore Liberty, I believe in France, I married a Frenchman, for Thomas Jefferson told me I was coming to a great nation and might trust both its government and its generosity.' They asked her then if she had been used kindly in prison, and she told them her jailor had been to her very unkind, and that he had taken from her the pearl necklace which was her wedding gift, and if you can believe Arenta, they were all extremely polite to her, and gave her at once the papers which permitted her to leave France. The next day a little money she got from Minister Morris, but a

Amelia E. Barr

very hard passage she had home. And listen now, her jailor was guillotined before she left, and she declares it was the necklace—very unfortunate beads they were, and Madame Jacobus said when she heard of their fate, 'let them go! With blood and death they came, it is fit they should go as they came!' Arenta thinks as soon as Fouquier-Tinville heard of them, he doomed the man, for she saw in his eyes that he meant to have them for himself. Well, then, she is also sure that they will take Fouquier-Tinville to the guillotine."

"After all, it was a lie she told, Joris."

"That is so, but I think her life was worth a few words. And Thomas Jefferson says she was ten thousand times welcome to the protection his name gave her. I thank my God I have never had such temptation. I will say one thing though, Lysbet, that if coming home some night, a thief should say to me 'your money I must have' and if in my pocket I had some false money, as well as true money, the false money I would give the thief and think no shame to do it. Overly righteous we must not be, Lysbet."

"I am astonished also. I thought Arenta would cry out and that only."

"What a man or a woman will do and suffer, and how they will do and suffer, no one knows till comes some great occasion. When the water is ice, who could believe that it would boil, unless they had seen ice become boiling water? All the human heart wants, is the chance."

"As men and women have in Paris to live, I wonder me, that they can wish to live at all! Welcome to them must be death."

"So wrong are you, Lysbet. Trouble and hardship make us

love life. A zest they give to it. It is when we have too much money, too much good food and wine, too much pleasure of all kinds, that we grow melancholy and sad, and say all is vanity and vexation. You may see that it is always so, if you look in the Holy Scriptures. It was not from the Jews in exile and captivity, but from the Jews of Solomon's glory came the only dissatisfied, hopeless words in the Bible. Yes, indeed! it is the souls that have too much, who cry out vanity, vanity, all is vanity! For myself, I like not the petty prudencies of Solomon. There is better reading in Isaiah, and in the Psalms, and in the blessed Gospels."

"To-morrow, Joris, I will go and see Arenta. She is fair, and she knows it; witty, and she knows it; of good courage, and she knows it; the fashion, and she knows it; and when she speaks, she speaks oracles that one must believe, even though one does not understand them. To Aurelia Van Zandt she said, my heart will ache forever for my beloved Athanase, and Aurelia says, that her old lover Willie Nicholls is at her feet sitting all the day long—yet for all these things, she is a brave woman and I will go and see her."

"Willie Nicholls is a good young man, and he is rich also; but of him I saw nothing at all. Cornelia Moran was there and no flower of Paradise is so sweet, so fair!"

"A very proud girl! I am glad she said 'no' to my Joris."

"Come, my Lysbet, we will now pray and sleep. There is so much NOT to say."

CHAPTER XIII

THE NEW DAYS COME

One afternoon in the late autumn Annie was sitting watching Hyde playing with his dog, a big mastiff of noble birth and character. The creature sat erect with his head leaning against Hyde, and Hyde's arm was thrown around his neck as he talked to him of their adventures on the Broad that day. Annie's small face, though delicate and fragile looking was full of peace, and her eyes, soft, deep and heavenly, held thoughts that linked her with heaven.

Outside there was in the air that November feeling which chills like the passing breath of death, the deserted garden looked sad and closed-in, and everywhere there was a sense of the languishing end of the year, of the fading and dropping of all living things. But in the house Annie and Hyde and the dog sat within the circle of warmth and light made by the blazing ash logs, and in that circle there was at least an atmosphere of sweet content. Suddenly George looked up and his eyes caught those of Annie watching him. "What have you been reading, Annie?" he asked, as he stooped forward and took a thin volume from her lap. "Why!" he cried, "'tis Paul and Virginia. Do you indeed read love stories?"

"Yes. The mystery of a love affair pleases every one; and I think we shall not tire of love stories till we tire of the mystery of spring, or of primroses and daffodils. Every one I know takes their tale of love to be quite a new tale."

"Love has been cruel to me. It has made a cloud on my life that will help to cover me in my grave."

"You still love Cornelia?"

"I cannot cure myself of a passion so hopeless. However, as I see no end to my unhappiness, I try to submit to what I cannot avoid. What is the use of longing for that which I have no hope to get?"

"My uncle grows anxious for you to marry. He would be glad to see the succession of Hyde assured."

"Oh, indeed, I have no mind to take a wife. I hear every day that some of my acquaintance have married, I hear of none that have done worse."

"You believe nothing of what you say. My uncle was much pleased with Sarah Capel. What did you think of the beauty?"

"Cornelia has made all other women so indifferent to me, that if I cannot marry her, my father may dispose of me as he chooses."

"Cannot you forget Cornelia?"

"It is impossible. Every day I resolve to think of her no more, and then I continue thinking; and every day I am more and more in love with her. Her very name moves me beyond words."

"There is no name, George, however sweet and dear, however lovingly spoken, whose echo does not at last grow faint."

"Cornelia will echo in my heart as long as my heart beats."

Then they were silent, and Hyde drew his dog closer and watched the blaze among some lighter branches, which a servant had just brought in. At his entrance he had also given Annie a letter, which she was eagerly reading. Hyde had no speculation about it; and even when he found Annie regarding him with her whole soul in her face, he failed to understand, as he always had done, the noble love which had been so long and so faithfully his—a love holding itself above endearments; self-repressed, self-sacrificing, kept down in the inmost heart-chamber a dignified prisoner behind very real bars. Yet he was conscious that the letter was of more than usual interest, and when the servant had closed the door behind him, he asked, "Whom is your letter from, Annie? It seems to please you very much."

She leaned forward to him with the paper in her little trembling hand, and said,

"It is from Cornelia."

"My God!" he ejaculated; and the words were fraught with such feeling, as could have found no other vehicle of expression.

"She has sent you, dear George, a copy of the letter you ought to have received more than two years ago. Read it."

His eyes ran rapidly over the sweet words, his face flamed, his hands trembled, he cried out impetuously—

"But what does it mean? Am I quite in my senses? How has this letter been delayed? Why do I get only a copy ?"

"Because Mr. Van Ariens has the original."

"It is all incredible. What do you mean, Annie? Do not keep me in such torturing suspense."

"It means that Mr. Van Ariens asked Cornelia to marry him on the same day that you wrote to her about your marriage. She answered both letters in the same hour, and misdirected them."

"GOD'S DEATH! How can I punish so mean a scoundrel? I will have my letter from him, if I follow him round the world for it."

"You have your letter now. I asked Cornelia to write it again for you; and you see she has done it gladly."

"Angel of goodness! But I will have my first letter."

"It has been in that man's keeping for more than two years. I would not touch it. 'Twould infect a gentleman, and make of him a rascal just as base."

"He shall write me then an apology in his own blood. I will make him do it, at the point of my sword."

"If I were you, I would scorn to wet my sword in blood so base."

"Remember, Annie, what this darling girl suffered. For his treachery she nearly died. I speak not of my own wrong—it is as nothing to hers."

"However, she might have been more careful."

"Annie, she was in the happy hurry of love. Your calm soul knows not what a confusing thing that is—she made a mistake, and that sneaking villain turned her mistake into a crime. By a God's mercy, it is found out—but how? Annie! Annie, how much I owe you! What can I say? What can I do?"

"Be reasonable. Mary Damer really found it out. His guilty restless conscience forced him to tell her the story, though to be sure he put the wrong on people he did not name. But I knew so much of the mystery of your love sorrow, as to put the two stories together, and find them fit. Then I wrote to Cornelia."

"How long ago?"

"About two months."

"Why then did you not give me hope ere this?"

"I would not give you hope, till hope was certain. Two years is a long time in a girl's life. It was a possible thing for Cornelia to have forgotten—to have changed."

"Impossible! Quite impossible! She could not forget. She could not change. Why did you not tell me? I should have known her heart by mine own."

"I wished to be sure," repeated Annie, a little sadly.

"Forgive me, dear Annie. But this news throws me into an unspeakable condition. You see that I must leave for America at once."

"No. I do not see that, George."

"But if you consider—"

"I have been considering for two months. Let me decide for you now, for you are not able to do so wisely. Write at once to Cornelia, that is your duty as well as your pleasure. But before you go to her, there are things indispensable to be done. Will you ask Doctor Moran for his child, and not be able to show him that you can care for her as she deserves to be cared for? Lawyers will not be hurried, there will be consultations, and engrossings, and signings, and love—in your case—will have to wait upon law."

"'Tis hard for love, and harder perhaps for anger to wait. For I am in a passion of wrath at Van Ariens. I long to be near him. Oh what suffering his envy and hatred have caused others!"

"And himself also. Be sure of that, or he had not tried to find some ease in a kind of confession. Doctor Roslyn will tell you that it is an eternal law, that wherever sin is, sorrow will answer it."

"The man is hateful to me."

"He has done a thing that makes him hateful; but perhaps for all that, he has been so miserable about it, as to have the pity of the Uncondemning One. I hear your father coming. I am sure you will have his sympathy in all things."

She left the room as the Earl entered it. He was in unusually high spirits. Some political news had delighted him, and without noticing his son's excitement he said—

"The Commons have taken things in their own hands,

George. I said they would. They listen to the King and the Lords very respectfully, and then obey themselves. Most of the men in the Lower House are unfit to enter it."

"Well, sir, the Lords as a rule send them there—you have sent three of them yourself—and unfit men in public places, suppose prior unfitness in those who have the places to dispose of. But the government is not interesting. I have something else, father, to think about."

"Indeed, I think the government is extremely interesting. It is very like three horses arranged in tandem fashion—first, you know, the King, a little out of the reach of the whip; then the Lords follow the King, and the Commons are in the shafts, a more ignoble position, but yet—as we see to-day, possessing a special power of upsetting the coach."

"Father, I have very important news from America. Will you listen to it?"

"Yes, if you will tell it to me straight, and not blunder about your meaning." "Sir, I have just discovered that a letter sent to me more than two years ago, has been knowingly and purposely detained from me."

"By whom?"

"A man into whose hands it fell by misdirection."

"Did the letter contain means of identifying it, as belonging to you?"

"Ample means."

"Then the man is outside your recognition. You might as well go to the Bridewell, and seek a second among its riffraff of scoundrels. Tell me shortly whom it concerns."

"Miss Moran."

"Oh indeed! Are we to have that subject opened again?"

His face darkened, and George, with an impetuosity that permitted no interruption, told the whole story. As he proceeded the Earl became interested, then sympathetic. He looked with moist eyes at the youth so dear to him, and saw that his heart was filled with the energy and tenderness of his love. His handsome face, his piercingly bright eyes, his courteous, but obstinately masterful manner, his almost boyish passion of anger and impatience, his tall, serious figure, erect, as if ready for opposition; even that sentiment of deadly steel, of being impatient to toss his sheath from his sword, pleased very much the elder man; and won both his respect and his admiration. He felt that his son had rights all his own, and that he must cheerfully and generously allow them.

"George," he answered, "you have won my approval. You have shown me that you can suffer and be faithful, and the girl able to inspire such an affection, must be worthy of it. What do you wish to do?"

"I am going to America by the next packet."

"Sit down, then we can talk without feeling that every word is a last word, and full of hurry and therefore of unreason. You desire to see Miss Moran without delay, that is very natural."

"Yes, sir. I am impatient also to get my letter."

"I think that of no importance."

"What would you have done in my case, and at my age, father?"

"Something extremely foolish. I should have killed the man, or been killed by him. I hope that you have more sense. Society does not now compel you to answer insult with murder. The noble not caring of the spirit, is beyond the mere passion of the animal. What does Annie say?"

"Annie is an angel. I walk far below her—and I hate the man who has so wronged—Cornelia. I think, sir, you must also hate him."

"I hate nobody. God send, that I may be treated the same. George, you have flashed your sword only in a noble quarrel, will you now stain it with the blood of a man below your anger or consideration? You have had your follies, and I have smiled at them; knowing well, that a man who has no follies in his youth, will have in his maturity no power. But now you have come of age, not only in years but in suffering cheerfully endured and well outlived; so I may talk to you as a man, and not command you as a father."

"What do you wish me to do, sir?"

"I advise you to write to Miss Moran at once. Tell her you are more anxious now to redeem your promise, than ever you were before. Say to her that I already look upon her as a dear daughter, and am taking immediate steps to settle upon you the American Manor, and also such New York property as will provide for the maintenance of your family in the state becoming your order and your expectations. Tell her that my lawyers will go to this business to-morrow, and that as soon as the deeds are in your hand, you will come and ask for the interview with Doctor Moran, so long and cruelly delayed."

"My dear father! How wise and kind you are!"

"It is my desire to be so, George. You cannot, after this unfortunate delay, go to Doctor Moran without the proofs of your ability to take care of his daughter's future."

"How soon can this business be accomplished?"

"In about three weeks, I should think. But wait your full time, and do not go without the credentials of your position. This three or four weeks is necessary to bring to perfection the waiting of two years."

"I will take your advice, sir. I thank you for your generosity."

"All that I have is yours, George. And you can write to this dear girl every day in the interim. Go now and tell her what I say. I had other dreams for you as you know—they are over now—I have awakened."

"Dear Annie!" ejaculated George.

"Dear Annie!" replied the Earl with a sigh. "She is one of the daughters of God, I am not worthy to call her mine; but I have sat at her feet, and learned how to love, and how to forgive, and how to bear disappointment. I will tell you, that when Colonel Saye insulted me last year, and I felt for my sword and would have sent him a letter on its point—Annie stepped before him. 'Forget, and go on, dear uncle,' she said; and I did so with a proud, sore heart at first, but quite cheerfully in a week or two; and at the last Hunt dinner he came to me with open hand, and we ate and drank together, and are now firm friends. Yet, but for Annie, one of us might be dead; and the other flying like Cain exiled and miserable. Think of these things, George. The good of being a son, is to be able to profit from your father's mistakes."

They parted with a handclasp that went to both hearts, and as Hyde passed his mother's loom, he went in, and told her all that happened to him, She listened with a smile and a heartache. She knew now that the time had come to say "farewell" to the boy who had made her life for twenty-seven years. "He must marry like the rest of the world, and go away from her," and only mothers know what supreme self-sacrifice a pleasant acquiescence in this event implies. But she bravely put down all the clamouring selfishness of her long sweet care and affection, and said cheerfully—

"Very much to my liking is Cornelia Moran, She is world-like and heaven-like, and her good heart and sweet nature every one knows. A loving wife and a noble mother she will make, and if I must lose thee, my Joris, there is no girl in America that I like better to have thee."

"Never will you lose me, mother."

"Ah then! that is what all sons say. The common lot, I look for nothing better. But see now! I give thee up cheerfully. If God please, I shall see thy sons and daughters; and thy father has been anxious about the Hydes. He would not have a stranger here—nor would I. Our hope is in thee and thy sweet wife, and very glad am I that thy wife is to be Cornelia Moran."

And even after Joris had left her she smiled, though the tears dropped down upon her work. She thought of the presents she would send her daughter, and she told herself that Cornelia was an American, and that she had made for her, with her own hands and brain, a lovely home wherein HER memory must always dwell. Indeed she let her thoughts go far forward to see, and to listen to the happy boys and girls who might run and shout gleefully through the fair large rooms, and the sweet shady gardens her skill and taste had ordered and planted. Thus her generosity made her a partaker of her children's happiness, and whoever partakes of a pleasure has his share of it, and comes into contact—not only with the happiness—but with the other partakers of that happiness—a divine kind of interest for generous deeds, which we may all appropriate.

Nothing is more contagious than joy, and Hyde was now a living joy through all the house. His voice had caught a new tone, his feet a more buoyant step, he carried himself like a man expectant of some glorious heritage. So eager, so ardent, so ready to be happy, he inspired every one with his buoyant gladness of heart. He could at least talk to Cornelia with his pen every day, yes, every hour if he desired; and if it had been possible to transfer in a letter his own light-heartedness, the words he wrote would have shone upon the paper.

The next morning Mary Damer called. She knew that a letter from Cornelia was possible, and she knew also that it would really be as fateful to herself, as to Hyde. If, as she suspected, it was Rem Van Ariens who had detained the misdirected letter, there was only one conceivable result as regarded herself. She, an upright, honourable English girl, loving truth with all her heart, and despising whatever was underhand and disloyal, had but one course to take—she must break off her engagement with a man so far below her standard of simple morality. She could not trust his honour, and what security has love in a heart without honour?

So she looked anxiously at Annie as she entered, and Annie would not keep her in suspense. "There was a letter from Miss Moran last night," she said. "She loves George yet. She re-wrote the unfortunate letter, and this time it found its owner. I think he has it next his heart at this very moment."

Amelia E. Barr

"I am glad of that, Annie. But who has the first letter?"

"I think you know, Mary."

"You mean Mr. Van Ariens?"

"Yes."

"Then there is no more to be said. I shall write to him as soon as possible."

"I am sorry—"

"No, no! Be content, Annie. The right must always come right. Neither you nor I could desire any other end, even to our own love story."

"But you must suffer."

"Not much. None of us weep if we lose what is of no value. And I have noticed that the happiness of any one is always conditioned by the unhappiness of some one else. Love usually builds his home out of the wrecks of other homes. Your cousin and Cornelia will be happy, but there are others that must suffer, that they may be so. I will go now, Annie, because until I have written to Mr. Van Ariens, I shall not feel free. And also, I do not wish him to come here, and in his last letter he spoke of such an intention."

So the two letters—that of Hyde to Cornelia, and that of Mary Darner to Van Ariens, left England for America in the same packet; and though Mary Darner undoubtedly had some suffering and disappointment to conquer, the fight was all within her. To her friends at the Manor she was just the same bright, courageous girl; ready for every emergency, and equally ready to make the most of every pleasure.

And the tone of the Manor House was now set to a key of the highest joy and expectation. Hyde unconsciously struck the note, for he was happily busy from morning to night about affairs relating either to his marriage, or to his future as the head of a great household. All his old exigent, extravagant liking for rich clothing returned to him. He had constant visits from his London tailor, a dapper little artist, who brought with him a profusion of rich cloth, silk and satin, and who firmly believed that the tailor made the man. There were also endless interviews with the family lawyer, endless readings of law papers, and endless consultations about rights and successions, which Hyde was glad and grateful to leave very much to his father's wisdom and generosity.

At the beginning of this happy period, Hyde had been sure that the business of his preparations would be arranged in three weeks; a month had appeared to be a quite unreasonable and impossible delay; but the month passed, and it was nearly the middle of November when all things were ready for his voyage. His mother would then have urged a postponement until spring, but she knew that George would brook no further delay; and she was wise enough to accept the inevitable cheerfully. And thus by letting her will lead her, in the very road necessity drove her, she preserved not only her liberty, but her desire.

Some of these last days were occupied in selecting from her jewels presents for Cornelia, with webs of gold and silver tissues, and Spitalfields silks so rich and heavy, that no mortal woman might hope to outwear them. To these Annie added from her own store of lace, many very valuable pieces; and the happy bridegroom was proud to see that love was going to send him away, with both arms full for the beloved.

The best gift however came last, and it was from the Earl. It was not gold or land, though he gave generously of both these; but one which Hyde felt made his way straight before him, and which he knew must have cost his father much self-abnegation. It was the following letter to Dr. John Moran.

MY DEAR SIR:

It seems then, that our dear children love each other so well, that it is beyond our right, even as parents, to forbid their marriage. I ask from you, for my son, who is a humble and ardent suitor for Miss Moran's hand, all the favour his sincere devotion to her deserves, We have both been young, we have both loved, accept then his affection as some atonement for any grievance or injustice you remember against myself. Had we known each other better, we should doubtless have loved each other better; but now that marriage will make us kin, I offer you my hand, with all it implies of regret for the past, and of respect for the future. Your servant to command,

RICHARD HYDE.

"It is the greatest proof of my love I can give you, George," said the Earl, when the letter had been read; "and it is Annie you must thank for it. She dropped the thought into my heart, and if the thought has silently grown to these written words, it is because she had put many other good thoughts there, and that these helped this one to come to perfection."

"Have you noticed, father, how small and fragile-looking she is? Can she really be slowly dying?"

"No, she is not dying; she is only going a little further away—a little further away, every hour. Some hour she will be called, and she will answer, and we shall see her no more—HERE. But I do not call that dying, and if it be dying,

Annie will go as calmly and simply, as if she were fulfilling some religious rite or duty. She loves God, and she will go to Him."

The next morning Hyde left his father's home forever. It was impossible that such a parting should be happy. No hopes, no dreams of future joy, could make him forget the wealth of love he was leaving. Nor did he wish to forget. And woe to the man or woman who would buy composure and contentment by forgetting!—by really forfeiting a portion of their existence—by being a suicide of their own moral nature.

The day was a black winter day, with a monotonous rain and a dark sky troubled by a ghostly wind. Inside the house the silence fell on the heart like a weight. The Earl and Countess watched their son's carriage turn from the door, and then looked silently into each other's face. The Earl's lips were firmly set, and his eyes full of tears; the Countess was weeping bitterly. He went with her to her room, and with all his old charm and tenderness comforted her for her great loss.

At that moment Annie was forgotten, yet no one was suffering more than she was. Hyde had knelt by her sofa, and taken her in his arms, and covered her face with tears and kisses, and she had not been able to oppose a parting so heart-breaking and so final. The last tears she was ever to shed dropped from her closed eyes, as she listened to his departing steps; and the roll of the carriage carrying him away forever, seemed to roll over her shrinking heart. She cried out feebly—a pitiful little shrill cry, that she hushed with a sob still more full of anguish. Then she began to cast over her suffering soul the balm of prayer, and prostrate with closed eyes, and hands feebly hanging down, Doctor Roslyn found her. He did not need to ask a question, he had long known the brave self-sacrifice that was consecrating the child-heart suffering so sharply that day; and he said only—

"We are made perfect through suffering, Annie."

"I know, dear father."

"And you have found before this, that the sorrow well borne is full of strange joys—joys, whose long lasting perfumes, show that they were grown in heaven and not on earth."

"This is the last sorrow that can come to me, father."

"And my dear Annie, you would have been a loser without it. Every grief has its meaning, and the web of life could not be better woven, if only love touched it."

"I have been praying, father."

"Nay, but God Himself prayed in you, while your soul waited in deep resignation. God gave you both the resignation and the answer."

"My heart failed me at the last—then I prayed as well as I could."

"And then, visited by the NOT YOURSELF in you, your head was lifted up. Do not be frightened at what you want. Strive for it little by little. All that is bitter in outward things, or in interior things, all that befalls you in the course of a day, is YOUR DAILY BREAD if you will take it from His hand."

Then she was silent and quite still, and he sat and watched the gradual lifting of the spirit's cloud—watched, until the pallor of her face grew luminous with the inner light, and her wide open eyes saw, as in a vision, things, invisible to mortal sight; but open to the spirit on that dazzling line where mortal and immortal verge.

And as he went home, stepping slowly through the misty world, he himself hardly knew whether he was in the body or out of it. He felt not the dripping rain, he was not conscious of the encompassing earthly vapours, he had passed within the veil and was worshipping

"In dazzling temples opened straight to Him, Where One who had great lightnings for His crown Was suddenly made present; vast and dim Through crowded pinions of the Cherubim."

And his feet stumbled not, nor was he aware of anything around, until the Earl met him at the park gates and touching him said reverently—

"Father, you are close to the highway. Have you seen Annie?"

"I have just left her."

"She is further from us than ever."

"Richard Hyde," he answered," she is on her way to God, and she can rest nothing short of that."

CHAPTER XIV

"HUSH! LOVE IS HERE!"

On the morning that Hyde sailed for America, Cornelia received the letter he had written her on the discovery of Rem's dishonourable conduct. So much love, so much joy, sent to her in the secret foldings of a sheet of paper! In a hurry of delight and expectation she opened it, and her beaming eyes ran all over the joyful words it brought her—sweet fluttering pages, that his breath had moved, and his face been aware of. How he would have rejoiced to see her pressing them to her bosom, at some word of fonder memory or desire.

There was much in this letter which it was necessary her father and mother should hear—the Earl's message to them—Hyde's own proposition for an immediate marriage, and various necessities referring to this event. But she was proud and happy to read words of such noble, straight-forward affection; and the Doctor was especially pleased by the deference expressed for his wishes. When he left the house that day he kissed his daughter with pride and tenderness, and said to Mrs. Moran—

"Ava, there will be much to get, and much to do in a short time, but money manages all things Do not spare where it is necessary." And then what important and interesting consultations followed! what lists of lovely garments became imperative, which an hour before had not been dreamed of! what discussions as to mantua makers and milliners! as to guests and ceremonies! as to all the details of a life unknown, but invested by love and youth, with a delightfully overwhelming importance.

Cornelia was so happy that her ordinary dress of grey camelot did not express her; she felt constrained to add to it some bows of bright scarlet ribbon, and then she looked round about her room, and went through her drawers, to find something else to be a visible witness to the light heart singing within her. And she came across some coral combs that Madame Jacobus had given her, and felt their vivid colouring in the shining masses of her dark hair, to be one of the right ways of saying to herself, and all she loved, "See how happy I am!"

In the afternoon, when the shopping for the day had been accomplished, she went to Captain Jacobus, to play with him the game of backgammon which had become an almost daily duty, and to which the Captain attached a great importance. Indeed, for many weeks it had been the event of every day to him; and if he was no longer dependent on it, he was grateful enough to acknowledge all the good it had done him. "I owe your daughter as much as I owe you, sir," he would say to Doctor Moran, "and I owe both of you a bigger debt than I can clear myself of."

This afternoon he looked at his visitor with a wondering speculation. There was something in her face, and manner, and voice, he had never before seen or heard, and madame—who watched every expression of her husband—was easily led to the same observation. She observed Cornelia closely, and her gay laugh especially revealed some change. It was

Amelia E. Barr

like the burst of bird song in early spring, and she followed the happy girl to the front door, and called her back when she had gone down the steps, and said, as she looked earnestly in her face—

"You have heard from Joris Hyde? I know you have!" and Cornelia nodded her head, and blushed, and smiled, and ran away from further question.

When she reached home she found Madame Van Heemskirk sitting with her mother, and the sweet old lady rose to meet her, and said before Cornelia could utter a word:

"Come to me, Cornelia. This morning a letter we have had from my Joris, and sorry am I that I did thee so much wrong."

"Madame, I have long ago forgotten it; and there was a mistake all round," answered Cornelia, cheerfully.

"That is so—and thy mistake first of all. Hurry is misfortune; even to be happy, it is not wise to hurry. Listen now! Joris has written to his grandfather, and also to me, and very busy he will keep us both. His grandfather is to look after the stables and the horses, and to buy more horses, and to hire serving men of all kinds. And a long letter also I have had from my daughter Katherine, and she tells me to make her duty to thee my duty. That is my pleasure also, and I have been talking with thy mother about the house. Now I shall go there, and a very pleasant home I shall make it. Many things Joris will bring with him—two new carriages and much fine furniture—and I know not what else beside."

Then Cornelia kissed madame, and afterwards removed her bonnet; and madame looked at her smiling. The vivid coral in her dark hair, the modest grey dress with its knots of colour, and above all the lovely face alight with love and hope, delighted her.

"Very pretty art thou, very pretty indeed!" she said, impulsively; and then she added, "Many other girls are very pretty also, but my Joris loves thee, and I am glad that it is thee, and very welcome art thou to me, and very proud is my husband of thee. And now I must go, because there is much to do, and little time to do it in."

For nearly a week Cornelia was too busy to take Arenta into her consideration. She did not care to tell her about Rem's cruel and dishonourable conduct, and she was afraid the shrewd little Marquise would divine some change, and get the secret out of her. Indeed, Arenta was not long in suspecting something unusual in the Doctor's household—the number of parcels and of work people astonished her; and she was not a little offended at Madame Van Heemskirk spending a whole afternoon so near to her, and "never even," as she said to her father, "turning her head this way." For Arenta had drunk a rather long draught of popular interest, and she could not bear to believe it was declining. Was she not the American heroine of 1793? It was almost a want of patriotism in Madame Van Heemskirk to neglect her.

After a week had elapsed Cornelia went over one morning to see her friend. But by this time Arenta knew everything. Her brother Rem had been with her and confessed all to his sister. It had not been a pleasant meeting by any means. She heard the story with indignation, but contrived to feel that somehow Rem was not so much to blame as Cornelia, and other people.

"You are right served," she said to her brother, "for meddling with foreigners, and especially for mixing your love affairs up with an English girl. Proud, haughty creatures all of them!

And you are a very fool to tell any woman such a—crime. Yes, it is a crime. I won't say less. That girl over the way nearly died, and you would have let her die. It was a shame. I don't love Cornelia—but it was a shame."

"The letter was addressed to me, Arenta."

"Fiddlesticks! You knew it was not yours. You knew it was Hyde's. Where is it now?"

She asked the question in her usual dominant way, and Rem did not feel able to resist it. He looked for a moment at the angry woman, and was subdued by her air of authority. He opened his pocketbook and from a receptacle in it, took the fateful letter. She seized and read it, and then without a word, or a moment's hesitation threw it into the fire.

Rem blustered and fumed, and she stood smiling defiantly at him. "You are like all criminals," she said; "you must keep something to accuse yourself with. I love you too well to permit you to carry that bit of paper about you. It has worked you harm enough. What are you going to do? Is Miss Darner's refusal quite final?"

"Quite. It was even scornful."

"Plenty of nice girls in Boston."

"I cannot go back to Boston."

"Why then?"

"Because Mary's cousin has told the whole affair."

"Nonsense!"

"She has. I know it. Men, whom I had been friendly with, got out of my way; women excused themselves at their homes, and did not see me on the streets. I have no doubt all Boston is talking of the affair."

"Then come back to New York. New Yorkers attend strictly to their own love affairs. Father will stand by you; and I will."

"Father will not. He called me a scoundrel, when I told him last night, and advised me to go to the frontier. Joris Van Heemskirk will not talk, but madame will chatter for him, and I could not bear to meet Doctor Moran. As for Captain Jacobus, he would invent new words and oaths to abuse me with, and Aunt Angelica would, of course, say amen to all he says;—and there are others."

"Yes, there is Lord Hyde."

"Curse him! But I intended to give him his letter—now you have burnt it."

"You intended nothing of the kind, Rem. Go away as soon as you can. I don't want to know where you go just yet. New York is impossible, and Boston is impossible. Father says go to the frontier, I say go South. What you have done, you have done; and it cannot be undone; so don't carry it about with you. And I would let women alone—they are beyond you—go in for politics."

That day Rem lingered with his sister, seeing no one else; and in the evening shadows he slipped quietly away. He was very wretched, for he really loved Mary Damer, and his disappointment was bitterly keen and humiliating. Besides which, he felt that his business efforts for two years were forfeited, and that he had the world to begin over again.

Without a friend to wish him a Godspeed the wretched man went on board the Southern packet, and in her dim lonely cabin sat silent and despondent, while she fought her way through swaying curtains of rain to the open sea. Its great complaining came up through the darkness to him, and seemed to be the very voice of the miserable circumstances, that had separated and estranged his life from all he loved and desired.

This sudden destruction of all her hopes for her brother distressed Arenta. Her own marriage had been a most unfortunate one, but its misfortunes had the importance of national tragedy. She had even plucked honour to herself from the bloody tumbril and guillotine. But Rem's matrimonial failure had not one redeeming quality; it was altogether a shameful and well-deserved retribution. And she had boasted to her friends not a little of the great marriage her brother was soon to make, and even spoken of Miss Damer, as if a sisterly affection already existed between them. She could anticipate very well the smiles and shrugs, the exclamations and condolences she might have to encounter, and she was not pleased with her brother for putting her in a position likely to make her disagreeable to people.

But the heart of her anger was Cornelia—" but for that girl," Rem would have married Mary Damer, and his home in Boston might have been full of opportunities for her, as well as a desirable change when she wearied of New York. Altogether it was a hard thing for her, as well as a dreadful sorrow for Rem; and she could not think of Cornelia without anger, "Just for her," she kept saying as she dressed herself with an elaborate simplicity, "Just for her! Very much she intruded herself into my affairs; my marriage was her opportunity with Lord Hyde, and now all she can do is to break up poor Rem's marriage."

When Cornelia entered the Van Ariens parlour Arenta was already there. She was dressed in a gown of the blackest and softest bombazine and crape. It had a distinguishing want of all ornament, but it was for that reason singularly effective against her delicate complexion and pale golden hair. She looked offended, and hardly spoke to her old friend, but Cornelia was prepared for some exhibition of anger. She had not been to see Arenta for a whole week, and she did not doubt she had been well aware of something unusual in progress. But that Rem had accused himself did not occur to her; therefore she was hardly prepared for the passionate accusations with which Arenta assailed her.

"I think," she said, "you have behaved disgracefully to poor Rem! You would not have him yourself, and yet you prevent another girl—whom he loves far better than ever he loved you—from marrying him. He has gone away 'out of the world,' he says, and indeed I should not wonder if he kills himself. It is most certain you have done all you can to drive him to it,"

"Arenta! I have no idea what you mean. I have not seen Rem, nor written to Rem, for more than two years."

"Very likely, but you have written about him. You wrote to Miss Darner, and told her Rem purposely kept a letter, which you had sent to Lord Hyde,"

"I did not write to Miss Damer. I do not know the lady. But Rem DID keep a letter that belonged to Lord Hyde."

Then anger gave falsehood the bit and she answered, "Rem did NOT keep any letter that belonged to Lord Hyde. Prove that he did so, before you accuse him. You cannot."

"I unfortunately directed Lord Hyde's letter to Rem, and

Rem's letter to Lord Hyde. Rem knew that he had Lord Hyde's letter, and he should have taken it at once to him."

"Lord Hyde had Rem's letter; he ought to have taken it at once to Rem."

"There was not a word in Rem's letter to identify it as belonging to him."

"Then you ought to be ashamed to write love letters that would do for any man that received them. A poor hand you must be, to blunder over two love letters. I have had eight, and ten, at once to answer, and I never failed to distinguish each; and while rivers run into the sea I never shall misdirect my love letters. I do not believe Rem ever got your letter, and I will not believe it, either now or ever. I dare be bound, Balthazar lost it on the way. Prove to me he did not."

"Oh, indeed! I think you know better."

"Very clever is Lord Hyde to excuse himself by throwing the blame on poor Rein. Very mean indeed to accuse him to the girl he was going to marry. To be sure, any one with an ounce of common sense to guide them, must see through the whole affair."

"Arenta, I have the most firm conviction of Rem's guilt, and the greatest concern for his disappointment. I assure you I have."

"Kindly reserve your concern, Miss Moran, till Rem Van Ariens asks for it. As for his guilt, there is no guilt in question. Even supposing that Rem did keep Lord Hyde's letter, what then? All things are fair in love and war, Willie Nicholls told me last night, he would keep a hundred letters, if he thought he could win me by doing so. Any man of sense would."

"All I blame Rem for is—"

"All I blame Rem for is, that he asked you to marry him. So much for that! I hope if he meddles with women again, he will seek an all-round common-sense Dutch girl, who will know how to direct her letters—or else be content with one lover."

"Arenta, I shall go now. I have given you an opportunity to be rude and unkind. You cannot expect me to do that again."

She watched Cornelia across the street, and then turned to the mirror, and wound her ringlets over her fingers. "I don't care," she muttered. "It was her fault to begin with. She tempted Rem, and he fell. Men always fall when women tempt them; it is their nature to. I am going to stand by Rem, right or wrong, and I only wish I could tell Mary Damer what I think of her. She has another lover, of course she has—or she would not have talked about her 'honour' to Rem."

To such thoughts she was raging, when Peter Van Ariens came home to dinner, and she could not restrain them. He listened for a minute or two, and then struck the table no gentle blow?

"In my house, Arenta," he said, "I will have no such words. What you think, you think; but such thoughts must be shut close in your mind. In keeping that letter, I say Rem behaved like a scoundrel; he was cruel, and he was a coward. Because he is my son I will not excuse him. No indeed! For that very reason, the more angry am I at such a deed. Now then, he shall acknowledge to George Hyde and Cornelia Moran the wrong he did them, ere in my home and my heart, he rights himself."

"Is Cornelia going to be married?"

"That is what I hear."

"To Lord Hyde?"

"That also, is what I hear."

"Well, as I am in mourning, I cannot go to the wedding; so then I am delighted to have told her a little of my mind."

"It is a great marriage for the Doctor's daughter; a countess she will be."

"And a marquise I am. And will you please say, if either countess or marquise is better than mistress or madame? Thank all the powers that be! I have learned the value of a title, and I shall change marquise for mistress, as soon as I can do so."

"If always you had thought thus, a great deal of sorrow we had both been spared."

"Well, then, a girl cannot get her share of wisdom, till she comes to it. After all, I am now sorry I have quarrelled with Cornelia. In New York and Philadelphia she will be a great woman."

"To take offence is a great folly, and to give offence is a great folly—I know not which is the greater, Arenta."

"Oh, indeed, father," she answered, "if I am hurt and angry, I shall take the liberty to say so. Anger that is hidden cannot be gratified; and if people use me badly, it is my way to tell them I am aware of it. One may be obliged to eat brown bread, but I, for one, will say it is brown bread, and not white."

"Your own way you will take, until into some great trouble you stumble."

"And then my own way I shall take, until out of it I stumble."

"I have told Rem what he must do. Like a man he must say, 'I did wrong, and I am sorry for it,' and so well I think of those he has wronged, as to be sure they will answer, 'It is forgiven.'"

"And forgotten."

"That is different. To forgive freely, is what we owe to our enemy; to forget not, is what we owe to ourselves."

"But if Rem's fault is forgiven, and not forgotten, what good will it do him? I have seen that every one forgives much in themselves that they find unpardonable in other people."

"In so far, Arenta, we are all at fault."

"I think it is cruel, father, to ask Rem to speak truth to his own injury. Even the law is kinder than you, it asks no man to accuse himself."

"Right wrongs no man. Till others move in this matter, you be quiet. If you talk, evil words you will say; and mind this, Arenta, the evil that comes out of your lips, into your own bosom will fall. All my life I have seen this."

But Arenta could not be quiet. She would sow thorns, though she had to walk unshod; and her father's advice moved her no more than a breath moves a mountain. In the same afternoon she saw Madame Jacobus going to Doctor Moran's, and the hour she remained there, was full of misery to her impetuous self-adoring heart. She was sure they were talking of Rem and herself; and as she had all their conversation to imagine, she came to conclusions in accord with her suspicions.

But she met her aunt at the door and brought her eagerly into the parlour. She had had no visitors that day, and was bored and restless and longing for conversation. "I saw you go to the Doctor's an hour ago, aunt," she said. "I hope the Captain is well."

"Jacobus is quite well, thank God and Doctor Moran—and Cornelia. I have been looking at some of her wedding gowns. A girl so happy, and who deserves to be so happy, I never saw. What a darling she is!"

"It is now the fashion to rave about her. I suppose they found time enough to abuse poor Rem. And you could listen to them! I would not have done so! No! not if listening had meant salvation for the whole Moran family."

"You are a remarkably foolish young woman. They never named Rem. People so happy, do not remember the bringer of sorrow. He has been shut out—in the darkness and cold. But I heard from Madame Van Heemskirk why Cornelia and that delightful young man were not married two years ago. I am ashamed of Rem. I can never forgive him. He is a disgrace to the family. And that is why I came here to-day. I wish you to make Rem understand that he must not come near his Uncle Jacobus. When Jacobus is angry, he will call heaven and earth and hell to help him speak his mind, and I have nearly cured him of a habit which is so distressing to me, and such a great wrong to his own soul. The very sight of Rem would break every barrier down, and let a flood of words loose, that would make him suffer afterwards. I will not have Jacobus led into such temptation. I have not heard an oath from him for six months."

"I suppose you would never forgive Jacobus, if you did hear one?"

"That is another matter. I hope I have a heart to forgive whatever Jacobus does, or says—he is my husband."

"It is then less wicked to blaspheme Almighty God, than to keep one of Lord Hyde's love letters. One fault may be forgiven, the other is unpardonable. Dear me! how religiously ignorant I am. As for my uncle swearing—and the passions that thus express themselves—everybody knows that anything that distantly resembles good temper, will suit Captain Jacobus."

"You look extremely handsome when you are scornful, Arenta; but it is not worthwhile wasting your charms on me. I am doing what I can to help Jacobus to keep his tongue clean, and I will not have Rem lead him into temptation. As for Rem, he is guilty of a great wrong; and he must now do what his father told him to do—work day and night, as men work, when a bridge is broken down. The ruin must be got out of the way, and the bridge rebuilt, then it will be possible to open some pleasant and profitable traffic with human beings again—not to speak of heaven."

"You are right—not to speak of heaven, I think heaven would be more charitable. Rem will not trouble Captain Jacobus. For my part I think a man that cannot bear temptation is very poorly reformed. If my uncle could see Rem, and yet keep his big and little oaths under bonds, I should believe in his clean tongue."

"Arenta, you are tormenting yourself with anger and ill-will, and above all with jealousy. In this way you are going to miss a deal of pleasure. I advise you not to quarrel with Cornelia. She will be a great resource. I myself am looking forward to the delightful change Jacobus may have at Hyde Manor. It will make a new life for him, and also for me. This afternoon something is vexing you. I shall take no offence. You will regret your bad temper to-morrow."

To-morrow Arenta did regret; but people do not always say they are sorry, when they feel so. She sat in the shadow of her window curtains and watched the almost constant stream of visitors, and messengers, and tradespeople at Doctor Moran's house; and she longed to have her hands among the lovely things, and to give her opinion about the delightful events sure to make the next few weeks full of interest and pleasure. And after she had received a letter from Rem, she resolved to humble herself that she might be exalted.

"Rem is already fortunate, and I can't help him by fighting his battle. Forgetfulness, is the word. For this wrong can have no victory, and to be forgotten, is the only hope for it. Beside, Cornelia had her full share in my happiness, and I will not let myself be defrauded of my share in her happiness —not for a few words—no! certainly not."

This reflection a few times reiterated resulted in the following note—

MY DEAR CORNELIA: I want to say so much, that I cannot say anything but—forgive me. I am shaken to pieces by my dreadful sufferings, and sometimes, I do not know what I say, even to those I love. Blame my sad fortune for my bad words, and tell me you long to forgive me, as I long to be forgiven.

Your ARENTA.

"That will be sufficient," she reflected; "and after all, Cornelia is a sweet girl. I am her first and dearest friend, and

I am determined to keep my place. It has made me very angry to see those Van Dien girls, and those Sherman girls, running in and out of the Moran house as if they owned Cornelia. Well then, if I have had to eat humble pie, I have had my say, and that takes the bitter taste out of my mouth— and a sensible woman must look to her future. I dare warrant, Cornelia is now answering my letter. I dare warrant, she will forgive me very sweetly."

She spent half-an-hour in such reflections, and then Cornelia entered with a smiling face. She would not permit Arenta to say another word of regret; she stifled all her self-reproaches in an embrace, and she took her back with her to her own home. And no further repentance embarrassed Arenta. She put her ready wit, and her clever hands to a score of belated things; and snubbed and contradicted the Van Dien and Sherman girls into a respectful obedience to her earlier friendship, and wider experience. Everything that she directed, or took charge of, went with an unmistakable vigour to completion; and even Madame Van Heemskirk was delighted with her ability, and grateful for her assistance.

"The poor Arenta!" she said to Mrs. Moran; "very helpful she is to us, and for her brother's fault she is not to blame. Wrong it would be to visit it on her."

And Arenta not only felt this gracious justice for herself, she looked much further forward, for she said to her father, "It is really for Rem's sake I am so obliging. By and by people will say 'there is no truth in that letter story. The Marquise is the friend of Lady Hyde; they are like clasped hands, and that could not be so, if Rem Van Ariens had done such a dreadful thing. It is all nonsense.' And if I hear a word about it, I shall know how to smile, and lift my shoulders, and kill suspicion with contempt. Yes, for Rem's sake, I have done the best thing."

So happily the time went on, that it appeared wonderful when Christmas was close at hand. Every preparation was then complete. The Manor House was a very picture of splendid comfort and day by day Cornelia's exquisite wardrobe came nearer to perfection. It was a very joy to go into the Moran house. The mother, with a happy light upon her face, went to-and-fro with that habitual sweet serenity, which kept the temperature of expectant pleasure at a degree not too exhausting for continuance. The doctor was so satisfied with affairs, that he was often heard timing his firm, strong steps to snatches of long forgotten military songs; and Cornelia, knowing her lover was every day coming nearer and nearer, was just as happy as a girl loving and well beloved, ought to be. Sorrow was all behind her, and a great joy was coming to meet her. Until mortal love should become immortal, she could hope for no sweeter interlude in life.

Her beauty had increased wonderfully; hope had more than renewed her youth, and confident love had given to her face and form, a splendour of colour and expression, that capti-vated everybody; though why, or how, they never asked—she charmed, because she charmed. She was the love, the honey, the milk of sweetest human nature.

One day the little bevy of feminine councillors looked at their work, and pronounced all beautiful, and all finished; and then there was a lull in the busy household, and then every one was conscious of being a little weary; and every one also felt, that it would be well to let heart, and brain, and fingers, and feet rest. In a few days there would likely be another English letter, and they could then form some idea as to when Lord Hyde would arrive. The last letter received from him had been written in London, and the ship in which he was to sail, was taking on her cargo, while he impatiently waited at his hotel for notice of her being ready to lift her anchor. The doctor thought it highly probable Hyde would follow this letter in a week, or perhaps less.

During this restful interval, Doctor and Mrs. Moran drove out one afternoon to Hyde Manor House. A message from Madame Van Heemskirk asked this favour from them; she wished naturally that they should see how exquisitely beautiful and comfortable was the home, which her Joris had trusted her to prepare for his bride. But she did not wish Cornelia to see it, until the bride-groom himself took her across its threshold. "An old woman's fancy it is," she said to Mrs. Moran; "but no harm is there in it, and not much do I like women who bustle about their houses, and have no fancies at all."

"Nor I," answered Mrs. Moran with a merry little laugh. "Do you know, that I told John to buy my wedding ring too wide, because I often heard my mother say that a tight wedding ring was unlucky." Then both women smiled, and began delightedly to look over together the stores of fine linen and damask, which the mother of Joris had laid up for her son's use.

It was a charming visit, and the sweet pause in the vivid life of the past few weeks, was equally charming to Cornelia. She rested in her room till the short daylight ended; then she went to the parlour and drank a cup of tea, and closed the curtains, and sat down by the hearth to wait for her father and mother. It was likely they would be a little late, but the moon was full and the sleighing perfect, and then she was sure they would have so much to tell her, when they did reach home.

So still was the house, so still was the little street, that she easily went to the land of reverie, and lost herself there. She thought over again all her life with her lover; recalled his sweet spirit, his loyal affection, his handsome face, and enchanting manner. "Heaven has made me so fortunate," she thought, "and now my fortune has arrived at my wishes. Even his delay is sweet. I desire to think of him, until all other thoughts are forgotten! Oh, what lover could be loved as I love him!"

Then with a soft but quick movement the door flew open, she lifted her eyes, to fill them with love's very image and vesture; and with a cry of joy flew to meet the bliss so long afar, but now so near. "O lovely and beloved! O my love!" Hyde cried, and then there was a twofold silence; the very ecstasy that no mortal words can utter. The sacred hour for which all their lives had longed, was at last dropt down to them from heaven. Between their kisses they spoke of things remembered, and of things to be, leaning to each other in visible sweetness, while

"Love breathed in sighs and silences Through two blent souls, one rapturous undersong."

Other books by this author

The Bow of Orange Ribbon

The Man Between

The Squire of Sandal-Side

A Knight of the Nets

Amelia E. Barr

Choose from Thousands of 1stWorldLibrary Classics By

A. M. Barnard
Ada Leverson
Adolphus William Ward
Aesop
Agatha Christie
Alexander Aaronsohn
Alexander Kielland
Alexandre Dumas
Alfred Gatty
Alfred Ollivant
Alice Duer Miller
Alice Turner Curtis
Alice Dunbar
Allen Chapman
Alleyne Ireland
Ambrose Bierce
Amelia E. Barr
Amory H. Bradford
Andrew Lang
Andrew McFarland Davis
Andy Adams
Angela Brazil
Anna Alice Chapin
Anna Sewell
Annie Besant
Annie Hamilton Donnell
Annie Payson Call
Annie Roe Carr
Annonaymous
Anton Chekhov
Archibald Lee Fletcher
Arnold Bennett
Arthur C. Benson
Arthur Conan Doyle
Arthur M. Winfield
Arthur Ransome
Arthur Schnitzler
Arthur Train
Atticus
B.H. Baden-Powell
B. M. Bower
B. C. Chatterjee
Baroness Emmuska Orczy
Baroness Orczy
Basil King
Bayard Taylor
Ben Macomber
Bertha Muzzy Bower
Bjornstjerne Bjornson

Booth Tarkington
Boyd Cable
Bram Stoker
C. Collodi
C. E. Orr
C. M. Ingleby
Carolyn Wells
Catherine Parr Traill
Charles A. Eastman
Charles Amory Beach
Charles Dickens
Charles Dudley Warner
Charles Farrar Browne
Charles Ives
Charles Kingsley
Charles Klein
Charles Hanson Towne
Charles Lathrop Pack
Charles Romyn Dake
Charles Whibley
Charles Willing Beale
Charlotte M. Braeme
Charlotte M. Yonge
Charlotte Perkins Stetson
Clair W. Hayes
Clarence Day Jr.
Clarence E. Mulford
Clemence Housman
Confucius
Coningsby Dawson
Cornelis DeWitt Wilcox
Cyril Burleigh
D. H. Lawrence
Daniel Defoe
David Garnett
Dinah Craik
Don Carlos Janes
Donald Keyhoe
Dorothy Kilner
Dougan Clark
Douglas Fairbanks
E. Nesbit
E. P. Roe
E. Phillips Oppenheim
E. S. Brooks
Earl Barnes
Edgar Rice Burroughs
Edith Van Dyne
Edith Wharton

Edward Everett Hale
Edward J. O'Biren
Edward S. Ellis
Edwin L. Arnold
Eleanor Atkins
Eleanor Hallowell Abbott
Eliot Gregory
Elizabeth Gaskell
Elizabeth McCracken
Elizabeth Von Arnim
Ellem Key
Emerson Hough
Emilie F. Carlen
Emily Bronte
Emily Dickinson
Enid Bagnold
Enilor Macartney Lane
Erasmus W. Jones
Ernie Howard Pie
Ethel May Dell
Ethel Turner
Ethel Watts Mumford
Eugene Sue
Eugenie Foa
Eugene Wood
Eustace Hale Ball
Evelyn Everett-green
Everard Cotes
F. H. Cheley
F. J. Cross
F. Marion Crawford
Fannie E. Newberry
Federick Austin Ogg
Ferdinand Ossendowski
Fergus Hume
Florence A. Kilpatrick
Fremont B. Deering
Francis Bacon
Francis Darwin
Frances Hodgson Burnett
Frances Parkinson Keyes
Frank Gee Patchin
Frank Harris
Frank Jewett Mather
Frank L. Packard
Frank V. Webster
Frederic Stewart Isham
Frederick Trevor Hill
Frederick Winslow Taylor

Friedrich Kerst	Hayden Carruth	James Branch Cabell
Friedrich Nietzsche	Helent Hunt Jackson	James DeMille
Fyodor Dostoyevsky	Helen Nicolay	James Joyce
G.A. Henty	Hendrik Conscience	James Lane Allen
G.K. Chesterton	Hendy David Thoreau	James Lane Allen
Gabrielle E. Jackson	Henri Barbusse	James Oliver Curwood
Garrett P. Serviss	Henrik Ibsen	James Oppenheim
Gaston Leroux	Henry Adams	James Otis
George A. Warren	Henry Ford	James R. Driscoll
George Ade	Henry Frost	Jane Abbott
Geroge Bernard Shaw	Henry James	Jane Austen
George Cary Eggleston	Henry Jones Ford	Jane L. Stewart
George Durston	Henry Seton Merriman	Janet Aldridge
George Ebers	Henry W Longfellow	Jens Peter Jacobsen
George Eliot	Herbert A. Giles	Jerome K. Jerome
George Gissing	Herbert Carter	Jessie Graham Flower
George MacDonald	Herbert N. Casson	John Buchan
George Meredith	Herman Hesse	John Burroughs
George Orwell	Hildegard G. Frey	John Cournos
George Sylvester Viereck	Homer	John F. Kennedy
George Tucker	Honore De Balzac	John Gay
George W. Cable	Horace B. Day	John Glasworthy
George Wharton James	Horace Walpole	John Habberton
Gertrude Atherton	Horatio Alger Jr.	John Joy Bell
Gordon Casserly	Howard Pyle	John Kendrick Bangs
Grace E. King	Howard R. Garis	John Milton
Grace Gallatin	Hugh Lofting	John Philip Sousa
Grace Greenwood	Hugh Walpole	John Taintor Foote
Grant Allen	Humphry Ward	Jonas Lauritz Idemil Lie
Guillermo A. Sherwell	Ian Maclaren	Jonathan Swift
Gulielma Zollinger	Inez Haynes Gillmore	Joseph A. Altsheler
Gustav Flaubert	Irving Bacheller	Joseph Carey
H. A. Cody	Isabel Cecilia Williams	Joseph Conrad
H. B. Irving	Isabel Hornibrook	Joseph E. Badger Jr
H. C. Bailey	Israel Abrahams	Joseph Hergesheimer
H. G. Wells	Ivan Turgenev	Joseph Jacobs
H. H. Munro	J. G.Austin	Jules Vernes
H. Irving Hancock	J. Henri Fabre	Julian Hawthrone
H. R. Naylor	J. M. Barrie	Julie A Lippmann
H. Rider Haggard	J. M. Walsh	Justin Huntly McCarthy
H. W. C. Davis	J. Macdonald Oxley	Kakuzo Okakura
Haldeman Julius	J. R. Miller	Karle Wilson Baker
Hall Caine	J. S. Fletcher	Kate Chopin
Hamilton Wright Mabie	J. S. Knowles	Kenneth Grahame
Hans Christian Andersen	J. Storer Clouston	Kenneth McGaffey
Harold Avery	J. W. Duffield	Kate Langley Bosher
Harold McGrath	Jack London	Kate Langley Bosher
Harriet Beecher Stowe	Jacob Abbott	Katherine Cecil Thurston
Harry Castlemon	James Allen	Katherine Stokes
Harry Coghill	James Andrews	L. A. Abbot
Harry Houidini	James Baldwin	L. T. Meade

L. Frank Baum
Latta Griswold
Laura Dent Crane
Laura Lee Hope
Laurence Housman
Lawrence Beasley
Leo Tolstoy
Leonid Andreyev
Lewis Carroll
Lewis Sperry Chafer
Lilian Bell
Lloyd Osbourne
Louis Hughes
Louis Joseph Vance
Louis Tracy
Louisa May Alcott
Lucy Fitch Perkins
Lucy Maud Montgomery
Luther Benson
Lydia Miller Middleton
Lyndon Orr
M. Corvus
M. H. Adams
Margaret E. Sangster
Margret Howth
Margaret Vandercook
Margaret W. Hungerford
Margret Penrose
Maria Edgeworth
Maria Thompson Daviess
Mariano Azuela
Marion Polk Angellotti
Mark Overton
Mark Twain
Mary Austin
Mary Catherine Crowley
Mary Cole
Mary Hastings Bradley
Mary Roberts Rinehart
Mary Rowlandson
M. Wollstonecraft Shelley
Maud Lindsay
Max Beerbohm
Myra Kelly
Nathaniel Hawthrone
Nicolo Machiavelli
O. F. Walton
Oscar Wilde

Owen Johnson
P.G. Wodehouse
Paul and Mabel Thorne
Paul G. Tomlinson
Paul Severing
Percy Brebner
Percy Keese Fitzhugh
Peter B. Kyne
Plato
Quincy Allen
R. Derby Holmes
R. L. Stevenson
R. S. Ball
Rabindranath Tagore
Rahul Alvares
Ralph Bonehill
Ralph Henry Barbour
Ralph Victor
Ralph Waldo Emmerson
Rene Descartes
Ray Cummings
Rex Beach
Rex E. Beach
Richard Harding Davis
Richard Jefferies
Richard Le Gallienne
Robert Barr
Robert Frost
Robert Gordon Anderson
Robert L. Drake
Robert Lansing
Robert Lynd
Robert Michael Ballantyne
Robert W. Chambers
Rosa Nouchette Carey
Rudyard Kipling
Saint Augustine
Samuel B. Allison
Samuel Hopkins Adams
Sarah Bernhardt
Sarah C. Hallowell
Selma Lagerlof
Sherwood Anderson
Sigmund Freud
Standish O'Grady
Stanley Weyman
Stella Benson
Stella M. Francis

Stephen Crane
Stewart Edward White
Stijn Streuvels
Swami Abhedananda
Swami Parmananda
T. S. Ackland
T. S. Arthur
The Princess Der Ling
Thomas A. Janvier
Thomas A Kempis
Thomas Anderton
Thomas Bailey Aldrich
Thomas Bulfinch
Thomas De Quincey
Thomas Dixon
Thomas H. Huxley
Thomas Hardy
Thomas More
Thornton W. Burgess
U. S. Grant
Upton Sinclair
Valentine Williams
Various Authors
Vaughan Kester
Victor Appleton
Victor G. Durham
Victoria Cross
Virginia Woolf
Wadsworth Camp
Walter Camp
Walter Scott
Washington Irving
Wilbur Lawton
Wilkie Collins
Willa Cather
Willard F. Baker
William Dean Howells
William le Queux
W. Makepeace Thackeray
William W. Walter
William Shakespeare
Winston Churchill
Yei Theodora Ozaki
Yogi Ramacharaka
Young E. Allison
Zane Grey